Love in

"Saranne Da ... ames in futuristic romance."
—*Romantic Times*

CLOSE ENCOUNTER

Something jolted Zachary: a sudden, almost painful awareness of her. Rowena stopped, then raised her face to stare at him.

"You seem to have been rather unnerved by the storm yourself, Commander," she taunted.

Later, Zachary would tell himself that he'd never intended what happened. He'd even try to convince himself that it was she who had initiated the kiss. But in this moment, all he knew was that she would be his, that he had to have her.

Rowena made no attempt to get away from him as his head lowered to hers, and the lips he covered with his own were parted and pliant. He drew her against him and she arched, curving her body to his.

Star-Crossed

Saranne Dawson

LOVE SPELL ✦ NEW YORK CITY

LOVE SPELL®

November 1994

Published by

Dorchester Publishing Co., Inc.
276 Fifth Avenue
New York, NY 10001

Copyright © 1994 by Saranne Dawson

Cover Art by John Ennis

Printed in the United States of America.

Prologue

The first curling tendrils of ghostly mist appeared as the army made its way up the steep hillside. Long lines of men with lances and bows advanced toward the valley, frightened but determined. This time, they would be victorious—or so their leaders told them. This time, traditional enemies had joined forces to defeat a common foe. This time they would eliminate the accursed sorcerers who'd held them in thrall.

Then the mist began to thicken, spilling down the long hillside to swarm over the army, touching it with cool, invisible fingers. In the ranks, there was an uneasy stirring. Brave men felt those icy fingers play along their spines, and those who had never seen the accursed sorcerers were as frightened as those who had. The stories about them whispered through their brains, weakening their resolve.

The sky was—or had been—blue, as clear a day as one could want. Now it was no longer possible to see that sky because the pale fog covered everything. And so gradually, the entire army came to a halt, blinded by the ever-thickening mist.

The leaders had reached the crest of the hill before the fog forced them to stop. Brightly colored pennants drooped in the damp chill as they sat astride their magnificent horses, frowning in frustration. All of them were members of the proud Warrior clans and had fought many battles—often against each other.

In their arrogance, they had believed that victory was assured this time. Not even their enemy's sorcery could overcome the sheer numbers they commanded this time. They would rid the world once and for all of the sorcerers. But beyond and below them, it was as though the valley had ceased to exist.

Temporarily stymied in their quest, the army waited. Horses whickered and stamped impatiently. Men talked in voices that were muffled by the fog. The leaders dismounted and paced along the top of the hill, discussing the situation. Was the fog a natural occurrence, requiring only that they wait it out—or was it the result of Dazhinn sorcery?

And what if it *was* sorcery? they asked themselves and others. Even their magic had its limits and the fog would lift sooner or later. They would simply wait it out and victory would still be theirs.

The light began to dim still further; night was now approaching. And then suddenly the mist vanished even more quickly than it had come. A full moon poured silver light over the landscape. Millions of stars glittered against the black canopy of the heavens. But in the valley below them, not a single light was visible.

The commanders sneered at this foolish trick. Could the Dazhinn actually believe that they would be fooled? They knew full well that there were houses and barns and stables and granaries down there. The valley had been home to the accursed Dazhinn since time began.

So they waited for dawn, confident that victory would still be theirs. But when the first pale light of the rising sun washed over the valley, nothing remained—not even a sign that anyone had ever lived there. Land that had been cleared centuries ago for grazing and for the growing of crops was now covered again by forest. A thriving town had vanished as well—home to more than 2000 people.

It's an illusion, one of them said—and his words were echoed by the others. A small, elite force was sent into the valley as daylight flooded the world. On the hilltop, the commanders watched as they made their way through the thick forest that couldn't be there. Any moment, they expected the signal that would tell them that the Dazhinn were indeed still there.

Then the war party was lost to view for a time as they made their way through the uneven floor of the valley. And still the commanders waited, confident that the sorcery would be exposed. But then the soldiers reappeared, and when they had returned to the hilltop, they informed the commanders that the valley was as it now seemed: empty, uninhabited forest. Not one trace of the Dazhinn had been found.

The army turned back reluctantly, neither defeated nor victorious, but suspended somewhere in between. Within weeks, all but a small force had returned to their scattered homes, spreading the strange tale, building the legend.

For years and then decades, they kept watch on the valley, building a great stone fortress on the hilltop that eventually came to be surrounded by a small village. But years passed and the century turned and the valley remained as it was. The soldiers from the fortress made regular trips down into the valley to hunt, but they reported that there was never any game to be found, despite the lushness of the valley that was bisected by a sparkling, swift-running stream. Besides that, they didn't like the place, though none of them could—or would—say why that was so.

More than 200 years after the army had turned back, there was a revival of interest in the place. The old fortress had been abandoned for some time, and the village surrounding it had dwindled. But men of a different age went down into the valley again, this time searching for any evidence that it had once been inhabited.

All myths have some basis in fact, said scholars. So *something* must have existed there at one time.

But they found nothing, and reported that while some game had returned, it was still not as plentiful as might have been expected. Nevertheless, interest in the place, once reawakened, did not subside—at least for the scholars. So eventually, the fortress was brought back to life, this time as a seat of learning. Ancient manuscripts were gathered from their various storage places and brought there. The leading scholars of the time took up residence and the little village began to thrive again, becoming first a town and then a small city.

Generations of students came and went: the best and brightest in the land. Spending a night in the valley, where the mists still came quickly and without warning, became a rite of passage. A few claimed to have "felt something." The others laughed at them. Sorcery belonged to a less enlightened past.

Chapter One

Rowena Sandor squinted at the horizon, where the dark, fir-covered mountains met the sky. She hated it when she did this, but she found herself doing it more and more frequently, They all did, though they rarely talked about it.

The sky was a deep, clear blue, and the dark mountains should have been sharp and clearly defined against that heavenly backdrop. But instead it was smudged, blurred. Black faded to charcoal and then to paler gray and finally to blue. It looked like a painting not quite finished.

She kicked her mare's flanks and rode on toward town, taking care not to look that way again. There was nothing to be done about it, so it must be ignored. Or so the Council and most of the others said. Rowena herself had never been comfortable with such self-deception, even though she had no answers to the problem, either.

The breeze swept her long, pale gold hair across her face and she put up a slim, long-fingered hand to brush it away. She was quite lovely, but her hands were her special gift: hands that could weave intricate tapestries, turning multicolored threads into scenes of magical beauty that drew the viewer into them. The women of her family had been weavers of tapestries for centuries. Sandor tapestries were highly prized among her people.

Rowena was making the rounds of the market stalls when the Council aide found her and requested that she accompany him to Council Hall.

She was both surprised and annoyed to be taken away from her shopping. What could the Council possibly want with her? They were known to consult regularly with various people, but of what use to them was a weaver? They surely couldn't intend to commission another tapestry. The walls of Council Hall were already well filled with Sandor tapestries, the most recent of which she had worked on as a child, together with her mother and grandmother.

Soon she was passing by that tapestry in the large anteroom to the Council's chambers, thinking sadly of her long-dead grandmother, who hadn't lived to see its completion, and her more recently departed mother, whose wish for a granddaughter to teach had gone unfulfilled because Rowena had refused to marry any of the suitors who had presented themselves.

Surely, she thought, the Council hadn't called her here to harangue her about *that*. From what she'd heard, they had given up exhorting people to increase the population. Her friend Freda, a midwife, said that people were afraid to have children now, because their future was so uncertain.

Still, it was possible that they were worried about the continuity of her family line—especially since she was the last of the skilled weavers. She had a few cousins who'd tried the work, but they lacked the talent to infuse magic into their craft, and so contented themselves with making pillows and cushions, leaving the weaving of the tapestries to her hands alone.

Such arts were of great importance to her people, who worshiped beauty in all its forms. Painters, sculptors, composers, and all artisans were revered among them and accorded places of high honor in their society. The union of magic and art was seen as the most noble of endeavors.

Still, she thought, if I were the Council, I would certainly not be wasting my time worrying about one family—or even about tapestries—when the very future of their people might be at stake.

She entered the Council chamber, announced by the aide. They were all there, seated at their long, curved table. Behind them, the largest of the Sandor tapestries filled the wall. Its weaving had taken place long before Rowena's time, but she still thrilled to see it, having been raised on

14

tales of the three generations who had labored for so many years on it.

Every chair was filled and all of the Council members stared at her as she took the proffered chair: the visitor's chair that was placed within the curve and opposite the Council leader. The leadership rotated among the various members, and the current leader was an imperious woman, the mother of one of Rowena's rejected suitors.

At present, there were five men and seven women on the Council—all of them elected for staggered three-year terms. Rowena knew them all, of course, and was related to four of them. In fact, she was related to *all* of them if one cared to trace things back that far.

Alma, the current leader, thanked her formally for coming—as though she had any choice, Rowena thought sourly. She knew Alma had felt personally affronted when Rowena had turned down her son's proposal of marriage. But perhaps if he'd had a less unpleasant mother, he might have been more acceptable himself. The fruit, as her Gran had frequently observed, never fell far from the tree.

"We have a very grave matter to discuss with you, Rowena," Alma intoned, to the accompaniment of somber nods all around. "We have reached a most difficult decision."

Rowena said nothing. What difficult decision could they have reached that had anything to do with her?

"As you know," Alma continued in her slightly reedy, officious tone, "the Council has never asked anyone to descend, preferring instead to accept volunteers."

Of course she knew that. Why did this unpleasant woman feel it necessary to remind her of that—unless . . . No, that was clearly impossible. Her skills were too valuable.

"But we are faced now with a situation that has forced us to reconsider that policy," Alma went on. "In fact, we face very grave danger. Our very survival may be at stake."

Rowena's green eyes scanned the table as she wondered if Alma were being overly dramatic. But all the eyes that met hers were troubled and she saw many nods of agreement, even among those she knew disliked the Council leader as much as she did. What was going on here? What was this grave danger? And why had they called her here to hear this?

"The reports we have received indicate that the Cassatans are preparing for war again," Alma said. "And while this is, of course, not at all unusual for them, this particular war could pose a very great danger to us. We have every reason to believe that it could be carried to the valley."

Rowena stared at her. The valley? *Their* valley? "But there is nothing in the valley," she protested. "Why would they make war there?"

"The valley lies quite near the border between the two nations that are likely to make war upon each other. It would be the first time that war has come to that region since our Ascent, and we believe that capturing Ashwara is certain to be a top priority because of its ancient symbolic value."

Ashwara. The fortress that was erected many centuries ago by the Cassatans to keep watch on the valley after her people had ascended. She'd never seen it, of course, but she understood the symbolism because it had become symbolic for her people as well: a symbol of the warmongering Cassatans who had forced them to leave that world.

"As you know, Rowena, we have struggled to put our people into positions where they can prevent such a thing from happening—but it appears that we have failed. The Descenders have managed to get into very high positions, or to influence those in high positions, but gaining entry into the top ranks of the military has been impossible. Those positions are reserved for descendants of the old Warrior class.

"At the present time, the Cassatans are in effect being ruled by one man: the military commander. The king is weak and defers to him, and the parliament, which we have managed to infiltrate, has only limited powers. We even have control over several of the king's closest advisers, but that hasn't been enough, either. And the commander is making plans for war."

Alma paused, her expression grim. Then she went on. "And if war comes to the valley, it may well break the spell. They have developed very powerful war machines, and the spell, as we all know, grows weaker by the year."

Rowena said nothing. She was naturally horrified by this news, but she still couldn't understand why they were telling it to her.

"We ordered that this man should be assassinated. Two attempts were made, and both failed. Now he lives beyond our reach in a well-guarded military compound, and when he leaves it, he is always surrounded by his Warrior guards.

"There's no way to cast a spell over him, either, since the Warriors have always been immune to our magic, save for that used in self-defense."

Rowena was shocked that the Council had actually ordered someone's death—even the death of a Warrior. Such things were more of the nature of the Cassatans than of her people, and therefore surely proved the desperation of their situation.

"So we turned to the astrologers, hoping that by charting his stars, they would find a way for us to prevent him from going to war. And that is how we came to ask you here."

The truth had begun to dawn on Rowena the moment Alma mentioned the astrologers. From the most ancient of times, her people had sought guidance from the stars. Many among them still continued to have charts done to find themselves a suitable mate. Rowena herself had never done so because she disliked believing that such things could be ordained.

"What they found," Alma continued, "is extremely rare. In fact, no one now alive remembers such a powerful conjunction. But they saw such a conjunction in his chart. He can be influenced—and the source of that influence is you, Rowena. Your own stars prove that. He will be completely unable to resist you even if magic doesn't work on him. Therefore, you will be able to accomplish what the others could not.

"You alone have the ability to get close to Commander MacTavesh—and kill him."

Rowena sat before the fire, shivering. The fire had long since driven the evening chill from the small room, but the coldness was deep within her and could not be driven out so easily.

They had given her time to think it over, but she knew that they'd already determined that she must descend. And how could she refuse, when the lives of all her people were at stake?

They had promised her that she could return once her mission had been completed, and assured her that it could be done—even though it had never been done before. Always before, those who descended had lived out their lives among the Cassatans, in service to her people. It was necessary because one could not hope to rise to a position of prominence and influence among the barbarians that quickly.

After she left Council Hall, Rowena had spent hours trying to think of a way to say no—a way to remain here, weaving her tapestries and tending her garden. But now she was forced to the unhappy conclusion that there was no other way. She must descend—and then she must kill this man who threatened their enchanted existence.

19

Nearly 500 years ago her people, the Dazhinn, had combined the powerful forces of their ancient magic to lift themselves out of a world grown too evil for them to tolerate. Surrounded by enemies and pursued relentlessly by the Warriors, they had called upon their sorcery to remove themselves, together with their beloved valley, into a different plane: an enchanted place suspended in time and space, forever safe from their bloodthirsty neighbors.

The spell had held all these years, keeping them safe and allowing them to live out their lives in peace. But about 50 years ago, they began to see the first signs that the spell was weakening. The most powerful sorcerers among them had sought a way to reinforce it, but they'd failed. By now, a second generation was trying to find a way to hold the spell, but so far without success.

In the meantime, their enchanted world drifted closer to that other world and a Gateway opened between them. The Council of that time decided that they could ill afford to place all their hopes on the possibility of reinforcing the spell, so a momentous decision was made. They would send people to the world of the barbarians and try to put them into positions of power, so that if they were forced to return to it, they could do so without fear of more wars.

"Descending" thus became the most noble of undertakings: sacrificing the happiness of their magical world in order to help future generations if that dreaded time came.

They were few in numbers to begin with, so the Descenders were of necessity a tiny group. But they had become well entrenched among the Cassatans, which was their name for the people of the world the Dazhinn had left behind. The word meant "barbarians" and was always spoken with the contempt they felt toward the warmongering people who had driven them to such extremes.

Blending in wasn't that difficult, since the Dazhinn shared a common language and cultural heritage with the most powerful groups of the barbarians: the Warriors and the Siletians. But it was the Warriors they hated most. Their battles went back to the beginning of time.

The earliest Descenders had had a difficult time indeed, but by now the newly descended had a secret network to draw upon in the society that now combined the ancient Warrior clans and the Siletians.

Among the Descenders, there were a few exceptionally powerful telepaths who could communicate with their like here, and through them, the Council monitored the other world.

Rowena sat huddled miserably before the fire, thinking about their promise that she could return once her mission was completed. They seemed quite certain that it could be done, but it took little intelligence on her part to understand the uncertainty.

Still, in the end, what did it matter? If she alone could reach this Warrior, MacTavesh, then she must go.

I don't want to do this, she thought again. How can I kill—even to save my people?

Perhaps when she met him, she would feel differently. After all, he was a Warrior, the descendant of those who'd driven out her people. When she saw him for what he was, she would be able to do it.

She'd made one last attempt to get out of this by reminding the Council that if she killed him, another would take his place and nothing would change. But they'd disputed that. Certainly, they said, another commander would be named, but he wouldn't be nearly as powerful as Zachary MacTavesh, and the king's advisers—among them some of her own people—would be able to control him.

Night fell and the stars came out, and Rowena stood there staring up at them, wondering how those tiny, cold bits of light could have ordained such a future for her.

Commander-in-Chief Zachary MacTavesh didn't need to crane his neck as others did to see the newest arrivals at the large, crowded gathering. At six feet four inches, he stood head and shoulders above the crowd—a crowd that would certainly have noticed him even if it hadn't been for his height.

He presented a commanding figure indeed: the very epitome of the Warrior with his harshly handsome aquiline features and his pale gray-blue eyes that seemed always to be taking the measure of those around him.

He detested these parties, but he attended them anyway. It was useful to be seen—now more than ever—and occasionally he could pick up some interesting information from men who overindulged in the excellent spirits served at such occasions. Given his size, he could match them drink for drink and suffer no mental impairments himself.

The real tedium of gatherings such as this came from the endless parade of women presented for his inspection. Ever since the formal period of mourning following Miriam's death and the death of their two children, well-intentioned matrons had been bringing forth prospective wives for him.

Zachary had no real antipathy to marriage and knew he would marry again at some point. After all, he was now childless, and continuing his proud line was very important. But the truth was that he found the demands of marriage and family tiresome, and was therefore resolved to postpone the inevitable as long as possible. He had just passed his forty-third birthday, but he was as physically fit as a man half his age.

The matrons whispered that despite his appearance, he must surely still be mourning the loss of his Miriam—but they were wrong. He was quite content without her. They'd seen little of each other in any event, given his responsibilities, and the marriage had been one of convenience. Miriam, who had come from the mercantile class, had had higher aspirations, while Zachary, descendant of a long, proud line of

Warriors, had gained the benefit of her family's largess.

His gaze traveled now over the heads of the glittering crowd to the couple now arriving: his closest friend, Duncan Wengor, and Duncan's wife, Paulena. Duncan caught his eye and started toward him, trailed by the elegant Paulena. At least, Zach thought gratefully, Paulena hadn't tried to foist some female protégé off on him. He would grant her that, although she still bothered him in a way he'd never quite been able to define.

The Wengors joined the group around him and they all made polite conversation for a time. Then they caught their host's eye and retreated to his comfortable, paneled study, followed by a few others who knew without being asked that their presence would be welcome.

"So, how do the preparations go?" their host inquired of Zach. He wasn't of the nobility himself, and therefore inclined toward a bluntness that Zach liked. The man had made such a huge fortune that his lowly birth could no longer be held against him.

"Well enough," Zach told him and the others. "I've at least persuaded His Majesty to part with some money for the arms makers."

"For which we are all suitably grateful," said another man with a slight bow in Zach's direction. He owned the largest munitions plant in the land.

"What will it take to persuade him to declare war?" another man asked in exasperation. "How much proof does he need?"

24

"He will agree when the time is right," Zach replied. "For now, we must build up our forces."

"The garrison at Ashwara has been reinforced," Duncan told them.

"So you think they will strike there first?" someone asked.

Zach nodded. "Our agents tell me that they are trying to secretly increase their forces on the other side of the mountain. They want Ashwara."

Their host frowned into his whiskey. "Damned foolish of them, if you ask me. The fortress guards nothing except for a valley that isn't even good for hunting."

"There's the university," someone pointed out. They had all been students there at some point.

Duncan chuckled. "I don't think they want Ashwara so they can capture a bunch of woolly-headed scholars. It's the symbolic value they want, my friend."

"A load of rubbish, that." Their host grimaced, blowing out a perfect smoke ring from his cigar. "Sorcerers and all that rot."

"Otherwise intelligent men have been known to follow just such irrational impulses," Zach replied. "The legend of the Dazhinn is our most enduring myth."

"Your aunt Paulena will meet you," the white-bearded Gatekeeper told Rowena as they rode toward the Gateway. "She looks forward to this reunion, though of course she wishes it were under more pleasant circumstances."

Rowena merely nodded. The opportunity to

see her favorite aunt again was the only pleasure that awaited her on the far side of the Gateway. Paulena was her mother's younger sister, and until her descent 14 years ago, when Rowena herself was 14, they'd been very close.

Paulena had descended later than most, having reached that momentous decision after her husband was killed in an accident. The marriage had been a very happy one—the result of a horoscope casting—and in her grief, Paulena had once again gone to the astrologers, who told her that her future happiness lay in the other world.

Rowena's mother had been openly skeptical. She didn't hold much with horoscope casting and suspected the astrologers of being in league with the Council to send as many people as possible through the Gateway. But Paulena had persisted, and six months after her husband's death, she had descended.

Rowena wondered what her mother would have to say if she knew that her only child was about to follow her beloved sister's path. She'd always been distrustful of the Council's plans, though she'd never said exactly why.

They rode on through the newly planted fields. With Rowena were the three Gatekeepers, two men and a woman—the most powerful sorcerers among them. The trio would use their combined powers to open the Gate and then to close it again behind her. The Gateway itself lay some distance ahead of them, cut off from the main valley by a sheer wall of rock that seemed to trap the thick mists that were ever present there.

Rowena was making her Descent without the normal lengthy preparations. Descenders were usually given all the information they needed to survive after their Descent, even though they were always met by someone. But the Council had decided to dispense with that because they considered the situation too urgent for her to wait any longer.

She had tried her best to avoid the celebration that always preceded a Descent, but of course word had spread, and in the end she had been forced to endure the ritual congratulations of all her extended family and friends.

The celebration had been difficult—chiefly because all of them, Rowena included, had felt it necessary to keep up the pretense that she would be returning. Despite the insistence of the Gatekeepers that such a thing could be done, they all knew it had never happened before.

She fought down her tears as she thought about it now. She wasn't given to premonitions like others among them, but when she'd left her cottage this morning, she'd had the very strong feeling that she was seeing it for the last time.

Then she frowned, recalling her one cousin's strange words last night. Seitha was often given to premonitions, and when Rowena had seen her last night, her somber expression had immediately suggested that she knew Rowena wouldn't return. Not sure that she wanted to know, Rowena had nevertheless asked her if she "saw" anything.

Seitha had nodded solemnly. "Yes, but I don't really understand it. I believe you will come back—but there will be a very great difference."

Pressed by Rowena to explain her strange words, Seitha had merely shrugged. She could tell her no more than that.

Difference, she thought now. What difference could there be? Either I will return or I won't. Could Seitha have meant that she would return, but would somehow be different herself?

She wished that she'd been able to learn what other Descenders learned before they left. Paulena had shrugged away the preparations, saying merely that it was a matter of speaking the proper dialect and knowing the conditions in the other world, but Rowena's mother had remarked sadly that she believed she'd lost her sister even before she descended, because there were things she was withholding.

No one other than the Council and the telepaths who communicated with their counterparts on the other side paid all that much attention to the world they'd left behind. Their attitude, even after all these centuries, continued to be one of "good riddance." They had no need to know anything more than that the people there were barbarians.

Rowena suppressed a shiver and at the same time thanked the stars that Paulena would be there—and the others as well. At least she wouldn't be alone in the world of the Cassatans.

About her mission she thought nothing at all. She had decided that it would do no good to fret about that now. She would do what must be done and then hope that she could return to her life.

They reached the rocky cliffs faster than she'd expected, then veered off to the south toward the narrow opening into the mist-filled Gateway.

Having tried without success to engage her in conversation, the Gatekeepers had finally fallen silent. Rowena could feel their uneasiness— and their disapproval as well. Even though they were always careful not to invade each other's privacy, some emotions could not be avoided. But she understood their disapproval. After all, for everyone else who came this way, it was a joyous time.

Too joyous, Rowena thought. They behaved as though they were Warriors, setting off to a great battle with visions of glory in their minds. That had always troubled her, since it seemed to suggest that they had something in common with their ancient enemies.

They reached the narrow pass and dismounted. The Gatekeepers immediately started along the well-worn path, but Rowena paused to take one last look at her beloved home. This end of the broad valley was slightly elevated, affording a panoramic view of rolling fields and distant mountains. The town was a faint smudge of gray stone near the center of the valley. Her own cottage was invisible, hidden behind a small hill.

The tears that had been threatening now spilled over onto her cheeks, and she quickly wiped them away. She would be back. She *must* believe that.

The three Gatekeepers were waiting for her and she let them lead her along the narrow path through the towering stone cliffs. The mists began to close around them, moving in with a suddenness that startled Rowena, even though she had known to expect this. One moment, they were walking in bright sunshine, and in the next, they were enveloped in the chill, damp fog. She'd been told to wear a heavy cloak, but it seemed to afford little protection. She was already shivering.

They had gone only a short distance when the Gatekeepers came to a halt. She was told that she must go on from here alone.

"What will happen?" she asked as she stared nervously at the nearly invisible path. She realized now that she'd given little thought to the actual Descent. Her mind had been focused on her mission and her fears at encountering the hated Cassatans.

"You will continue along the path while we open the Gateway," the eldest of them told her. "After a time, you will feel it drop away beneath you. I'm told that the sensation is a pleasant one, but you might feel somewhat dizzy. Some feel this more than others. But your aunt will be there to help you."

It seemed too easy, she thought suspiciously, but she could ask nothing more, since they had already begun their ritual chants—perhaps as a way of forestalling more questions.

She turned away from them and began to walk slowly along the path. She'd worried that she might not be able to see it well enough to follow it, but as she moved along cautiously, she realized that it was always visible for a short distance—almost as though an invisible broom were sweeping away the mists.

With each step, she kept expecting to feel the sensation they'd warned her about. For a time she could still hear their chanting behind her and the sounds reassured her. But then it faded away and she was totally alone in a thick, dank mist that obscured everything except for the dark, glistening stones of the path.

Her soft leather shoes continued to strike the stones even as the mist closed in around her feet. Then suddenly, the stones were no longer there! She stumbled to a halt, but it was too late. Her feet now touched nothing at all. She was floating in the impenetrable mist!

Terrified, she tried to turn back—only to discover that she could no longer command her own body. She sank to what should have been the ground, but nothing was there, and now she'd lost all sense of up and down. She cried out and drew herself into a tight ball, fighting waves of dizziness.

She was falling—and not falling. Winds whipped at her cloak, but there was no sound. Darkness had replaced the soft gray of the mist: a blackness darker than the darkest night.

The falling/not falling sensation continued and the invisible winds tore at her ever more strongly as she huddled into a still tighter ball. She was cold, colder than she'd ever been before. And then, just when she was certain that she could endure no more, her knees slammed painfully against something hard.

She cried out as she fell forward, and her hands touched smooth, wet stone. When she dared to open her eyes, she saw the same dark stones as before. But then the dizziness overcame her again and she was forced to close her eyes.

Was she there? Had she passed through the Gateway? What if she were trapped somewhere in between—left forever in some nameless place?

She began to crawl slowly along the path, discovering to her horror that she was not only dizzy, but also very weak. The effort required to drag her body along the path seemed nearly beyond her.

Around her, blackness had slowly given way to gray mist once again, but it was a mist as cold as the dark had been. Her teeth were chattering from the tremors that shook her body. Twice, she tried to pull herself to her feet, and both times she sank quickly to her knees again.

"Paulena!" she cried desperately, her voice muffled by the fog. "Polly! Are you there?"

"Coming, dear."

The voice seemed to be coming from a very great distance, but it was clearly her aunt's voice.

Rowena sobbed with relief and stopped trying to move her leaden body.

Then suddenly, Paulena was there—or rather, she was being embraced by a woman who resembled her aunt. Before she lapsed into unconsciousness, Rowena realized that she'd failed to take into account the passage of the years. Instead, she'd kept Polly in her heart at the age she'd been when she'd descended. Twenty-eight: the same age Rowena herself was now.

She awoke to a sense of motion and a blurry view of her surroundings. She blinked several times, trying to see more clearly as she heard the rhythmic clip-clop of horses' hooves. She was in a carriage, but it was unlike any carriage she'd ever seen before.

A single lamp lit the small, luxurious space. Everything was a deep wine-red color: the fabric-covered walls, the deeply cushioned seats that faced each other. Even the woman who sat across from her wore a rich, fur-trimmed cloak of that color.

And now the woman was leaning toward her, smiling. Yes, it was definitely Paulena. She'd know that smile anywhere, even if time had subtly rearranged the familiar features. She tried to return her aunt's smile.

"Don't try to talk yet, dear. I'm afraid that you might have had a worse time of it than most, although everyone feels a bit weak and dizzy at first."

Rowena's blurred vision was gradually clearing and she turned her head carefully to gaze at her surroundings. The opulence amazed her. Even the gently swinging lantern was finely wrought brass and etched glass. She was astounded to think that glass was so plentiful here that it would be used in carriage lanterns. And the fabrics were so rich and heavy.

"This is my carriage," Paulena told her. "The driver is Abner Fogal. We're taking you to my country home by the sea. It's not far, and it will be a good place for you to rest and regain your strength."

Abner, Rowena thought muzzily. He was one of her rejected suitors. He'd descended less than a year ago, and at the time she'd wondered if he'd done so because she'd refused his offer of marriage.

"How lovely you are, Rowena," her aunt continued. "But then you always were. You look so much like Mother."

Rowena tried to smile again. She knew that she bore a very strong resemblance to her grandmother. She'd seen that for herself, even though her Gran's looks had faded somewhat by the time Rowena could first remember her.

She drifted off to sleep again, lulled by the swaying movement of the carriage and her aunt's soothing voice. And then she awoke with a start as the movement stopped and light suddenly flooded into the curtained carriage. The door had opened and Abner stood there staring at her.

Rowena started to greet him, but the words died on her lips as she saw the cold anger in his eyes: the same anger she'd seen when she'd rejected his suit. Until then, he'd kept it hidden, but she'd still sensed a rage in him before that, a hatred just waiting for something to fix upon. Apparently, he'd now found something: her!

However, she was too dizzy and weak to dwell upon the matter now, and in any event his expression was quickly transformed into blandness as he helped her from the carriage. Then it took both him and Paulena to hold her upright. In her mind, she was still falling or not falling through that blackness, and not even the solid ground beneath her feet could convince her brain otherwise.

She was concentrating so much on simply putting one foot before the other that she was inside the house before she'd even gotten a look at it, other than to register a vague impression of enormous size.

As they led her up a wide staircase into a sumptuous bedroom, Rowena realized that what her aunt had described as being her "country house" was larger and more lavish than anything she'd ever seen—larger even than Council Hall.

And before she tumbled into a big canopied bed and fell asleep, Rowena had begun to understand just how little she knew of the world of the Cassatans.

There was simply too much for her to take in: huge rooms, most of them larger than her

35

entire cottage, richly carved and polished furniture of a style far grander than anything she'd ever seen, thick, jewel-tone rugs in strange patterns, walls covered with patterned paper, long windows set with glass so clear that she at first thought nothing was there.

She looked down at the soft blue dressing gown her aunt had given her, fingering its smooth, delicate fabric and thinking about the wardrobe upstairs filled with similarly luxurious and strange clothing.

She was seated in a many-windowed room Paulena called a "conservatory." It was filled with strange plants in huge pots, some of them taller than she was.

But wondrous as all this was, it was the scene beyond the long windows that had captured and held her attention. The house, Paulena had explained, was perched on a cliff on a narrow strip of land that jutted out into the sea—and it was the sea that so fascinated her.

A seemingly endless stretch of blue-gray water rose and fell in a steady rhythm, crashing against the rocks far below the house. The sound was the first thing she'd heard when she'd awakened, and it continued to delight her.

She'd heard of the sea, of course, but she knew now that she'd never understood its vastness, and neither had she known of its restless movements. She'd always assumed that it must simply be a larger version of the lake at home where they all swam in the summer.

She wanted very much to go out there, to see it more closely. But she was so weak—and still dizzy as well. Paulena had said that she must be patient and it would go away in a few days. For once, it wasn't all that difficult for her to be patient because she felt so lethargic, so drained of all her normal energy.

She sipped fragrant tea from a delicate cup and nibbled at some delicious pastries that had been brought to her by a young girl. The girl's appearance had startled her, since she hadn't realized that anyone else was here. Now she began to wonder if the girl could possibly be a slave. She knew that the Cassatans often enslaved the people they conquered; they'd intended to do just that to her people. But surely her aunt wouldn't countenance such a thing—not even to fit herself into their accursed world!

She set down the teacup and got up slowly, then made her way just as slowly to the windows. Far below her, waves crashed upon the dark rocks, sending plumes of spray high into the air. The spray reminded her of the mists and she shivered involuntarily from the memory.

"Oh, dear, are you cold? Let me have Maddie build up the fire."

Rowena turned at the sound of her aunt's voice, then had to brace herself against a table as the sudden movement brought on another dizzy spell. Paulena was at her side quickly to help her back to her chair. Then she pulled a long cord that was half-hidden behind the draperies. Almost immediately, the same young girl appeared.

"Maddie, please build up the fire. My niece is chilled."

Rowena watched as the girl did her aunt's bidding, then left. "Is . . . is she a *slave?*"

Paulena laughed. "No, of course not. She's a paid servant. She lives in a cottage on the property with her family. They take care of the house. There are no slaves here, Rowena."

"There aren't?" Rowena frowned. "But . . ."

Paulena waved a bejeweled hand impatiently. "Yes, I know what you've been told—but it isn't true." Her expression became grim. "I'm afraid that you've been told many things that are not true."

"What do you mean?" Rowena asked, confused.

"This world is not what you were taught it is. Some things I will explain to you when you're feeling better. Other things you must judge for yourself in time."

"Do you mean that we've been lied to?" Rowena asked, thinking about how her mother had distrusted the Council.

"Yes," Paulena stated succinctly. "The Council would prefer that we believe nothing has changed here. Normally, they make some effort to correct that before one descends, though their version of the truth even then leaves much to be desired.

"However, in your case, they were so eager to

get you here that they failed to prepare you— and perhaps for good reason."

Rowena wasn't at all sure what her aunt meant by that, but she let it go for now. The truth was that she wasn't yet ready to face up to her mission here. So instead, she turned her attention to the house.

"Does everyone live like this here?" she asked curiously, scarcely able to believe it.

"No—and this home is modest by comparison with our home in the city."

"*Our* home, you said. Do you share it with other Descenders?"

"No, I meant my husband and me. He's a very wealthy man."

"You've married again? Oh, Polly, I'm so happy for you! Who is he?"

"You don't know him, dear. He's not one of us."

"Not one of us?" Rowena echoed in shock. "You mean that you've married one of *them*— a Cassatan?"

Paulena got up from her chair and came over to take Rowena's hands in hers. "Please don't use that term again, Rowena. It doesn't exist here. And yes, I'm married to one of them."

Rowena started to say how terrible it was that her aunt should be forced to do such a thing. But she stopped herself at the last possible moment as it occurred to her that Paulena didn't seem at all unhappy. Still, she surely couldn't have *chosen* to marry a barbarian. It had to be part of a plan.

"As I said, there is much you need to learn. We will stay here until you're feeling well again. My husband is in the city. He's quite accustomed to my spending time here, and he knows that my long-lost niece will be joining me."

Lost. Rowena thought that there was much truth in her aunt's words. She *was* lost—in more ways than one. She didn't understand anything—and worst of all, she feared that the answers Paulena was promising her would not be at all to her liking.

Chapter Two

"Our people continue to live very much as we did five hundred years ago, Rowena—while here, many things have changed. When I descended, I felt as though I'd traveled through time itself."

Rowena nodded. She couldn't deny the truth of Polly's words. In the past four days, she'd seen so many wonders—and heard about even more.

Hot water came from taps. Heat was provided by things called radiators, which Paulena explained were filled with steam piped in from something in the basement called a boiler. The lamps here were oil lamps like those at home—though much more elegant—but Polly said that in her city home, there were gaslights—gas being something else that came through pipes.

The sheer volume and variety of clothing was also quite overwhelming. When she'd protested that her aunt had provided her with far too much,

41

Paulena had laughed and said that it was only the beginning, and she would need much more in the city.

Even the food was overabundant in its variety, though again her aunt had said that meals were much simpler here than they would be when they returned to the city.

And according to Paulena, there were still more wonders that were being invented every day. Something she called electricity, which Paulena herself didn't understand, would soon be transforming this world yet again. And her husband and his friends were talking about conveyances that moved themselves and even messages that traveled through the air, though not by means of the telepathy some of the Dazhinn used.

Rowena was fascinated but very uneasy about all this. It seemed to her that the Cassatans had found magic of their own, even though, according to her aunt, they called it "science."

"I can see that many things have changed," she told Paulena now, choosing her words with care. "But I can't believe that Cass—that the people could have changed so much. After all, if they'd changed, we wouldn't be sending *our* people here."

Paulena said nothing, and Rowena realized that they had yet to talk of her mission. "You do know why I've been sent?" she asked.

Her aunt nodded and her expression gave nothing away. "Zachary MacTavesh is my husband's closest friend and a frequent guest in our homes—both here and in the city."

Rowena thought that Paulena was maintaining a very careful neutrality, and she felt that uneasiness stir a bit more. She wondered how Polly could possibly stand to be in the company of one of their ancient enemies, but something held her back. There was much about Paulena she didn't understand—not the least of which were the occasional references to her husband that seemed to be almost affectionate.

So instead, she plied her aunt with more questions about how the Cassatans lived. Paulena had already told her that there was much she would need to learn before she could mingle freely with them without drawing unwelcome attention to herself.

Paulena sighed. "The most important thing you must learn will surely be the most difficult—especially for you, since you're so very independent and strong-willed, much like your mother and grandmother, I might add.

"Life here is very difficult for our women. This world is dominated by men. The only way that we women who've descended have been able to serve our people is to marry powerful men and then use our spells to affect their decisions."

Rowena stared at her in shock and horror. But at least now she understood why Paulena had married one of them. Obviously, she'd been badly mistaken to believe that her aunt was happy in her marriage.

"Women cannot own property and they cannot divorce their husbands, no matter how cruel they might be. Husbands, on the other hand, can and do divorce their wives—and the children remain with them if they want them. Many, if not most, men have mistresses as well, though no woman could ever take a lover openly.

"What I'm speaking of is, of course, the upper classes: the nobility like my husband, the Warriors, and the wealthy merchant class. But the laws apply to all.

"There is an elected parliament, similar to our Council but very much larger. Of course they are all male and women are not even permitted to vote." She had recited all this without emotion, but now she gave Rowena a defiant look.

"Some of us are working very hard to change that now.

"The king still has great power, but he is a weak, silly man who sits on the throne only because he was born to it. There is great concern because he has three daughters and no sons and only a male can rule."

Rowena could contain herself no longer. "And you say that things have *changed*? It seems to me that if they have, they have only gotten worse. You told me that slavery does not exist here— but what else would you call it when women are forced to live like this? And why do they accept it?"

"I have asked myself that question many times, dear—but I have no answer. They have always lived this way. In fact, one of the reasons our people were so reviled by them is that we have always treated men and women equally. They believe that to be unnatural, and as you will soon see for yourself, most women accept it as well. It's a very strange society." She paused and regarded Rowena thoughtfully.

"You're very beautiful and beauty often allows a woman to speak her mind more freely. Women are not prized here for their intelligence or their abilities, but rather for their beauty alone. Still, you must learn to defer to men and hold your tongue."

"I will do no such thing!" Rowena stated hotly. Her hatred for the accursed barbarians had grown even greater.

"Then despite what the astrologers say, your mission may well fail. Your spells will not work on a Warrior. They alone have always been immune to our enchantments. Throughout our long history, the reason we were able to defeat them—or at least to hold them off—was that the spells *did* work against the men under their command."

Once again, the subject of Zachary MacTavesh had been broached, but as before, Rowena declined to pursue it. She knew that she could not avoid the Warrior much longer, but at the moment, she was far more interested in this enslavement of women. She asked her aunt what she'd meant when she said that there were some who were working to change things.

Paulena told her about what she called a "suffrage movement" that was pressuring men to grant women the right to vote. They believed that this was the necessary first step to improving the general lot of women here.

"Those who oppose it understand that it's only a first step." Paulena smiled. "They say that if we gain the right to vote, we will never cease our demands—and they are right, of course. But we will still win in the end."

Several more days passed as Paulena taught Rowena what she must know before they went to the city. She explained that Rowena would be excused any small mistakes because she was supposed to have come from a backward rural area far from the city.

So they spent many hours playacting polite social conversation, with Paulena showing her how to be a "proper lady"—small dramas that invariably ended with Rowena feeling frustrated and angry at such shallowness.

But repugnant as all of this was, by far the worst were the hideous undergarments Paulena told her she must wear—especially a horrible device called a corset that was laced so tightly she could barely breathe.

"Why must I wear it?" she demanded. "And why should I wear dresses that leave me half-naked? This makes no sense, Polly! First you say that ladies must be demure—and then you put me into a dress that no woman in our world would ever wear!"

Paulena laughed. "I know it sounds strange, but you forget how it is here. Women dress to attract men, and men like low-cut dresses and tiny waists."

"And do they also like it when women faint because they cannot breathe properly?" Rowena demanded.

"Actually, they do. Some women 'swoon' regularly. Remember what I said: it's very fashionable to be delicate and empty-headed."

Rowena sank onto the sand in the shelter of two huge rocks. She'd walked too far along the shore, and now that accursed weakness was back again. Paulena had told her that most Descenders got over it within a few days, but she'd been here a week and she was still being plagued by spells of dizziness and weakness. It was made all the worse by the fact that she'd never known a day's sickness in her life, save for the occasional sniffles that everyone experienced.

She wanted to go home. She wanted this to be over, even though it had not yet actually begun. She would not allow herself to think that she might not be able to go home because the thought of being forced to spend the rest of her life in this horrible world was not to be borne.

Neither she nor Paulena had mentioned her mission again, and she was still loath to bring it up because she no longer believed she could possibly succeed—astrologers or no astrologers.

She wondered if her aunt could be deliberately avoiding the subject as well. Despite the fact that Paulena must have married her husband to accomplish her own mission, Rowena had yet to see any evidence that she was unhappy with him. And the Warrior, MacTavesh, was his best friend.

Rowena was deeply worried about her aunt. She had no experience at meeting people again after so many years and therefore didn't really know if someone could change—become a stranger with a familiar face. She knew she could trust Polly, but she was still very concerned.

Polly had said this morning that they must return to the city soon, even if Rowena wasn't quite ready to be "presented to society," as she put it. She had obligations there, and while her husband was quite tolerant of her absences, knowing how much she enjoyed coming here, his patience would soon wear thin.

I don't want to leave here, Rowena thought—except to go home. She'd grown to love the sea with its wonderful smells and sounds. There was even a large sailboat tied up at the dock. They had small sailboats at home and Rowena had often sailed on the lake, but this one was too large for her to sail alone. Besides, Paulena told her that women did not sail and the boat could be taken out only when her husband was here.

This business of things that men could do and women could not do vexed her greatly. At home, people did as they pleased. Naturally, there were some things that required a man's greater strength, but many women compensated for their lesser strength by using magic.

She sighed, staring out from her shelter at the restless sea. She supposed that if Polly knew she'd come down here and put on her own clothes, she'd be upset. She was trying so hard to turn Rowena into a "proper lady" by insisting that she behave in that absurd manner even here. But the thought of being forced to wear those tight, constricting, indecent garments had sent her rummaging through her wardrobe for the loose, comfortable shirt and trousers she'd worn here.

She knew she should get up and start back to the house, but she was so tired and it was so very peaceful here. And in any event, the moment she got back, she would have to play her new role again. Polly would insist that she dress for dinner, even though there were only the two of them. And then she would want her to practice her "social conversation," which was nothing more than simpering silliness.

Even as she thought unhappily about what lay in store for her, Rowena drifted off to sleep and dreamed of her little cottage and her enchanted home—now jeopardized by Zachary MacTavesh.

Zach stood at the edge of the precipice behind the house and breathed deeply of the salt air. He was grateful to his old friend Duncan for inviting him here so often, although he suspected that Duncan had an ulterior motive this time.

Paulena had been here for a week, and though Zach knew Duncan would never admit it to him, he was sure Duncan had suggested the trip because he couldn't stand being separated from her any longer. Even after 12 years of marriage, the man was still besotted. No doubt he was in there now, telling Paulena that the visit was Zach's idea.

Zach smiled and shook his head. *You think you know everything there is to know about someone, and then you find out how wrong you are.*

During his first marriage, Duncan had behaved like most other men, maintaining a civil relationship with his wife, while picking up and discarding mistresses on a regular basis. Then Paulena had walked into his life barely two months after Marya's death—and they'd been married a scandalous month later. Furthermore, Zach was certain that Duncan had remained faithful to her all these years.

He liked Paulena well enough, he supposed, but something about her had always made him slightly uncomfortable. He guessed it was probably because of the hold she had over his old friend, but sometimes he was convinced that there was more to it than that.

He stared down at the boat as it bobbed gently alongside the pier. If the weather held, they could take it out tomorrow. He needed some peace of mind right now, and he could think of no better place to find it than out there on the sea.

He turned away from the cliff's edge and started down the steep path that led to the rocky shore, his mind on his many problems of the moment, despite his attempts to set them aside for now.

Forces were gathering against him and his plans, and while he was confident that he would prevail in the end, he was annoyed that he had to deal with them.

People seemed to have grown too soft in recent years. They'd forgotten the proud traditions that had made them supreme in the world. That was the only explanation he could come up with for their willingness to put up with the outrages their neighbors were perpetrating on them. The damned diplomats with their soothing words and their womanlike meekness were gaining too much credibility. They were convincing too many people that war wasn't the solution to their problems, and by so doing were only delaying the inevitable and allowing the enemy to build up its own forces.

Power not exercised, he'd said often, is weakness. And right now, his beloved country was looking very weak indeed. Not only would it encourage their current enemy, but it also gave hope to potential enemies elsewhere.

Sometimes Zach wasn't even sure about Duncan's position in this matter. Duncan would support him, of course, but the fact that Zach was even questioning his support had to be the result of Paulena's pillow talk. Lately, Duncan had even begun to make the case for letting women vote— Paulena's latest cause.

Zach wasn't opposed to reforms in the property laws and the divorce laws; he'd even told Paulena that. But if women ever got the right to vote, an already bad situation would become even worse—especially with the growing strength of the parliament.

A few years ago, Zach had lent his powerful support to the new laws that gave Parliament a stronger voice—but he'd counted on the right sort of men getting elected. And now he wasn't so sure about that. Too many of them were already weak, and if women got the right to vote and they had to be accountable to them as well . . .

He continued along the shore, now well out of sight of the house. His shoulder began to ache a bit. The wound had completely healed, but the dampness here must be aggravating it. And that got him to thinking about those two attempts on his life.

Everyone else seemed certain that they were two isolated incidents, not at all related and undoubtedly the work of two madmen—but Zach himself wasn't so sure.

The first one—the one who'd managed to wound him—had never been caught. The second one Zach had wounded and then captured himself. The man was dying when he questioned him, and all he'd gotten out of him was some nonsense about "defenders" and a valley, which meant nothing to anyone.

Still, the incidents nagged at him. Despite what his men had said about the would-be assassins being madmen, the facts they had on the second one just didn't bear that out.

The man he'd shot had been working for nearly two years for a family Zach knew well and trusted. They'd never seen any sign of madness in him and had, in fact, quite liked him. But they knew nothing at all about his background and Zach's men had been unable to find out anything, either. What little the dead man had said to others about his past had proved to be untrue.

So Zach was left with an uneasiness that wouldn't go away. He'd never talked to anyone—not even Duncan—about the feelings he'd gotten about things from time to time throughout his life. But he'd always been right—and once, such a feeling had saved his life and the lives of the men under his command.

There were stories, passed down from father to son, about such feelings. They'd always happened from time to time among the fierce Warrior clans who traced their origins back to the dawn of time. Once they'd been accepted, but now, in this more enlightened age, they seemed suspect.

Zach had had one of those feelings after the second assassination attempt—but not before, when he might have expected it. The problem this time was that the feeling was very vague: no more than a sense that something was about to happen.

In any event, he thought as he continued his stroll along the shore, he'd taken all the steps necessary to guarantee that there'd be no third attempt on his life, even if doing so had made him a virtual prisoner much of the time.

He walked around a huge boulder, one of many strewn along this rugged coastline—and stopped in his tracks. A girl lay curled up in the shelter of the boulders—either sound asleep or dead!

No, not a girl—clearly a woman. He amended his thoughts as he noted the womanly curves just barely visible beneath her loose, coarse clothing. And not dead, either, he realized a moment later. He could see the faint rise and fall of her breathing.

Zach stood there, frozen in a strange sort of confusion, unable to take his eyes off her, but unwilling to approach her, either. Maybe it was the odd intimacy of the scene—the way she slept curled up, with her pale golden hair unbound and falling across her face. Women never let their hair down like that, except in the privacy of their boudoirs. And neither did any of the women he knew dress like a poor farmboy.

By now, his initial confusion was edging closer to something very familiar indeed. The hot fires of lust were surging through him, shocking him with their intensity. In fact, he had to struggle against it, to put from his mind the image of her naked in his arms, her golden hair spilling all around them.

Who was she? There were no other houses for miles, and she couldn't be a servant at Duncan's home. He knew them all well.

Suddenly, he recalled that Paulena had a niece here—but hadn't she said that the girl was resting, recuperating from some illness? A long-lost niece who had recently contacted her and come to visit from some godforsaken corner of the country.

This has to be her, he decided, glad to be able to force away his untoward thoughts. But what was she doing out here—too far from the house for someone supposedly recovering from an illness?

Then it occurred to him that she might not have simply fallen asleep, but instead could have fallen ill again. The sun was gone behind the hills now, and the breeze off the water was cool—far too cool for the light clothing she wore.

Still, he approached her cautiously, without quite understanding why he felt the need for caution. And when he was less than six feet from her, she began to stir. He stopped, and for one incredible moment, he had a nearly overwhelming urge to turn and flee from her.

She shuddered lightly, then raised a delicate hand to brush the spun gold from her eyes. A heartbeat later, he was staring into a pair of green eyes so brilliant that he could almost feel himself falling into them.

A sharp jolt of awareness shot through him, and with it a return of that heat, but he managed to conceal it as he met her stare.

"Hello. I'm sorry if I frightened you, but I didn't expect to find you here, either."

Several strange seconds passed between the moment when Rowena first opened her eyes, caught on the very edge of some momentous but unremembered dream, and the moment when her gaze became focused enough to make out the figure of a man.

He was very tall and broad-shouldered with streaks of gray through his black hair—shorter hair than she was accustomed to seeing on men and slightly curled as it swept back from a harsh, aquiline face with a very square jaw and a deeply cleft chin. His very pale eyes pierced her as he spoke, and she felt that gaze deep within her.

Altogether, he presented a figure that, despite his soft, slightly husky voice, bespoke power and authority—and she knew even before he identified himself who he must be.

"I'm Zachary MacTavesh, and I assume that you must be Paulena's niece, although she seemed to believe you were resting upstairs."

The Warrior, she thought with all the ancient hatreds that name implied: the man I must kill. And yet, overlaying that hatred was a fascination. An ancient legend had sprung to life before her very eyes—and before his as well, she thought with satisfaction, even if he didn't yet know it. Or perhaps he did know it at some hidden level. Despite his polite words, he seemed uneasy somehow.

Through her mind whispered the tales of ancient battles, where Dazhinn magic had clashed with Warrior power. The Warrior clans had lived in the high mountains surrounding her people's beloved valley, and time and time again throughout history, they'd tried to conquer and enslave her people.

She shivered—not from the chill, but from her memories—and then he was suddenly removing his jacket, a dark blue woolen thing with brass buttons.

"You're cold," he said, his voice more normal now—a voice that brooked no dissent. "Allow me to offer you this. Are you feeling all right? Your aunt said that you've been ill. You *are* Paulena's niece, aren't you?"

"Yes," she replied as she started to get to her feet. "I'm Rowena Sandor, and I'm fine, thank you. I merely fell asleep."

She was determined to show no weakness to this man, but as soon as she stood, she was overcome with dizziness and would certainly have fallen if he hadn't moved quickly to grasp her arms.

"Steady there," he said in a voice that was trying for gentleness but not really succeeding. The huskiness was back in his voice and she thought that he seemed reluctant to touch her.

She felt the heat and strength of him through her light shirt and wanted to pull away, but the dizziness persisted for another long moment. Their eyes met again and time seemed to spin out forever—all the way back to dark, jagged mountains and a mist-filled valley. Then, just when she saw something else glitter in the depths of his dark eyes, he abruptly let her go.

"Can you walk back to the house, or shall I carry you?" he asked in a voice that had again retreated into polite formality.

"I'm fine now," she told him, grateful that the dizziness had passed.

He placed the jacket carefully around her shoulders, his movements suggesting that he was afraid to touch her again. She began to walk beside him back along the shore, wondering how he had come to be here. Polly couldn't have been expecting him. They hadn't even discussed him yet.

"Will you be visiting your aunt long?" he inquired, his tone that of an adult speaking to a child.

"I'm not sure," she replied. "Perhaps for a few months."

"I see. And where are you from?"

She named a distant part of the country, grateful that at least she and Paulena had worked out her story.

"Ahh," he said, nodding. "Perhaps that explains your accent, then. I couldn't quite place it."

She was annoyed, since she'd been working very hard to match her speech to Polly's. But at least he didn't seem suspicious about it. She knew she had to be extremely careful not to arouse any suspicion at all on his part, because she was already certain that her presence had had an effect upon him.

"I believe my aunt has mentioned you," she told him in an attempt to deflect any further questions about herself. "You are a friend of her husband's and the commander of the army."

"Yes, that's correct. You must find this very different from your home—and you have yet to see the city, I assume?"

"No, I haven't seen it yet, but I'm looking forward to it."

"And no doubt the city will be looking forward to seeing you as well, Miss Sandor."

She gave him a sharp look that seemed to confuse him. Then she realized that this was merely part of the silly games men and women played here, and that she was expected to blush or make some inane remark. She did neither.

There was an unreality to all this. Here they were, ancient enemies, walking along the shore and pretending to be what neither of them was. He was no more the fine gentleman than she was a proper lady, and she had a nearly overwhelming urge to show him just who and what she was. Her talents weren't as great as some—except, of course, when it came to her tapestries—but like all her people, she possessed some abilities.

Would he believe it even if he saw it with his own eyes? she wondered. In the few conversations she'd had with Paulena on the subject, she'd learned that the barbarians no longer believed that the Dazhinn had possessed magic, if indeed they'd existed at all.

But we do exist, she thought, and you will learn that, Warrior.

They had reached the steep path that led up to the house, and as she stepped from the hard-packed sand along the shore to the softer sand near the path, Rowena stumbled. Immediately, his arm shot out to encircle her waist. She flinched at the sudden contact with the rock-hardness of his arm and the firm pressure of his hand. He let her go quickly, then gestured to the path.

"Will you be able to climb the path?"

"Yes," she said, hoping it was true.

"It seems to me, Miss Sandor, that it wasn't very wise for you to be out here alone, given the fact that you don't know this place and you've been ill."

She had already started up the path, but his words and his tone stopped her and she turned to face him. "I'm not a child—and I've been out here before."

Then she turned abruptly and resumed her climb up the path—but not before she saw the astounded look on his face. It was a look she sincerely hoped she would see again.

Perhaps, she thought, I can make him really dislike me. Then I can go home and let the Council figure out some other way to deal with him.

The climb was very tiring, but she kept putting one foot before the other, determined not to need his help again. About halfway up, the path made a sharp turn, and she paused there to catch her breath, cursing the weakness that made her feel like an old woman.

She had been conscious every moment of his presence behind her, and she hoped now that he would continue on his way. But he stopped, too, and they stood there side by side, both of them staring at the wild beauty of the scene below them.

"I like it here," he said in a gentler tone. "This is a very peaceful place."

She turned to him sharply. "Peaceful?"

"Yes. Don't you think so?"

"Yes, I do—but why would a Warrior like a peaceful place?" The words were out before she could stop them: the first in what she feared might be a long line of mistakes.

Those strange, colorless eyes bored into her. "Do you think, then, that a Warrior can be happy only in battle?"

"Of course. What other reason is there for Warriors?"

If he took offense, he didn't show it. "The true reason for a strong army is to *prevent* war, not to fight it," he said, once again adopting that paternal tone.

"I find that very difficult to believe, Commander MacTavesh," she replied as she resumed her walk up the path. "Your history would argue otherwise."

"You're very outspoken," he observed mildly.

"So Polly tells me. But I am who I am, and I have no intention of changing to suit the fashion of the times."

"I see. So Paulena has been trying to mold you into a proper lady?" he asked, the amusement plain in his voice as he followed her up the path.

"Yes—and with very little success, as you can see," she replied.

He chuckled, a deep and surprisingly pleasant sound that seemed to vibrate through her. She was greatly relieved to see her aunt appear at the edge of the terrace behind the house, just as they reached the top of the cliff. And with her was her husband. Rowena refused to think of him as being her uncle, even though she knew she would be forced to address him as such.

He was a tall, rather thin man: nearly as tall as Zachary MacTavesh, but far less powerful in appearance. His dark hair was thinning on top and he had a lean but attractive face, one that was wreathed in a welcoming smile at the moment as he stood with one arm possessively around Paulena's waist.

"Rowena! I thought you were resting!" her aunt gasped in astonishment.

"She was," Zachary MacTavesh said with another chuckle. "But it seems she prefers the beach to a bed."

"Oh, dear. Are you all right?" Paulena peered at her closely and managed at the same time to convey her concern about the men's presence.

"I'm fine—perhaps just a bit tired. I walked too far."

Paulena introduced her to her "uncle," who greeted her with what seemed like genuine warmth. "Welcome to Cliff House, Rowena," he said. "Polly tells me that you're quite taken with the place—as she herself is."

"Thank you. It's very beautiful here. I'd never seen the sea before."

Duncan smiled at her, then turned to the sea and breathed deeply. "It's the smell, you know. When I'm in the city too long, I think of Cliff House, and it's always the smell I imagine. Polly says she does, too." He glanced toward his wife with affection, then turned back to Rowena.

"But you will like the city as well, I think," he told her. "So much to do." His eyes twinkled mischievously.

"Has Polly recruited you yet for her latest crusade—the suffrage movement?"

Rowena exchanged a quick glance with her aunt. "We've discussed it."

"And you don't agree with her?" He frowned.

"Oh yes, of course I do. How could I not agree?"

"Strangely enough, there are some women who don't agree," Duncan replied.

"And many men—probably most men," Rowena stated, not bothering to hide her contempt.

"That is true enough—including one who is present among us at the moment," Duncan said, turning to the silent Warrior with an arched brow. "Perhaps *you* can persuade him, Rowena."

"Since he's a Warrior, that's rather unlikely," she replied acerbically.

"Oh ho! I see she has your measure already, Zach." Duncan smiled at her. "Zach and I have been friends since childhood, and I have yet to change his mind about anything, although I confess that the opposite has not been true."

Rowena joined in the general laughter, but she was beginning to understand—and to have sympathy for—her aunt's difficulties. Duncan Wengor was the battleground upon which the war between Paulena and Zach must be playing itself out.

And she discovered that she had sympathy for Duncan as well, despite the fact that he was a Cassatan. Torn between loyalty to his oldest friend and the gentle spells cast upon him by his wife, his life must be difficult indeed.

Chapter Three

"I had no idea that they were coming here," Paulena told her the moment she came into Rowena's room. "Duncan found it necessary to say that the visit was Zach's idea, but it was his own."

"Then why didn't he say that?" Rowena asked curiously.

Paulena sighed. "Because Duncan is uncomfortable with his feelings for me. Men here are like that, Rowena. Feelings are the province of women, while action is the province of men. Now tell me what happened down there on the beach."

Rowena shrugged. "Nothing happened. I fell asleep and he found me."

"Something more happened. He hasn't taken his eyes off you. But if Duncan isn't always comfortable with his feelings, Zach is even less so.

"As Duncan told you, they have been best

friends since childhood. Duncan, too, is descended from the old Warrior clans, but on his mother's side. Zach, on the other hand, comes from an unbroken string of Warriors on both sides. In fact, he's a direct descendant of one of the leaders of the army that forced us from the valley."

All the more reason to hate him, Rowena thought. "He thinks of me as a child," she stated angrily.

"No doubt he does," Paulena nodded. "After all, there are fifteen years between you. He is a widower. His wife and sons were killed about a year ago in a tragic carriage accident. She was the only child of a very wealthy merchant. It was a marriage of convenience and nothing more— at least on his part. I do believe that she loved him. But what she wanted most was acceptance, and for members of the mercantile class, that means marrying either a member of the nobility or a Warrior."

Rowena found such things nearly impossible to comprehend. "But why was it a marriage of convenience for *him?*"

"Because although his family has an ancient and highly respected name, they haven't much money. Neither, for that matter, do many of the nobility. So it has become increasingly common for daughters of wealthy merchants and bankers to marry into those classes.

"And in Zach's case, I think it was also simply a matter of having a wife—and of course carrying on his name. Zach is a highly complex man,

Rowena—far more complicated than Duncan. Like others of the Warrior clans, he has a very strong sense of history and tradition and great patriotism. But unlike most of them, he also sees the need for change."

"It didn't sound that way to me."

"The suffrage movement, you mean?" Paulena smiled. "I think he is badly torn on that one. His strong sense of fairness dictates that he should support it, but he fears that allowing women to vote will weaken his causes in Parliament because women would be far less likely to support war.

"He did support other changes, though: the recently enacted laws to strengthen Parliament, for example. And he has spoken out on behalf of changing the divorce and property laws—much to the chagrin of his fellow Warriors.

"He is very determined to take us into war against the Atanians and their allies, the Gavese."

"The three who united against *us*," Rowena said disgustedly.

"Exactly. And since Zach, to all intents and purposes, is the *real* ruler, he will almost certainly get his way. He's very shrewd and knows just how to play both the king and the parliament. In fact, I wouldn't be surprised if he decided to provoke an incident that could be blamed upon the Atanians, just to guarantee war. He may even have had a hand in the border incidents that have already happened."

"Just because he wants war," she said with a grimace.

"No, because he believes they are planning to go to war in the future anyway, and he would rather it came now, before their forces pose a real threat."

"It sounds as though you support him in this." Rowena frowned.

"I understand his thinking, but how could I support him, when it poses such danger to our people?"

Paulena was silent for a moment and Rowena caught, quite without conscious intent, her thoughts about this quandary. Then she knew she was right. Paulena's loyalties no longer lay exclusively with her own people. She was greatly saddened by this sudden knowledge, but knew that she must not let herself forget it.

"I have had my doubts about the wisdom of sending you here," Paulena confessed quietly, "regardless of the astrologers' predictions. They don't know Zach—and I do. If there was ever a man who could resist his fate, it's him."

Rowena could not mistake the admiration in her aunt's voice. "You like him, don't you?"

Paulena nodded. "Yes, I do. He's a fascinating man, and I am not the only one among our people who knows him who feels that way. The Warriors are our oldest enemy, going back to the earliest times, and perhaps that's the reason. Haven't you felt that?"

"What I feel for him is contempt," Rowena stated with more firmness than she felt at the moment.

Paulena sighed. "Well, under the circumstances, that's for the best. But I must warn you, dear, that I am not convinced that the astrologers told you the full truth."

"What do you mean?"

"If you recall, I, too, once studied the stars, although I never achieved the proficiency to become a full-fledged astrologer. And the conjunction they spoke of regarding you and Zach cannot be entirely one-way. If you have the power to change the course of his life, he has that same power to change yours."

Rowena stared at her, aghast. Then into her mind came her cousin's prediction: that she would return, but she would be different. Could that be what she'd meant?

Polly left, after reminding her to change into something suitable for dinner, but Rowena stood there, lost in thought. Had the astrologers lied to her—or to put it more charitably, failed to tell her the whole truth? And if Polly was right, wasn't she placing herself in great danger?

Nonsense, she told herself. I've met him and I feel nothing for him. How could I? He's a Warrior—and it was one of his very own ancestors who drove us from this world.

And yet, as she summoned the maid and allowed herself to be laced into the hated corset, she kept thinking about Polly's statement. It seemed to have struck at a deep truth: the unholy attraction of ancient enemies.

"How very lovely you look, my dear," Duncan said, rising as she entered the smaller of the two parlors. "Polly will have every eligible young man in the city camped out on our doorstep—not to mention a few ineligible ones."

Rowena laughed—and for once, the laughter was genuine. Despite her attempts to remind herself that Duncan, too, was one of the enemy, she truly liked this man. And it was also not lost upon her that his words could merely amuse her, while the same words spoken by Zachary MacTavesh irritated her.

As for the commander, he said nothing—but his eyes spoke very eloquently. As Paulena had said, they rarely left her as the four of them sat down to a sumptuous dinner by candlelight at a table that glittered with crystal and silver.

Rowena was proud of her playacting, and several covert glances at her aunt confirmed that she, too, was proud. It wasn't all that difficult, since she'd often acted in various pageants and theater productions at home. She had only to convince herself that this was a stage set and the others were actors as well.

The conversation consisted largely of the various goings-on in the city, with either Paulena or Duncan carefully explaining backgrounds to her. She was intrigued despite herself. The foolishness these people were capable of apparently knew no bounds. At home, such complicated machinations were impossible, given the fact that everyone knew everyone else so well.

"Felice has wangled an invitation to my dinner for her niece, Zach," Paulena said after talking about an upcoming party. "And she inquired first if you were to be present."

The silent member of their group shifted his gaze from Rowena, who welcomed the move, to Paulena. "Then I might find it necessary to excuse myself at the last moment."

"Come now, Zach." Duncan laughed. "She's a very attractive young woman."

"That's true enough," he replied. "But between her charming ears lies nothing but empty space."

Rowena watched this exchange with interest, then could not resist asking what she knew was a very improper question. "But I understood that men prefer such women?"

The commander's pale gaze bored into her. "Some do," he stated succinctly before changing the subject.

After dinner, the men adjourned to Duncan's study and Rowena was left alone with her aunt. Paulena beamed at her.

"You did very well. I've no doubt that you're ready to come to the city."

"Was his wife an intelligent woman?" Rowena asked.

"Not particularly—but his mistresses have been. Or at least the ones I know. Several of them are active in the movement."

"How many does he have?" Rowena asked, appalled.

"Oh, only one at a time, as far as I know. And perhaps none at present, though not for a lack of candidates. Duncan said once that women are only of limited interest to Zach, and I think he's right. He says it's usually that way for men who wield great power and intend to keep it. But of course, that's what makes him so attractive to women."

"I don't find him attractive at all," Rowena replied, pulling a face.

"Nor did I when I first met him, even though I found him quite fascinating from the beginning. I think it was just because he's so different from our own men."

That was certainly true, Rowena reflected. "He's too . . ."

"Too *male*," Paulena finished for her. "We are accustomed to smaller men and men who are gentler."

Rowena nodded. That was it exactly. From the moment she'd opened her eyes and found him standing before her, she'd felt overwhelmed by an awareness of the difference between them—the contrast between men and women. It was something she'd never really thought about before.

"He's quite taken with you," Paulena went on. "I'm sure that Duncan noticed it, too. What remains to be seen is what he'll do about it."

Then she leaned forward, her expression clouded with worry. "Have you truly thought about the danger you are in, Rowena? I know it's unlikely that he will discover your true identity, but if he should . . ." She stopped abruptly, then continued. "If he does suspect you, he will kill you as he killed Lothar."

A chill swept through Rowena. "Lothar is dead?"

Paulena nodded sadly. "He was the second one to attempt to assassinate Zach, and Zach killed him."

Rowena's anger surged forth. Lothar was a distant cousin and a favorite childhood playmate: a laughing, daring boy who'd been only 18 when he descended.

"One can't blame Zach, of course," Paulena went on. "After all, it was his life or Lothar's. Through Duncan, I helped to convince Zach that he was simply the victim of two random attempts by madmen, but that's why there is such fear among us now. If a third attempt fails, no one could convince Zach that there isn't some sort of conspiracy.

"I know through Duncan that he already investigated the background of Lothar and found it to be false. Of course, there is no chance at all that he could guess the truth, but we are still in a dangerous position now. Artur Benlow, the first to attempt to kill Zach, got away, but we've had to send him to one of the outer provinces permanently."

Paulena looked at her for a long moment, her expression unreadable. "I told you before that you must judge some of the changes here for yourself—and so you must. But there are other judgments you may be forced to make as well."

"What judgments?" Rowena asked. Something in her aunt's tone was very troubling.

"We will discuss that later, after you have acquainted yourself with the situation."

At that moment, the men rejoined them and

Rowena was left to puzzle over Polly's words. It was becoming increasingly clear to her that her aunt was troubled and perhaps divided in her loyalties. Not that she believed for one moment that Polly would betray her own people, but the nagging thought remained that she was troubled by something.

Duncan suggested a stroll along the path that followed the cliff's edge, and Paulena summoned a maid to get their cloaks. The night was cool and clear with a nearly full moon that cast a silvered glaze over the sea spray far below them.

The path was just barely wide enough for two people to walk side by side and Duncan took his wife's arm, tucking it through his crooked elbow. Rowena thought it a rather strange gesture, but when she was forced to walk beside Zachary MacTavesh, he offered his arm and she followed her aunt's lead.

It is these small things that may yet catch me out, she thought nervously, unless I am to be excused by being thought an ignorant peasant who could have no knowledge of such behavior. Paulena had already suggested that some mistakes might be excused thusly, but it rankled nevertheless.

Walking beside the tall Warrior, Rowena's thoughts naturally turned again to poor Lothar, who had been killed by this man. Polly had seemed to be able to excuse him for it, but she herself wasn't so forgiving. Except for Polly herself, no one who'd descended had left such a hole in her life.

Lothar had been such a dear friend throughout her life. He would never have become a lover, because, as they'd both agreed, their friendship went too deep for them ever to make that transition.

And this man, this Warrior now beside her, had killed him.

The foursome talked as they strolled along the cliff, and at one point Duncan made a reference to his friend's restricted life since the assassination attempts. Given her thoughts at that very moment, Rowena could not resist speaking up, even though she was very much aware of the possible dangers.

"Have there been attempts on your life, Commander?" she asked in an astonished tone.

He nodded. "Twice in the past three months."

"And were they caught?" she asked, noting the suddenly rigid posture of her aunt as she walked slightly ahead.

"One escaped and has never been found," he told her. "The other one I shot myself. But he died before I could get any sense out of him."

By now, Paulena had stopped and was giving Rowena a subtle look of warning, but she ignored it. She found Zachary MacTavesh's phrasing rather interesting. Did he mean that Lothar had in fact told him something? Paulena hadn't given her any indication that that had happened.

"So you learned nothing from him?"

"Nothing that made sense, in any event," he replied disgustedly. "He kept talking about 'defenders' and 'the valley,' but that was all."

Defenders, Rowena thought. Fortunately, he had misunderstood—and he'd obviously made no connection to *their* valley.

By now, the foursome had stopped on the path, and Duncan spoke up. "You know," he said musingly, "I've been thinking about that, Zach, and it occurs to me that he could have been referring to the Valley of the Dazhinn."

Rowena struggled to hide her surprise, but fortunately, the Commander had turned to his old friend. She dared not look at Polly now, and guessed that was why she'd tried to warn her. Duncan had probably mentioned his thoughts to her.

"What makes you think of that?" Zach asked Duncan.

Duncan shrugged. "I thought of it only because of your family's connection to Ashwara, I suppose. It's said that there are still those who carry the Dazhinn blood living in the hills there, and I recall hearing once that some of them still believe the valley to be under a spell." He turned to Rowena.

"I'm sure you must recall from your studies the legend of the Dazhinn, even though it's far removed from your own home. Commander MacTavesh is the direct descendant of the man who led the armies in the great battle there—or perhaps I should say the battle that never happened, if one is to believe the old tales."

"Yes, of course." Rowena nodded. "Do you not believe those tales, then, Uncle Duncan?"

He chuckled. "I believe nothing that my senses

cannot confirm. There were many legends from that time—each of them more outrageous than the last, though I daresay the legend of the Dazhinn and their magic is the most outrageous of all.

"When we were students at Ashwara, Zach and I, together with some friends, spent a night in the valley. It was and is a ritual for new students."

Rowena glanced at Zachary MacTavesh curiously. No Warrior could have gone into that valley without sensing *something*. He was smiling at Duncan's reminiscences, but when their eyes met briefly, she saw something flicker there and she knew that whatever he might have said to Duncan and the others, he *had* felt something in their valley.

"If the Dazhinn possessed no magic, then what do you think happened in that battle, Commander?" she inquired.

"I think it likely that the Dazhinn simply fled into the hills under cover of fog. They were clearly outnumbered."

Once again, Rowena ignored the subtle warning from Paulena and persisted. "But what about the stories that even their homes vanished?"

"They didn't vanish," he stated succinctly. "The fog may have persisted for days or even weeks, as it frequently does in that valley. In all likelihood, the men sent down there simply couldn't find the village."

Rowena nodded. "Yes, I can see how that might

have happened, but then wouldn't it have been found later?"

"The Dazhinn undoubtedly returned under cover of those mists and destroyed every evidence of their existence there. It would not have been so difficult to do. Their homes were supposed to have been constructed of uncut stone with thatched roofs, and there are piles of such stones all over the valley to this day."

Duncan spoke up. "You must remember, my dear, that this was nearly five hundred years ago and there were few written records then. Everything was simply passed down from father to son, with considerable embellishment along the way."

Zach was frowning thoughtfully. "You know, Duncan, it occurs to me that the dead assassin might very well have come from that region. It hadn't really occurred to me before that anyone might still feel that way about the Valley of the Dazhinn. I will have someone look into it."

Duncan nodded. "Your plans might well have aroused such feelings."

"What plans are those?" Rowena asked innocently.

"War plans, my dear," Duncan told her. "Nothing you need to trouble your pretty head about."

Rowena felt her anger rising dangerously, but this time she did heed her aunt's silent warning. She might have walked along the very edge of danger, but she knew when to draw back.

They began to make their way back to the house, and she once again took the commander's proffered arm. He was strangely silent all the way back—a silence that made her nervous. He couldn't possibly find any connection between Lothar and the valley—or between *her* and the valley—but she was still filled with that uneasiness that resulted from treading too close to an abyss.

Later, when they had all retired for the night, there was a light knock at Rowena's door. Knowing it would be Paulena, she called to her to enter and Paulena lost no time in chastising her for her questions.

"I don't see what difference it made." Rowena shrugged. "I was just curious about what they thought about us."

"I could have told you that. They believe we're nothing more than silly old legends, as you saw."

"Which is, of course, exactly what we want them to believe." Rowena smiled. "But I was certainly tempted to show them a thing or two."

Paulena stared at her, aghast. "You know the rules, Rowena. Under no circumstances—not even under pain of death—can we reveal who we are or show them our magic. The only magic we can work here is our spells."

"Speaking of spells, how is it that you didn't make Duncan forget his thoughts about the valley? He must have told you about it."

Paulena nodded. "Yes, he told me." She was silent for a long time as she avoided Rowena's gaze. And when she finally did turn to her, her eyes were glazed by tears.

"I don't work any spells on him unless it's absolutely necessary. I . . . love him, Rowena. I know you must find that impossible to understand."

Rowena shook her head. "No, I don't find it impossible to understand, Polly. I like him, too." Even if he does sometimes treat me like a child, she added silently.

"Well, certainly no harm was done," she went on briskly, as much to reassure herself as to soothe her aunt. "They will find no connection between Lothar and the valley."

"No, we're always very careful to get everyone far from the valley quickly. An exception was made for you because I could easily bring you here without arousing suspicion. But usually Descenders are taken immediately to the city, to safe houses we've established there. And they are forbidden to go anywhere near the valley after that. I'm the only one who has, because my going there can easily be explained, since it's only several hours from here."

"Are there really people living in the hills there who have Dazhinn blood?" Rowena asked.

Paulena shrugged. "It's possible. I've heard that before. In general, as you know, our people didn't marry outside the clan, but a few might have. We've never dared to try to find out."

"Did Duncan ever say anything to you about that time he spent in the valley?"

"No more than he said tonight. But I know what you're thinking. Zach could not have gone into that valley without sensing *something*. Still, he must have managed to hide it from the others."

Zach lay in bed, listening to the distant sounds of the sea that had always lulled him to sleep very easily here. This night, however, sleep was eluding him.

In his mind's eye swam the golden-haired image of Rowena Sandor. He could even hear her voice with that slight accent he found charming. This was no empty-headed female; on the contrary, he had the distinct impression of a very clever mind.

He shifted about uncomfortably in the bed as he thought about her. At his age, he should be well past the hot-blooded lust of youth. There were many men who, when they reached his age, sought to recapture that lost youth with younger women, but he'd never been one of them and had always thought such behavior foolish. Had he now become such a fool himself?

It occurred to him that Rowena Sandor disturbed him in much the same way that Paulena did—though with the added perturbation of lust. What was it about them that seemed to touch something very deep and primitive within him?

Unable to find an answer, his thoughts drifted instead to the legend of the Dazhinn and yet another unexplained feeling. He'd never told anyone—not even Duncan—how he'd felt in that accursed valley, but he could recall it very clearly even now.

From the first moment he'd set foot in the

mist-shrouded valley, he'd felt himself to be an unwelcome intruder, a man among unseen enemies. And the feeling had persisted until they'd climbed back up to Ashwara.

But he reminded himself, as he'd done before, that they'd all been drinking quite a bit and the others had persuaded him to tell old stories of that battle that hadn't happened. Even the most commonsensical man could feel a certain chill around a campfire when ghost stories were told while a jug was being passed around.

As a child, Zach had heard the usual ghost stories, but the one that was told most often through the generations in his family was the Legend of the Dazhinn.

He fell asleep finally and dreamed of a mist-filled valley and frustrated Warriors on the hill above. And when he reached the deepest regions of sleep, the mists parted to reveal a golden-haired woman with eyes the color of precious emeralds.

But these were only dreams, bits of flotsam cast up from the sea, and when he awoke, he gave them no thought at all.

Rowena was feeling irritable—childishly so, she knew—but there it was. She had so hoped to have the opportunity to sail in the lovely boat, and her wish had been granted. But her pleasure was considerably diminished by being forced to wear all the tight, constricting garments that "ladies" apparently wore even on such an outing.

Her aunt had seemed quite surprised when Duncan had suggested at breakfast that the two of them join Zach and him. Rowena could only assume that it was customary for the men to sail alone. But here they were, the four of them, on a magnificent day with a strong breeze that billowed the white sails against a deep blue sky.

Her annoyance diminished rapidly though, as they moved away from the dock and she stood at the rail, staring back at the sheer cliffs and the grand house perched above them. Lovely white birds swooped and circled overhead, and she shaded her eyes, trying to see them more clearly.

"They're called gulls," said a voice in response to her silent question. "Scavengers, but still beautiful. If you fetch some of the bread from the picnic basket, you'll soon see them close up."

Rowena turned to see the commander standing just behind her. He seemed different this day, clad as he was in rough clothing. Apparently, it was acceptable for men to dress to suit the occasion, but not women.

She thanked him for his suggestion and made her way below to where the two huge picnic baskets had been stowed. After deciding that one loaf of bread wouldn't be missed, she went back up on deck. He turned to her with a smile.

"You would be more comfortable dressed as you were when we met," he remarked.

"I certainly would, but Polly seems determined to turn me into a lady."

He chuckled. "It occurs to me, Miss Sandor,

that not even your formidable aunt could force you to do that which you choose not to do."

"I wouldn't want to cause her any embarrassment—or Uncle Duncan, either," she replied as she began to break the loaf into smaller chunks.

"Why did you decide to come here?" he asked.

The question caught her off guard, but fortunately she and Polly had already worked out a story. "I wanted to see more of the world. I knew my mother had a sister, but I'd never met her. There was an estrangement between them long ago, but after Mother died, I discovered among her things old letters from Aunt Polly and I wrote to her."

"Was your mother by chance the weaver of tapestries whose work I've seen?"

Now he'd really caught her by surprise. She knew that Polly had taken a tapestry with her—a small one that she'd concealed beneath her cloak, since they were forbidden to take anything with them. But she was shocked that her aunt would have displayed it.

"Yes, she was a weaver—and so am I," Rowena replied as she began to toss the chunks of bread overboard.

"I was surprised when I saw it," he said as they both watched the gulls swoop down and snatch the bread. "I've never seen its equal—not even in the museums. Are you as good as your mother was?"

"Yes," she replied, even though many at home thought she was the most talented of all her family.

"Then I daresay you could become a wealthy woman by weaving them and selling them here—in the city, I mean."

She didn't answer him because one of the gulls had perched on the rail only a few feet away and was staring at her with its graceful head cocked inquiringly. She broke off another chunk, and without thinking about it, sent soothing thoughts to the bird that brought it to her unhesitatingly.

It took the chunk and gobbled it up quickly, then stared at her imploringly, so she gave it some more and then some more, until all was gone. Then it flew off with its shrill cry and joined its fellows.

"You seem also to have a certain talent with animals," he remarked, his pale gaze traveling from the disappearing bird to her. "They'll often come close, but I've never seen one eat out of someone's hands before."

She looked away quickly, hoping that he hadn't seen the sudden fear in her eyes. Like all of her people, she had a gift of communication with creatures, and using it with the gull had been second nature to her.

How many mistakes can I make before I've made one too many? she asked herself. But then, he didn't believe in Dazhinn magic, so she was probably safe enough. She even began to wonder wickedly what it would take to make him believe.

"Do you happen to have any tapestries with you?" he asked, returning to their earlier conversation.

"No, I'm afraid not."

"A pity. If you had, I would like to purchase one."

"Do you collect art, Commander?" she asked, her tone betraying her skepticism. They all knew that Warriors had no appreciation for such things. In fact, the Warrior clans had always belittled her people for their artistic talents.

"No, but my late wife did, and I've learned to appreciate at least some of it. That tapestry, though . . ." His voice trailed off strangely as he stared out to sea.

"Once I had seen it, I began to understand what Miriam, my late wife, meant when she said that certain paintings spoke to her."

"And what did my mother's tapestry say to you, Commander?" she asked, beginning once more to feel that slight dizziness from approaching a dangerous abyss.

He turned to her with a slight smile. "The tapestry hangs in Paulena's boudoir. I saw it only because Duncan was very ill at the time and I was with him. The physicians feared for his life and naturally, so did I. But I remember as I stood there staring at it, my fears were lessened, soothed away."

Exactly what it was intended to do, Rowena thought—though Mother would have been appalled to learn that a Warrior had benefited from it.

Then she wondered how it was that Paulena had allowed Duncan to come so close to death. Unless his illness was the result of a terrible wound, she could surely have healed him. That was another talent they all had, though some were better than others.

"Many people have felt what you felt," she told him. "It's a combination of the colors and the design. The talent has been passed down for many generations in my family." What she didn't say, of course, was that they employed their magic in the choosing of colors and designs, then wove that magic into the tapestry.

"I'm surprised that your family's talents haven't become more widely known," he said.

Now Rowena felt as though she were poised on the very edge of that precipice. She could not afford to encourage his interest too much. If she did, he might well make inquiries about her nonexistent family.

"They take very long to create and are generally sold to very few people, who collect as many as they can."

Thankfully, at that moment Duncan, who was at the helm, called out to his friend and he excused himself. Rowena, in turn, went to seek out her aunt, who was ensconced in one of the chairs that were bolted to the wooden deck.

"You should have warned me that he saw my mother's tapestry," she admonished her aunt.

Paulena looked surprised. "Oh, dear, I'd forgotten about that. It's in my boudoir, but he saw it when Duncan was so ill that time. What did he say about it? I remember that he was quite taken with it. I discovered him there, so entranced that he didn't hear me at first."

Rowena told her of the conversation. "We must hope that he doesn't become sufficiently curious to check up on my family."

Paulena looked troubled, but said that she doubted it. "He has too much else on his mind at the moment."

Rowena hoped that was so, though of course she certainly didn't like what was clearly on his mind. "Why did you allow Duncan to become so ill?"

Paulena cast a quick glance toward the men before responding. They were beyond earshot and deep in conversation as well. "It was a terrible time. Duncan had been visiting Straymouth, a city some distance away where he has business interests. He fell ill from a plague that had broken out there. By the time he was brought home, he was near death. The family physicians were hovering about, and I didn't dare cure him too quickly, though it hurt terribly to see him suffering. I wanted to scream at the physicians to get out and let me cure him, but of course I couldn't."

Rowena nodded sympathetically, only now beginning to truly understand how difficult it must be for Polly to love Duncan and yet be unable to reveal her secrets.

"Are there other marriages like yours?" she inquired, thinking about the other women who'd descended.

"A few, but most of us have married men simply to gain control over them." She gave Rowena a grim smile. "I can't prove it, of course, but I strongly suspect that at least a few of them have been making their husbands very miserable quite deliberately, as a way of getting even for being forced into the marriage.

"Carlotta Tavorin is married to a leader of Parliament—a truly unpleasant man. His greatest passion, apparently, was his gambling. There are elegant gaming houses all over the city and he patronized them all, and was apparently quite lucky most of the time.

"But since his marriage to her, his luck has dwindled and he can no longer afford to visit them as frequently. I suspect that Carlotta had a hand in that."

Rowena joined in her aunt's laughter. She didn't know Carlotta well, but she could certainly imagine her doing such a thing.

"Then there's Tabitha Weston. She's married to one of the king's advisers—an insufferably arrogant man who loves the sound of his own voice. I heard from Duncan that he was suddenly struck dumb in the midst of a heated debate in the King's Council. The physicians were never able to find the cause for it."

Rowena's laughter rang out again, this time causing the men to glance their way. She had known Tabby well as a child, and remembered her as a young woman with a mischievous turn of mind. Still, she thought, how miserable their lives must be, married to men such as Paulena had described.

"We're the leaders of the suffrage movement,"

Paulena told her. "If that ever became known, they'd have even more reason to hate us."

"Did you know what kind of life you would be leading before you descended?" Rowena asked.

Paulena shook her head. "No. The Council withheld that information—among other things. If they'd told us, not one of us women would have descended, and they knew that in many ways it would be easier for us to gain access to power than it would be for the men."

Rowena's jaw set firmly. "Well, you can rest assured that I'll put an end to it when I return. I'll tell everyone."

Paulena stared at her but said nothing. Rowena had lifted her head to stare at the ever-hopeful gulls, but she caught something from her aunt and jerked her attention back to her quickly, her face horror-stricken.

"You don't believe that I'll be going back, do you?" she asked in a choked voice.

"I know nothing," Paulena said hastily. "I was told you would be permitted to return."

"But you don't believe it!"

"The Council must have known they wouldn't be able to continue their deceptions if you return," she said hesitantly.

"But Seitha said I would return," Rowena protested weakly. "And she has the gift of farsight."

Paulena nodded, obviously relieved. "Then I am happy to leave off my worrying."

But Rowena didn't tell her the other part of Seitha's prediction: that there would be a "difference."

*   *   *

The day drifted by as they sailed through what Duncan described as calm waters, staying within view of the coastline as the winds pushed at the big sails. Two servants had been brought along, so that all the sailing chores weren't left to Zach and Duncan.

"I hadn't intended upon such a long journey," Duncan remarked as they finished off the banquet that had been prepared for them. "But on a day such as this, it seems a shame to go back."

Rowena's gaze was fixed upon the dark shape of mountains that rose only a few miles from the shoreline. She'd been staring at them for some time without understanding why—and then suddenly she knew. Beyond those mountains lay the valley! What she was seeing were the backsides of the mountains at home that were slowly fading as the spell weakened. But these mountains were sharp and distinct as they rose to meet the deep blue sky.

" . . . probably can. Let me get the glasses."

Rowena turned to Duncan as he rose and then disappeared below. Zach was standing at the rail, staring at the mountains as well, and she felt a shiver run through her. She glanced at Polly, but her head was turned, too, as she joined the Warrior at the rail.

A moment later, Duncan returned with a strange-looking device and lifted it to his eyes. "Yes. I see it."

He handed the device to Zach, who then raised it to his eyes. Rowena realized that it must be something to peer through, but what was it that they saw through it? She joined them at the rail.

Zach offered the device to her. "Have you ever used these?"

She shook her head and he held them up to her eyes, then explained the little wheel that she should turn until she could see clearly. But it wasn't necessary. The moment he held them to her eyes, she could see the distant mountains as though they were almost in front of her.

And then she saw what they'd been staring at: Ashwara. The old stone fortress sat atop the highest of the peaks, just barely visible even through the glasses.

"That's Ashwara," Zach told her. "The Valley of the Dazhinn lies just beyond it."

My home and not my home, she thought sadly, harking back to that disturbing conversation with her aunt.

"They were good days, Zach," Duncan said as he stared at the mountains. "Our last chance to be children, really."

Rowena glanced at the commander as she heard the wistful tone in Duncan's voice. His strong profile was softer somehow, as though he shared his friend's sentiments. She felt a surge of anger that they should have found pleasure in a place that was such a symbol of pain to her people.

"We haven't been back there for a long time," Duncan continued. "If the weather holds, why don't we visit it tomorrow?" He turned to Paulena.

"It might be an interesting outing for Rowena, don't you think?"

Paulena nodded, smiling too brightly at her. "Yes, it's a charming town and the view from the fortress is quite breathtaking."

"Then we'll go if the weather holds," Duncan stated, then gestured toward the mountains. "Perhaps we can call upon Dazhinn magic to guarantee that."

Soon after, they headed back to Cliff House, but not long after they had set a southerly course, Zach expressed a concern about the weather, pointing to the southeasterly sky.

"There's a storm brewing," he said, "and I'm afraid that we're headed right into it. We'd better try to stay closer to the shore in case we have to seek shelter."

"I think we can outrun it," Duncan said hopefully, "and be home before it reaches us."

But his prediction proved to be wrong. They were still some distance from Cliff House when the steadily rising wind gave way to a howling gale.

Chapter Four

The heavens had darkened to a smudgy charcoal, split with increasing frequency by jagged bolts of lightning. Thunder at first grumbled and then boomed as the storm rushed to meet them.

Duncan told Paulena and Rowena to go below. "Don't worry," he said soothingly. "We've been through storms before."

Rowena, who had since childhood been entranced by the great power contained in storms, wasn't overly concerned. But as they both went down to the small cabin, she saw that Paulena was trembling and pale.

"I hate storms," she said. "There was a violent storm the night Zeb died, and the healer was delayed. I've always blamed that storm for his death."

Rowena nodded sympathetically. Paulena's husband Zeb, whom she remembered with great fondness, had been badly injured when he was thrown from a horse he was attempting to break. His injuries were well beyond the capacity of Paulena's healing, so the village healer had been summoned. But Rowena could recall her mother's saying that not even that talented woman could have saved him.

"We can stop it," she told her aunt. "Together I'm sure we could do it, but we'd need to go back up on deck."

Paulena sank onto a bench, trembling. "No, we can't risk that. Both Duncan and Zach are expert sailors. They will manage."

But as the moments passed in agonizing slowness, the boat was lifted and tossed about. Rowena clung to a sturdy post, watching Polly with concern. By now, she was sobbing and her normally high color had become almost ghostly.

This is absurd, she thought. I could put an end to it myself. They all held certain talents in common, but each of them also had certain powers unique to them, and Rowena had discovered in her teens that she possessed the ability to tame great storms. She couldn't bring rain from a blue sky, as a few others could. Nor could she summon the mist. But when she stood in the midst of a thunderstorm, she could draw off its power, channeling it instead deep into the earth.

It was largely a useless talent—or so she'd thought in the past. Such storms passed on quickly in any event and often brought needed rains.

Saranne Dawson

Besides that, controlling the forces of nature was something her people rarely approved.

Her gaze fell on a dark cloak of oiled cloth that hung from a peg. The men were undoubtedly very busy at the moment. Surely she could sneak up there and put an end to this. She knew better than to try from down here. In order to draw off the storm's power, she had to feel it around her, and all she felt now was the heaving and bobbing of the boat.

Staggering like a drunk, she made her way across the cabin and put on the cloak. "I'm going to stop this," she told Polly as she started for the door.

"No!" her aunt said, trying to sound emphatic but succeeding only in a hoarse whisper. "They might see you!"

"If they do, I'll just tell them that I like storms. It's the truth." Then she left the cabin before Paulena could try again to stop her.

The power of the storm sang through her as she climbed up to the deck. She'd always liked that feeling—a feeling of great energy and well-being. When she'd described it once to a friend, her married friend had laughed and said that it sounded as though she made love with storms.

She emerged on the wildly heaving deck and looked around. Duncan and Zach and one of the two servants were clustered near the helm, fighting the big wheel. So she started toward the stern, moving carefully over the rain-slick deck, counting on the darkness and her dark cloak to hide her if they should turn that way.

96

Grasping the rail, she raised her face to the torrent of rain and sent her mind into the heart of the storm, trembling herself as she felt its force.

Down, she commanded silently. Down into the depths of the sea. And she felt the response: slowly at first and then more quickly. Her whole body sang with the power she invoked.

She had no idea how long she stood there, her face raised to the dark heavens, transported by the forces of the storm and by her own response. But it couldn't have been long, because the wind was still howling and the thunder and lightning had yet to cease. And then the spell was broken as she heard a scream.

She whirled about, sweeping her wet hair from her face, to see one of the servants sliding across the wet deck and under the railing. His hand reached out desperately to grab at the slick railing, then started to slip.

Rowena's reaction was instinctive: a reaching out to save a fellow human being. For one brief moment, the man was actually suspended in air between the boat and the water, and then he was moving upward again, and this time caught the rail with both hands.

No sooner had she released him to his own devices than she saw the tall dark figure of Commander Zachary MacTavesh, followed quickly by the other servant.

Zach heard the servant's scream and ran toward the stern. He saw the man sliding toward the rail, then slipping beneath it, his one hand waving frantically as he tried to grab the slippery rail. For a brief second, he caught it before slipping away again.

Then Zach's eyes played tricks on him. It seemed for one strange moment as though the man were suspended in midair, still struggling to reach the rail while his body floated free. Then he was moving upward slightly and this time, managed to grasp the rail with both hands.

Zach helped him back to the deck, that strange image still in his mind. The man thanked him profusely, but his eyes kept darting to the stern of the boat.

"What is it, man?" Zach asked impatiently, his thoughts still on that strange vision.

"Miss Sandor, sir. She was there. I saw her. Now she's gone."

"What?" Zach scanned the area, but saw no one. The worst of the storm was passing on— very quickly now, it seemed. "Where did you see her?"

"Right there, sir," the man said, pointing. "When I come back here, she was just standing there. Had her face raised, looking up."

Frightened now, Zach ran to the rail and searched the raging waters. Surely she hadn't been up here. The man must have suffered from the same sort of hallucination that had affected him. But fear was still twisting in his gut as he ran back to the steps that led down to the cabin.

The first thing he saw when he burst through the door was her, and his relief nearly weakened him. But her golden hair was wet and dripping, and a rain-slick cloak hung on a nearby peg.

"Were you up on deck?" he demanded, his voice harsher than he'd intended.

She gazed at him steadily with those brilliant green eyes. "Yes. I assume the man is all right. I came back down here when I saw that you'd arrived."

"What in hell were you doing there?" he thundered. "You could have been swept overboard like he was!"

"Well, as you can see, I wasn't," she stated coolly. "I was there because I like storms."

"I gave you credit for being more intelligent than that, Miss Sandor."

"I'm not one of your soldiers, Commander, so please don't use that tone of voice on me. And as I believe you yourself pointed out, no one can force me to do what I don't want to do."

In his relief and then his anger, he hadn't even seen Paulena in the cabin, but now a movement caught his eye and he turned to her and saw that she was pale and trembling.

"Are you all right, Paulena?" he inquired with concern.

"I'm fine, thank you, Zach. Rowena likes storms, but I don't. It seems to have passed, so I think I'll go up on deck for a breath of air."

She was past him and up the steps before he could offer his assistance, so he turned back to Rowena.

"Didn't it occur to you that your aunt might be needing your help?"

She gave him a strange smile. "I did help her, Commander, and I don't need you to remind me of my responsibilities. Please excuse me."

She started past him, but before he realized what he was doing, he'd reached out to grasp her arm. Something jolted him: a sudden, almost painful awareness of her. She stopped, then raised her face to stare at him.

"You seem to have been rather unnerved by the storm yourself, Commander," she taunted.

Later, he would tell himself that he'd never intended what happened. He'd even try to convince himself that it was she who had initiated the kiss. But in this moment, all he knew was that she would be his, that he had to have her.

She made no attempt to get away from him as his head lowered to hers, and the lips he covered with his own were parted and pliant. He drew her against him and she arched, curving her body to his, female softness to his male hardness.

His tongue found hers and teased it, dueled with it in a sensual dance. He was lost in her, oblivious to anything but her soft scent, her womanly curves he longed to free from their stiff coverings.

And then reality crashed upon him. The knowledge of what he was doing left him temporarily stunned, almost paralyzed. But still, his lips didn't want to leave hers and his arms refused to obey his command to let her go.

In the end, it was she who extricated herself from his embrace. She started up the steps, then paused for one brief moment and turned to stare at him. There was no mistaking the shock on her face before she fled.

Rowena stumbled onto the deck, then grasped the railing. Her body still felt the imprint of his. Her lips tingled still from his kisses. Her body felt heavy and achy and not quite hers. And she knew that Paulena had been right: the astrologers had lied to her.

She had no experience of men beyond a few stolen kisses beneath the moon—but she didn't need experience to know what she felt. She wanted this man, this Warrior—wanted to feel him deep inside her. The knowledge left her weak and terrified.

Thunder rumbled off in the distance as the storm moved on and she raised her head to stare at a far-off flash of lightning. Of course! What she'd felt was nothing more than the aftermath of the storm's power, combined with a residue of the magic she'd used to tame it.

She began to feel much better—at least until she remembered again her friend's teasing comparison with lovemaking.

The well-built boat was undamaged and they sailed the short distance to Cliff House with no difficulty. Zach emerged on deck to give Duncan a hand, but he spared her barely a glance. Only the servant whose life she'd saved kept watching her. They exchanged no words, but she could feel his eyes on her all the way home.

She worried for a time that the commander might have seen her save the man, or that the man himself might speak up, but before long, she dismissed both possibilities. The poor man had been in such a state of terror that he couldn't really know what had happened to him, and if Zachary MacTavesh had seen anything, he would surely dismiss it as a trick played on his eyes by the storm.

With the men busy tacking to port, Paulena and Rowena were left alone. Rowena saw that her aunt's color had returned, but she still seemed troubled.

"I've never seen Zach angry like that," Paulena said quietly.

"Well, I daresay he'll think twice before speaking to me like that again," Rowena responded, shooting a glance at his broad back as he stood at the helm.

"What you did was dangerous, Rowena."

"More dangerous than you know," she replied, then told her aunt what had happened. "The man keeps looking at me, but I think he was too frightened to know what really happened."

Paulena was looking pale again. "Rowena! How could you take such a risk?"

"What was I to do, Polly—let the man die? He was swept overboard."

"Yes, but—"

"Or does his life count for little because he's merely a servant?" she challenged.

"Of course not. But it is your own welfare that should concern you first. What if Zach saw it?"

Rowena shrugged. "If he did, he'll convince himself that he didn't. Besides, I think he has other things on his mind right now."

Fortunately, Paulena didn't pursue that as they reached the dock. Now that she had convinced herself that her reaction to his kiss was the result of the storm, Rowena was beginning to think about all those old stories of Warriors and their execrable behavior toward women. It was well-known that they often raped women they'd captured, although thankfully, her people could defend themselves.

She now understood this society well enough to know that such behavior—even his kiss—was unacceptable. She could almost feel sorry for him, caught as he was by his star-crossed attraction to her and his Warrior heritage, while at the same time he lived in a time when he could no longer act upon those base impulses.

But she reminded herself, too, that she dare not count upon the thin veneer of civility that was all that stood between them. If they had truly been alone . . .

Rowena rose to greet a sun-filled day with little enthusiasm. Duncan had repeated his intention that they should journey to Ashwara if the weather permitted—and it now seemed that it did. She was not looking forward to a long ride in the confines of the carriage with Commander MacTavesh, and her only consolation was that he was probably viewing the prospect with even less enthusiasm.

His behavior toward her during dinner and a foreshortened evening had been stiff and formal, and she was sure that Polly at least had noticed the tension in the air.

She sighed, wondering if she should pretend to be sick again. The truth was that she'd felt fine ever since his arrival, although she certainly didn't ascribe the improvement to his presence.

Besides, she wanted to see Ashwara, and this might be her only opportunity. She wanted to look down upon her people's true home: the home from which they'd been forced by the Warriors.

The carriage awaited them after breakfast, driven as before by Abner. Rowena hadn't seen him since her arrival, but Polly had explained that he was employed at their household in the city, where he served as a personal assistant to Duncan. When a desirable position opened up in another household, he would leave with a recommendation that would grant him instant entry into another important home.

He helped her into the carriage, his expression betraying no emotion, but Rowena again felt the anger in him, and as she took her seat, she saw the commander watching him. She decided that she'd better speak to Polly about it. She was sure that Abner wouldn't cause any problems, but she knew she'd feel better if he were elsewhere.

The two-hour journey was somewhat less unpleasant than she'd feared, owing largely to Duncan's storytelling. He regaled them with tales of his school days at Ashwara, showing a real talent for mimicry as he limited several of their professors.

"Some of them seem to truly believe they are living in the time of their teaching," he told Rowena. "When we were there, there was one man who actually affected the dress of the period. He was particularly fond of Zach because one of Zach's ancestors was his favorite figure from that time."

"That didn't stop him from wreaking havoc upon my treatises," Zach said with a smile—the first Rowena had seen from him since the outing yesterday.

Duncan chuckled. "Yes, I recall him saying once that a paper of yours looked as though it had been written at the Miscama."

"It was, as I remember," Zach replied with a chuckle.

"The Miscama?" Rowena frowned. It was the name of a festival her people celebrated each spring.

"The Miscama is a tavern," Duncan told her. "I believe the name derives from a pagan festival celebrated by the Dazhinn. You'll find many references to them at Ashwara. The myth lives on—especially as there's money to be made from it. People have never quite lost their fascination with the Dazhinn."

So we have become a sort of joke, Rowena thought angrily even as she smiled at Duncan. Once again, she felt a great urge to prove the powers of her people. How dare these barbarians make light of them!

Saranne Dawson

"I understand that some enterprising students have begun to collect stones from the valley and sell them, claiming that they have magic powers." Duncan chuckled.

Still seething over the ridicule of her people, Rowena was caught by surprise as they entered Ashwara. Paulena had described it as a "small city, really no more than a large town," but it was far larger and more crowded than anything she'd ever seen. The outer edges were filled with homes as large and even larger than Cliff House, some of them built in that style, while others were more plain in appearance.

Not until they reached the center of the town did she see evidence of anything old, and even then, she reflected wryly, they were new by comparison to the village of her people. For the first time since her Descent, she felt a jarring sense of dislocation in time, brought on now by the juxtaposition of the very old and the very new.

The streets were filled with people on this bright, sunny day, most of whom seemed to be young men: students at the university. Paulena had told her that Ashwara was the finest institution in the land, drawing the best and brightest young men. No women went there, of course. Women were considered to be unfit for the rigors of higher learning.

True to Duncan's word, the name "Dazhinn" figured prominently in many of the signs announcing various shops and eating places. She spotted the Miscama even before Duncan pointed it out to her. It was one of the oldest buildings:

stone with a red-tiled roof, and along the borders of the large sign above the entrance were drawings of scantily clad people with flowers woven into their hair, dancing with various animals.

Rowena was too angry to speak. Her people had never dressed like that and the ritual dances for Miscama bore no resemblance to the lewd portrayals on the garish sign. Denied a victory in battle over the Dazhinn, these barbarians had gained a different kind of victory by ridiculing them.

Then she saw a group of what she assumed must be soldiers in white uniforms decorated with various ribbons and braid. They weren't carrying weapons, but it was still obvious to her that they must be soldiers.

The commander remained silent, as he had for much of the trip, but Duncan saw her staring at them.

"There is a small garrison in the fortress," he told her. "As you probably know, the fortress was manned for many years after the Dazhinn disappeared. Finally, it was abandoned, and then much later, it became the university.

"Some years ago, the town fathers persuaded the king to bring back the soldiers. Ashwara was beginning to become a favorite summer vacation spot, drawing many visitors from all over. The town fathers thought it would be a good idea to bring back the soldiers and keep up the pretense that the valley needed to be guarded in case the Dazhinn should return. So far, they haven't," he finished with a chuckle.

Rowena risked a glance at Paulena, who was smiling at her husband's remark. Their eyes met briefly and communicated silently. The Dazhinn had indeed returned—but in a way these barbarians could never have anticipated.

The carriage began the long, winding ascent to the top of the mountain and Rowena leaned out the window to see the great fortress. It stood outlined sharply against the blue sky, a monument to a time when the Dazhinn had been taken seriously indeed.

When they reached the summit and alighted from the carriage, she saw that many buildings now crowded the hilltop, surrounding the original fortress. All of them, however, were built of the same pale gray stone, and they contrived to look as though they too had been there for 500 years.

No sooner had they gotten out of the carriage than a bell rang out. Rowena looked up at the nearest tower in the fortress and saw the huge, deep-throated bell as the sound dwindled away.

"The bell is as old as the fortress," Duncan told her. "It was put there to warn of the return of the Dazhinn and summon the soldiers to arms. Now it simply tolls at noon and midnight."

But this day, it also tolls for its original purpose, Rowena thought with some satisfaction.

They walked through a parklike area where students lounged beneath trees and families strolled about. Zach had offered his arm, and after a very deliberate moment of hesitation, she took it. A trio of soldiers approached them, laughing and talking among themselves.

Suddenly, one of them stared in their direction and said something to his fellows, whereupon they all fell silent and came to a halt. Rowena knew a moment of complete terror as she imagined that they had somehow recognized her as being Dazhinn.

But a moment later, she realized that it was the commander who had attracted their attention. They did a very strange thing—or strange to her eyes, at least. They drew themselves up rigidly and raised their arms with the palm of the hand extended and touching their brows.

"Sir!" they chorused, their bodies so stiff Rowena thought they had turned to stone.

"At ease, men," Zach said, returning the gesture.

They hurried away and she was curious enough to inquire how it was that they'd recognized him when he wasn't in uniform. But it was Duncan who answered her.

"It behooves all soldiers to recognize their commander, my dear, and I daresay that Zach is easily the most recognized man in the country, save perhaps for the king."

As they walked on, she saw further evidence that Duncan was right. People stared at them unabashedly as they made their way to the high stone arch that marked the entrance into the fortress, and the same routine was repeated with the two soldiers posted at either side of the wide gate.

"Perhaps you should have come in disguise,"

Duncan said wryly to Zach. "I've no doubt we'll soon be subjected to a visit by the dean."

"A pleasure to be avoided if at all possible." Zach chuckled, turning to Rowena. "Perhaps you could feel ill if that happens."

"You don't like him?" she asked.

"I don't dislike him. He's a highly intelligent man; otherwise he wouldn't have his position. But he's a well-known bore who can go on interminably on his favorite subject."

"And what is that?"

"The Dazhinn, of course," he replied with a smile. "That period of history is his specialty."

They walked on through the great courtyard, where trees and flowers had apparently long since replaced the weapons of war that must once have filled the space. Rowena rather hoped that the dean *would* put in an appearance, and if he did, she had no intention of feigning illness. She was greatly curious about what this man knew of her people.

The climb to the top of the fortress was long and arduous. Both Duncan and the commander inquired several times if she were up to the journey, but she assured them quite honestly that she was fine and had recovered fully from her illness.

And then, just when she thought that the climb would never end, they were there. A wide arched doorway opened onto the broad, flat roof of the fortress—and beyond it lay the Valley of the Dazhinn.

Rowena stood at the chest-high stone parapet

and stared at her people's true home. The view from here was spectacular, encompassing the entire wide valley and its surrounding hills. It was all thickly forested, whereas her home (the "other valley," as she now thought of it) had been partially cleared many centuries ago for grazing and crop growing.

But she saw the river threading its way through the forest, and the sun reflected off the lake where they all swam and sailed small boats. Using those as points of reference, she was able to orient herself despite the lack of buildings and other familiar landmarks.

The others were talking, but their words were no more than minor buzzing in her ears as she stared at her home. She became aware of a deep vibration within her that she'd never felt before, and knew it must be the power of the ancient spell that had separated this place from the other valley for 500 years.

How did they do it? she wondered in awe. *For all the magic we now possess, we could never accomplish something like this.* Had the gods granted her ancestors their own powers for long enough to allow them to save themselves? She could think of no other explanation.

Ignoring the others, she began to walk along the stone roof, peering down and seeking out familiar landmarks: a steep cliff of bare stone, a particular bend in the river. Then, after finding them, her gaze went to the far end of the valley, where the steep, forbidding cliffs hid the Gateway.

Even on this clearest of days, that portion of the valley was enshrouded in mists that lay like a gauzy cloth over the treetops, blurring the base of the cliffs.

If only I could walk down there now, she thought, and leave this world of barbarians. For all their luxuries and mechanical wonders, they were still as savage as before, even though that brutality was now overlaid with civility.

Tears stung her eyes as she remembered her conversation with Polly. Would the Council really force her to remain here forever? Surely they couldn't be that cruel.

Then she shivered, recalling the detestable Alma, the Council leader, and her lecture on subjugating one's own pleasure to the greater good of them all. She shivered, wondering if that was what she'd really meant.

"Are you feeling ill?" a deep voice inquired.

Startled, she turned before she realized he would see the tears in her eyes. Through the blur, she saw the commander, his rugged face frowning with concern.

"No, I'm fine. I was just . . . woolgathering." She tried to blink away the tears as best she could.

"This place appears to have affected you greatly, then," he said curiously.

She affected a shrug. "It's just that I've heard the tales so many times over the years."

He turned to stare out at the valley and his expression became grim. "Speaking for myself, I've had more than my fill of the Legend of the

Dazhinn. It always leaves me with the unpleasant thought that my ancestors must have been fools."

"Why do you say that?"

He swept an arm to encompass the valley. "There were surely no more than a thousand or so of them, while our army numbered three or four times that. And they were trapped in the valley. Fog or no fog, we should have beaten them."

"Then perhaps they *did* have magic," she suggested.

He smiled indulgently. "That, at least, would explain it."

"Why would people believe they were sorcerers if there wasn't some evidence?"

"You must remember, Miss Sandor, that those were far less enlightened times, when people could see magic in a sudden storm or the birth of a freak animal. Have you ever seen a magic performance?"

"No. What do you mean?"

"Then you must go to one. There are some men who have a talent to make things appear and disappear through sleight of hand or by drawing away the attention of the audience. And there are spiritualists who contrive to make it seem that the dead return to speak with their loved ones.

"It's all fakery, of course, but even in these times there are people who can convince others that magic exists. Many people *want* to believe, it seems. That's why the Legend of the Dazhinn holds such enduring interest."

They had begun to walk back toward Duncan and Paulena, who were at the other end of the wide roof. Suddenly he stopped. She glanced up at him and saw, to her amazement, that he looked very uncomfortable. Could the spell be affecting him? she wondered hopefully, thinking that he deserved to suffer.

"Miss Sandor, I have been struggling to find the words to express my deep regret over my behavior yesterday. I have no excuse to offer, however much I wish that I did. I can only assume that you didn't speak of it to your aunt, and I thank you for that."

His clipped speech came to an abrupt halt. He was clearly awaiting a response from her, but she said nothing. To her very great surprise, she was as uncomfortable as he was. The memory of that kiss was touching something deep inside her. She wanted only to forget about it, to pretend it hadn't happened at all.

"Will you forgive me?" he asked.

Pressed for a response, she gave him the standard reply used by her people in such a situation. "It is forgotten," she said, eager now to reach Paulena and Duncan, who were awaiting them at the far end of the roof.

"Forgotten?" he echoed, raising his dark brows in shock.

Abruptly, she realized that her innocent response had been misinterpreted. Clearly, this was a man who was unaccustomed to having his attentions dismissed so lightly. His reaction

114

would have been amusing under other circumstances. As it was, however, she sought a way to defuse the situation.

"I meant merely that I *do* forgive you, Commander. The storm had unnerved us all."

He seemed about to say something more, then apparently thought better of it and remained silent as they rejoined Paulena and Duncan. But as they began the long climb back down from the roof, Rowena could feel his eyes upon her.

Try as he surely did, Zach could not prevent his gaze from straying toward Rowena Sandor. A growing mystery lay inside that golden head and lithe body: a mystery he had to unravel.

It would have been easy for him to excuse his behavior as the result of being seduced by a highly practiced temptress—especially in view of her casual dismissal of his kiss—but Zach was not a man to engage in self-deception. For all her considerable self-possession and her candor, he was convinced that she didn't fit into that category.

The truth was that he had no answers to the questions that had been tormenting him since those moments in the boat's cabin. All he knew was that in that moment when he'd reached for her, he'd simply stopped thinking about anything other than having her. And despite his apology, he *still* hadn't stopped thinking about that.

He had never believed himself to be a man of strong appetites, unlike so many around him.

Not that women didn't appeal to him, of course, but even when he found one he wanted, she never occupied his mind to the exclusion of everything else. The need for women was to him like the need for food: an appetite to be sated before moving on to more important matters.

But at the moment, he was chagrined to realize that nothing in his life seemed quite so important as Rowena Sandor.

When they reached the main hall of the fortress, they were approached by a young man who identified himself as an aide to the dean, who was requesting the honor of their presence at tea. He then led them into the section of the old fortress that had been set aside as living quarters for the dean, where they met the man and his wife.

Rowena was very curious about this man, who was said to be such an expert on her people. In appearance, he was almost comical: a short, slight man with an oversize bald head that appeared to have swollen in an attempt to contain his considerable intellect.

As they feasted on a variety of delicacies, the commander asked the dean about the rural people in the hills surrounding the valley.

"Is it true that some of them still lay claim to being descended from the Dazhinn?"

"Oh, yes, absolutely!" the man replied, bobbing his large head. "They're quite proud of it, though when you ask them to expand upon the subject, they become very closed."

116

"Do they claim magic for themselves?" Rowena asked, drawing the attention of both men.

"Indeed they do, Miss Sandor, though any request to speak to those who have these supposed powers is invariably met with excuses. They're not unlike other rural folk: closed and secretive in all things. But I do know that they continue to celebrate Miscama and other festivals associated with the Dazhinn.

"I'm inclined to doubt the veracity of their tales, because my own studies indicate that the Dazhinn never married outside their own clan. They apparently believed that if they did, they would dilute their gifts.

"For many centuries, these people were protected by the Dazhinn who perhaps saw them as being a buffer against their enemies."

"A buffer that failed them in the end," Duncan put in.

"Perhaps," their host said. "Or perhaps it was they who saved the Dazhinn, by taking them into their homes and eventually into their clans—if we are to believe the Warriors' account of that final battle, that is."

"You don't believe that, do you?" Rowena asked, hearing the doubt in the man's voice.

He smiled at her. "The more I study the history of that time, such as it was, the less I know *what* I believe, Miss Sandor. It is difficult for me to imagine that the Warriors, who were so determined to conquer them, would have failed to seek them out among the clans in the hills.

"And they would have stood out, you know.

Saranne Dawson

The Dazhinn are invariably described as being a very handsome people. Indeed, Dazhinn women were considered to be the fairest in the land, giving rise to the later belief that witches were always beautiful and seductive.

"In any event, they should have been relatively easy to spot if the army had pursued them."

Rowena shifted her gaze briefly to the commander, curious about his reaction to all this. He had remained silent, but a slight frown creased his brow. Then finally—and reluctantly, she thought—he spoke.

"There were stories of hidden caverns in those hills—places where the Dazhinn could have hidden and been supplied by the hill clans."

"That is so, my dear Commander." The dean smiled, obviously enjoying himself. "But I ask the question I have asked of you in the past. If this was true, why did we never hear of them again? The Dazhinn, as we all know, were a proud people, quite capable of winning battles even given their small numbers. And in short order, the alliance forged by your ancestor fell apart. So why would they not have taken advantage of the situation?"

And with scarcely a pause to allow for a response, he added, "And then, of course, there is the fact that no such caverns have ever been found, despite the fact that several expeditions— including one headed by you—spent months searching for them."

A smile curved Zachary MacTavesh's wide

118

mouth, but Rowena saw that it didn't touch his eyes.

"Then perhaps they used their magic to remove themselves to a distant corner of the world—as you have so often suggested, Dean."

"Do you believe that?" Rowena asked, intrigued. If so, he must be the only one who had actually guessed—and accepted—the truth. Or very close to the truth, in any event.

"My dear, I simply don't know. When Commander MacTavesh was my student here, we had many long and ultimately pointless arguments on the subject. But unlike him, I do not rule out the possibility of magic."

Then he turned to Zach, his expression becoming solemn. "There are rumors that have reached me of the possibility of war with the Atanians, and perhaps the Gavese as well. I raise this issue because of my concern about our position here. I'm sure you realize that recapturing Ashwara would have great symbolic value to them, and the border is not so far away."

"If war comes, you will be adequately protected, Dean. The students, of course, will have to leave in order to make room for more soldiers."

The dean was visibly agitated. "The disruption of our nation's finest institution of higher learning would be a grave mistake, Commander."

Zach gave him a cold smile. "Then you'd better hope that our neighbors to the north behave themselves."

You want this war, Rowena thought with an

inner shiver. You don't want just any war. It is *this* one you seek—another battle for the Valley of the Dazhinn.

She had misjudged his interest in her people. Instead of dismissing them as being mere legend, he was obsessed with them. He wanted the battle denied to his ancestors, as though defeating his ancestors' former ally here could somehow make up for that.

She thought about what the dean had said: that he had led an expedition to find those nonexistent caverns. After all this time, he still felt the need to prove that her people had escaped by conventional means. What that suggested to her was that, despite his protests to the contrary, a part of Zachary MacTavesh did indeed believe in Dazhinn magic.

And now, if he was successful in bringing war to the valley, he might well have a far greater victory than even he could imagine.

No one really knew what would happen to her people if the spell failed, but it was generally assumed that they would return to their original home here. And even with her as yet limited knowledge of this world, Rowena knew that Dazhinn magic could not stand up to the weapons at the command of Zachary MacTavesh.

Furthermore, she had only to look into those pale, cold eyes to know that he would show them no mercy.

Chapter Five

Rowena escaped gratefully from the dress-makers and slipped out to the beautiful gardens behind Paulena's home, leaving her aunt to finish the instructions regarding her new wardrobe.

For the first time in her life, she felt over-whelmed. They'd arrived in the city yesterday and she'd been in a daze ever since. Nothing Polly had told her had prepared her for the reality: the sheer size of the city, the tall buildings, the throngs of people.

Even now, in the high-walled garden, the city was a constant presence, like a huge beast crouched just beyond the walls, waiting to devour her. How, she wondered, do people live in a place like this? At least here, she had the privacy of the garden and the wooded copse that bordered it. But out there, many of them lived quite literally on top of each other in the high buildings.

More shocking to her than any of it, though, were the contrasts. Duncan and Paulena lived in a section of the city where huge homes were surrounded by high walls enclosing large spaces. But she'd glimpsed other places where people lived in unimaginable squalor.

In her own world, there were certainly those who had more than their neighbors, but no one was in need. No one lacked a place to live or food to eat or any of the necessities. But here, she'd already seen malnourished children and men and women wearing rags. The wrongness of it ate at her, although Paulena had apparently long since accepted it.

This morning, Paulena had interviewed girls to find a maid for her—and this despite the fact that the huge house was overflowing with servants. And so was the garden. As she strolled along the white-pebbled paths, she could see three men busy at work in the flower beds or cleaning the numerous fountains.

She didn't like the way she felt here, as though the city had robbed her of her worth, rendered her invisible and unimportant. How could they hope to change the course of events here? Could the Council really know what it was like?

Maybe the commander was right, she thought, when he dismissed us as a part of a distant past. Maybe we *are* nothing more than a foolish legend. Certainly there is no place for us in a world such as this.

And yet there was her mission to consider. But she grew uncomfortable every time she thought about it, because each time she thought about him, it was his kiss she remembered. Even when she tried to focus on the danger he represented to her people, she kept reliving those moments in his arms until her thoughts would move beyond that and she forced herself to let it go.

In two days' time, Paulena was giving a dinner and he would be among the guests. Rowena had no doubt at all that he was very much attracted to her, but she also thought that Polly might have been correct when she said that if anyone could resist his fate, it was Zachary MacTavesh.

"Getting used to playing the lady of the manor, are you?" a familiar, mocking voice said behind her.

She turned to find Abner standing there, staring at her with his cold, angry eyes.

"You know why I've been sent here, Abner," she said, ignoring his rudeness.

"Sure. You're going to lure the big man into your bed and then stick a knife in his black heart," he said with a sneer. "I wish they'd given me a chance to kill him."

"If they had, you'd undoubtedly be dead now," she replied coldly, even as the image he'd invoked shuddered through her.

"So would he." His sneer became even more pronounced. "You don't really think they're going to let you go back, do you? Because they won't."

She said nothing because he had touched her darkest fear. But he couldn't know the truth any more than she herself did.

"You're going to have to learn to live like the other women here live," he went on. "At least until we take over—and maybe even after that."

"What are you talking about, Abner? We're not 'taking over.' How could we? There aren't enough of us, and that isn't the plan anyway."

"There's a lot you don't know," he replied smugly, then turned on his heel and disappeared.

Rowena stared after him. She would have to speak to Polly about getting him out of here. Maybe she was bringing out the worst in him. He knew perfectly well that they didn't intend to "take over." They were here to use their talents to change the barbarians, so that if the day ever came when they must return to this world, they could live here in peace.

And yet, after all that she'd seen, did she really believe that could happen? Certainly it couldn't happen if Zachary MacTavesh didn't die.

Abner's words came back to her and she shuddered again. Even if he were dangerous and even if she did hate him, could she actually kill him? It was a question that haunted her now as she heard Abner's words and unwillingly conjured up the images he'd invoked.

Rowena stared into the long mirror at a stranger that only vaguely resembled her. The result of the ministrations of her maid and the hairdresser was that she felt foolish.

True, the bright green gown she wore that matched her eyes was quite beautiful, and she'd convinced the maid not to lace the hated corset too tightly. But her long hair had been pushed and prodded and pinned into something so unnatural that it made the face beneath it unfamiliar. And to make matters worse, the maid had dabbed at her face and brushed it with an assortment of what Paulena called "cosmetics" so that her lashes were too dark and her cheeks were unnaturally rosy. She'd finally drawn the line at the prospect of having the girl pluck out some of the hairs in her eyebrows.

And now she must go downstairs and be introduced to some of the most important people in the land—and face Commander MacTavesh again. Her only consolation was that both Tabitha and Carlotta would be there as well, but Paulena had already warned her that she could not be too friendly toward them, since she wasn't supposed to know them.

With a sigh, she cast one last look at the stranger in the mirror and left her room. As she walked down the hallway, she could already hear the steady hum of conversation in the two huge drawing rooms. Polly had told her to make a late entrance, saying that this would be expected. Apparently, young women being "presented to society" were noted for making dramatic entrances.

She paused briefly at the polished railing, and then, when she realized that she was scanning the crowd gathered below for the commander, she started down the broad, curved staircase. A hush had fallen over the crowd before she was even halfway down, and for one irrational moment, she was sure they must have recognized her for what she truly was.

Both Duncan and Paulena had reached her by the time she had descended the stairs, and she was immediately swept up in a round of introductions. Carlotta and her husband were among the first to whom she was introduced, and she had already seen Tabitha across the room. But the commander was nowhere to be seen. She recalled that he'd threatened not to come because of a particular woman who was to be here, and she wondered if he'd made good on that threat.

She acquitted herself well enough, although she encountered several women younger than she whose friendliness was unmistakably false. She wondered why they should dislike her, but there was no opportunity to question Paulena about it.

Very soon, she noted that either Polly or Carlotta or Tabby were always there at her side—no doubt to cover up any mistakes she might make. Several young men also seemed to have taken up permanent residence near her, and it was clear that they were determined to impress her.

It all felt so false, so foolish. People either said things they clearly didn't mean or things that were in and of themselves meaningless. She said as little as possible and her face already ached with the effort required to smile as though she were enjoying all this.

Then she sensed a change in the atmosphere, a slight lowering of the level of conversation, a joint turning of heads. And as she, too, turned, she saw him. His height made him visible even over the heads between them—and his eyes met hers.

He was dazzling this night in a white uniform bedecked with gold braid that crisscrossed his broad shoulders and rows of colored ribbons and medals that seemed to cover half his chest. There was even a gold-handled sword at his side.

They stared at each other across the room, and then his attention was dragged away from her as someone spoke to him. Rowena turned her back on him and resumed the conversation she'd left off.

"The commander does have a way of filling a room, doesn't he?" an older woman said. "Have you met him yet, Miss Sandor? I know he's a regular visitor here."

"Yes, we've met," Rowena told her, then quickly returned to a discussion of the woman's charitable work. She'd already learned from Polly that she and many other women worked with the poor in places called "settlement houses."

But the woman appeared to be unable to let the subject of Zachary MacTavesh alone. "He's a widower, you know."

"Yes. My aunt told me."

"And certainly the most eligible man in the land," the woman persisted.

"I'm sure he must be," Rowena replied, then

resumed her questions about the settlement houses.

Suddenly, the woman broke off in the middle of a sentence and smiled brightly. "Good evening, Commander."

Reluctantly, Rowena turned to find herself staring at the rows of ribbons and medals. Slowly, she lifted her gaze until she was staring into pale gray-blue eyes that were focused on her with such intensity that it nearly took her breath away.

"Good evening, Miss Sandor. I trust you've been enjoying your first few days in the city."

"'Enjoyment' isn't exactly the word I would use," Rowena said. "I think 'overwhelmed' would describe it better."

"Somehow I doubt that," he replied, and she saw amusement glittering in his eyes. "I think it would take much more than the city to overwhelm *you.*"

"Perhaps you overestimate me, Commander."

He shook his head slowly. "No, I think I have it right."

Others began to crowd around them, but it took a while for Zach to notice that they weren't alone. From the moment he'd spotted her, there'd been no one else in the room.

She was beautifully dressed and her golden hair was styled in the latest fashion, but somehow none of it looked real. It was as though she'd been gotten up for a stage play. The real Rowena Sandor was the woman he'd first encountered on the beach, clad in a peasant boy's dress, her hair unbound and tumbling about her shoulders.

Scarcely an hour had passed since their parting that he hadn't thought about her. She was even there in his dreams. Earlier, he'd decided not to come tonight because he was deeply worried about his growing obsession with her. But then he'd found himself calling his valet to lay out his uniform even as he told himself he would stay home.

He must have her. Once he did, the obsession would surely fade. But he knew he must proceed carefully. This was no worldly woman with whom he could have a brief affair. Not only was he convinced of her innocence, but she was also Paulena's niece.

A hunger raged inside him as he stood there trying to focus on the conversation. He was truly shocked at the primitive beast that lurked inside him, urging him to carry her away right now.

It was impossible! He could not have her— and yet he *must* have her. The silent battle raging inside him now made light of all real battles he'd fought in his long and illustrious career. And yet none of this showed on his face as he stood there beside her, breathing in her soft scent.

Dinner was announced, and one of the young men who'd been dancing attendance upon her started to offer Rowena his arm. But before she could move, the smile on his face froze and then fell away, and he turned away from her.

"Will you do me the honor, Miss Sandor?"

said that now very familiar deep voice.

She turned to the commander. "It appears that I have no choice, Commander, since you've frightened him away. Do you enjoy making people fear you?"

If her impertinent question surprised him, he gave no indication. "Only when it seems necessary," he responded as they joined the line of people moving toward the large dining room.

She chose not to ask the obvious question about why he should think it necessary in this case. Instead, she chattered on about her first few days in the city. When she finally paused for a breath, he smiled and leaned close to her.

"It isn't necessary for you to play the game with me, you know."

She stared at him, temporarily struck speechless. He swept an arm around them.

"This is a stage set and you are an accomplished actress, thanks to Paulena's excellent tutelage. But the real Rowena Sandor despises all this as much as I do."

That he should have seen through her so easily terrified her, and her expression must have shown it because he laid a hand over hers that was wrapped about his arm.

"Don't worry. I won't give you away if you don't betray me."

She managed to smile, but that word "betray" was echoing loudly in her brain. She knew it was nothing more than a figure of speech, but coupled with his statement about her playacting, the effect upon her was devastating.

Very fortunately, they were quickly seated and surrounded by others and the necessity to carry on numerous conversations with those seated near her prevented her from dwelling on his remarks.

Tabby and her husband were seated directly across from them, and it took very little time for Rowena to confirm Polly's statements about the man. His overly loud, grating voice dominated the conversations—except, that is, when the mostly silent commander chose to speak.

The conversation turned to a ballet performance two weeks hence, a royal command performance that was part of the celebration to honor the king's birthday. Paulena had told her about it, explaining that ballet was a variation on the dances her people had performed for centuries, though certainly less spectacular. The top dancers among her own people were those who could augment their leaps through the use of magical talents, and the very best of them could actually remain suspended in air for a time. Rowena herself performed in these dances, although she was far from being the best, chiefly because her work kept her from having time for the grueling practice.

"You will be attending the ballet, won't you, Miss Sandor?" a woman inquired.

"Yes, I believe so. My aunt mentioned it to me."

"Will you be making your home here?" the woman inquired.

The innocent question sent a chill through

131

her and she shook her head. "No, not permanently."

A short time later, as the servants were removing the first of many dishes, Zachary MacTavesh leaned close to her.

"You said that you weren't sure how long you'd be staying—and now it sounds as though you intend to leave soon. Do you dislike the city that much?"

"I'm not sure how I feel about the city," she said honestly. "But I cannot stay forever. I have my work."

"Then you haven't come here to find yourself a husband, as I suspected?" he inquired.

"No, I haven't. I have no interest in marrying."

She turned away from him, but she could feel his eyes on her. His question, however, caught her by surprise.

"Why not?"

She reflected that since she had herself been guilty of impertinent remarks, she could scarcely fault him for the same thing. It brought back to her that thought about the very thin layer of civility that lay between them and their ancient heritages.

"My work is very important to me," she replied. "Therefore, I have no time for a husband and family."

"But your mother must have combined the two," he persisted.

"That's true enough—but I won't."

"Then there will be no daughters to whom you can pass on your talents."

In what she knew must be total innocence, he had struck a nerve. Rowena had indeed been thinking about that as the years passed and the likelihood of her ever having children diminished.

"That seems to me to be an insufficient reason to marry," she replied in a tone intended to end this particular conversation.

She was greatly relieved when it appeared that he had decided not to pursue the conversation. It disconcerted her to find that his curiosity about her was apparently as great as hers about him. She knew she should have expected that, but she hadn't. Somehow, she'd thought he would remain a remote figure: a Warrior and not an individual.

That is because you could kill a Warrior, she told herself, but you may not be able to kill a man.

The long dinner proceeded with no further intimate conversation between them, and Rowena breathed a small sigh of relief when the men adjourned to Duncan's spacious study for brandy and cigars.

But her relief was short-lived as she quickly found herself to be the object of much curiosity on the part of the other women present. Rowena spent an uncomfortable half hour being subjected to many questions and to the close scrutiny of several of the younger women present.

It didn't take long for her to guess which of them was the woman who had nearly caused the commander to change his mind about

133

attending this dinner. She was quite lovely, but almost unbelievably shallow. And she seemed determined to cast Rowena as an ignorant peasant.

Rowena tolerated this for some time, but soon grew tired of the woman's barbed chatter and her airs. When she lifted a small glass of sherry toward her lips, Rowena saw to it that instead of reaching those highly rouged lips, it spilled over the very low front of her dress. Then, as the woman sputtered and squealed, she sat there and sipped delicately at her own sherry, trying her level best not to smile.

The next time you decide to behave badly, be sure it isn't toward a Dazhinn, she thought wickedly as Paulena led Felice off to try to rescue the gown.

"Well done," said Tabby, who was seated next to her on the sofa. "I thought of doing the same thing myself."

The two exchanged smiles, and for the first time since her arrival here, Paulena felt the comfort of being with her own people. Paulena was kind and Rowena loved her dearly, but her aunt was badly torn between her competing loyalties.

"I know such things are forbidden here," she whispered to Tabby, "but I couldn't seem to help myself."

Tabby put her hand over Rowena's briefly. "Believe me when I say that I understand."

The tall and elegant Carlotta glided over to join them. She arched a pale brow at Rowena.

"How very strange that the usually perfect Miss Tamblen should have had such a terrible accident. Personally, I had considered the possibility that she might 'accidentally' fall out of that ridiculous gown."

The three women burst out laughing, and the warmth of their presence stayed with Rowena— at least until the men returned.

"The commander really is quite taken with you," Carlotta whispered. "His behavior is most uncharacteristic. Even my Henry, who rarely notices such things, commented on it. But you must take care, Rowena, that you are not attracted to him as well."

With Carlotta's warning ringing in her ears, Rowena's gaze unwillingly sought out the man in question, only to find those pale eyes meeting hers from across the room as he began to make his way toward her.

Once issued, the warning would not be denied. As conversational groups formed and reformed, he seemed always to be at her side. And even when he wasn't, she knew exactly where he was without seeking him out. She'd developed an awareness of him that was frightening.

She kept hoping that the guests would leave— or that at least one of them would—but when that didn't happen, she finally managed to slip away and escape into the garden. The doors that led to the terrace were open on this warm night, and people had spilled out there, but the extensive gardens, with their mazes of shrubbery and

135

many paths and bubbling fountains, were completely empty.

Rowena walked aimlessly along the paths with the vague intention of finding her way to the charming gazebo near the woods. She felt despair dogging her steps. Not once since agreeing to this mission had she seriously doubted her ability to carry it out. Now she was confronting for the first time the terrible reality of what she was expected to do.

Can I do this thing? she asked herself silently. Can I kill—even to save my people?

She paused, raising her eyes to the stars and hating them for putting her into this position. How could such tiny, distant, cold lights have wreaked such havoc upon her life?

"Are you one of those who believes that answers are to be found in the stars?"

She froze at the sound of his voice, wondering how he could have crept up on her like that—and how he had once again managed to make an innocent remark that was so close to the truth.

She turned to him slowly, and as she did, she realized that they were once more alone. At the time she'd slipped away from the others, his back had been turned and he was deep in conversation with several men. But it was obvious that he'd become aware of her absence very quickly.

"No, I don't believe that," she said in response to his question. "We make our own destinies." Except when we allow others to make them for us, she thought—as I so foolishly did.

He offered his arm. "Let's walk on to the gazebo. I, too, feel the need to escape."

"It seems to me, Commander, that you must have spent all your life at such events, while I have the excuse of having lived a rural existence."

"That's not true. I grew up in the mountains among my clan. Not until I was eighteen did I first encounter city life, and then only on occasion while I was a student at Ashwara."

"Oh. I just assumed you'd grown up here, since Uncle Duncan said you were lifelong friends."

"Duncan's mother is descended from the Warrior clan and he always spent his summers with us in the mountains."

"But surely by now you've grown accustomed to this kind of life."

"Growing accustomed to something and taking pleasure from it are two very different things. I do what I must do because of my position."

"Is it true that *you* are the real ruler?" she asked, curious about how he saw his position.

He chuckled. "His Majesty can overrule me anytime he chooses."

"But he doesn't."

"No, although sometimes he temporizes."

"And that is what he's doing now—when you want war?"

"I do not *want* war, Miss Sandor. But when I know that war is to come, I want to win."

"I don't believe that," she stated coldly. "You're a Warrior; therefore you must want war."

137

"No one wants to see good men die terrible deaths, Miss Sandor. It is true that in times past, my clan often sought war. But those days are long gone. The more we develop weapons of destruction, the less we want to use them. One day, we will probably invent a weapon so terrible that no one will dare go to war."

Rowena remained silent. All her instincts told her that he was speaking the truth—and yet, in the end, what difference did it make? Whether or not he wanted war, it seemed likely that it would come—and she would have to stop it to save her people.

They had reached the gazebo. Darkness surrounded them and the sounds of the party had faded away. The gazebo was lit by oil lamps suspended from the corners of the roof and they swung slightly in the evening breeze, casting an ever-changing light over the scene. Rosebushes climbed the trellises that formed the walls of the gazebo, and their lush scent hung in the air. Rowena touched their soft petals and breathed deeply of the fragrance, all the while aware of the tall, silent man behind her.

When she turned back to him, he was staring at her intently, his expression a mixture of desire and bewilderment. She took a few steps away, needing desperately to put some space between them. Carlotta's warning was still echoing through her head.

The moments filled up with tension, then spilled over. She felt strange: languorous, heavy, intensely aware of her own body and of his—and the differences between them.

"We should return to the house," she said.

"Yes." But he didn't move, either.

Then he took her hand, holding it lightly in his much larger one. His eyes roved over her face as though he were seeking an answer that must surely be there.

"What is it about you, Rowena Sandor?" he asked softly, almost as though he were thinking aloud. "Why do you seem so . . . different?"

She stiffened involuntarily and he let go of her hand immediately. "I did not mean to insult you. I'm afraid that your candor has provoked the same behavior in me."

"Then that is surely the difference you spoke of, Commander," she said quickly.

He nodded, but she thought that he looked doubtful. She was sure that he must feel what she felt: that call of ancient enemies to each other. Perhaps, she reflected, the bonds of hatred can be every bit as powerful as the bonds of love. As a Dazhinn, she quite naturally despised Warriors; all her people did. But it seemed to her now that she hadn't truly understood how deep that strange bond could be.

"Will you permit me to escort you to the ballet?" he inquired, reverting to his formal tone.

"Yes," she said. "I would like that—although I can't help wondering if you would enjoy such a thing."

He laughed. "I'm expected to be there. I promise that I will make every attempt to stay awake."

She smiled. She liked the sound of his laughter, and she liked, too, the fact that he hadn't gone on to say that her presence would surely make it worthwhile. Even with her limited exposure to this society, she had already seen how men were given to such flattery.

He may be right, she thought. We do share something. But it was still very difficult for her to accept that she could have anything at all in common with this Warrior.

They walked back to the house. Her hand rested lightly on his arm as they strolled through the fragrant gardens, and for one brief moment, Rowena found herself wishing that they could be two different people, not separated by the ancient hatreds of their people.

The feeling passed quickly, though, because she was not one to waste time pining for a world that couldn't be.

"This is a mistake, Rowena. Even if the Council is correct and our people are in danger, sending you here to kill Zachary MacTavesh was a mistake."

Carlotta's blue eyes flashed at her as she spoke. Rowena glanced around at the others: Polly and Tabby. They were all seated in the shaded gazebo on a warm afternoon. She couldn't tell if the other two agreed with Carlotta, but at least they didn't disagree.

"Do you mean you doubt that I can accomplish my mission?" she asked Carlotta.

"Oh, I've no doubt that you can get close

enough to him to have the opportunity—something no one else could accomplish. The commander is clearly besotted with you. It's the talk of the court since Polly's dinner party.

"What I meant was two things, really. Can you actually do it—and if you do, do you seriously believe that you'll get away with it?"

"I have no choice, Carlotta. Everyone seems certain that war will come to our valley—and the Council is equally certain that the spell will be broken if it does."

Tabby spoke up. "You could always marry him, Rowena. I know that our spells have no effect upon Warriors, but in this case, a spell might not even be needed. As Carlotta said, he's quite mad about you."

"You forget that I am here only temporarily. When I've accomplished my mission, I will go home."

Complete silence greeted that statement and gave rise once more to the fear that she'd been trying to ward off. She looked from one to the other of them and found that only the forthright Carlotta would meet her eye.

"You will not be permitted to return, Rowena. The Council lied to you—as they lie to everyone who's descended. Tabby may be right. If you marry him, you may be able to change his mind."

"I could not change his mind," Rowena stated firmly. "Regardless of his feelings for me, he believes that war is necessary. And I think he also looks forward to gaining a victory in the valley where his ancestor was denied one."

The conversation changed abruptly as a servant arrived with lemonade, and when he left, it seemed that none of them wanted to resume it. That included Rowena, who was too confused to think about it, let alone speak of it.

Instead, they began to talk about the ballet performance and the other events to celebrate the king's birthday. Rowena hadn't yet mentioned the commander's invitation to Paulena, so she now told all of them.

"Then you will be sitting in the royal box, instead of with us," her aunt said in surprise.

Rowena stared at her. "I . . . I just assumed that we would all be together."

Paulena shook her head. "No, we have our own box, but Zach will certainly be with the king as always."

Mention of the king reminded Rowena of something she'd wondered about before. "Why hasn't someone simply cast a spell on the king to prevent him from agreeing to this war?"

Carlotta rolled her eyes. "Don't think we haven't tried. Those of us who have access to him have done our best, and perhaps we've succeeded in postponing it, but Zach will win in the end. Spell or no spell, the king is no match for Zach.

"Our spells can be powerful, but they must be reinforced often if there is opposition to them, and none of us sees him all that much, whereas Zach is with him daily."

"Is there no one then, who has any influence

over Zach?" she inquired bleakly.

"No one," Paulena said succinctly. "Not even Duncan, who is his closest friend. Zach already believes I have too much influence over Duncan, although he doesn't know how, of course. And the only others who could possibly dissuade him are his officers—all of whom are Warriors themselves and therefore unreachable.

"There are a goodly number of men in the parliament who do not want war. A few have been influenced by us, but many have come to that position completely on their own. But not one of them is willing to stand up to Zach."

"This is such a strange and complicated place." Rowena sighed. "So many things seem wrong, and yet I've met some good people, too."

Once again, a heavy silence descended upon them and Rowena found herself looking from one to the other. Finally it was Paulena who spoke.

"You must decide for yourself how you feel about them, Rowena."

"But she should also know the truth," Carlotta stated.

"No," Paulena said quickly, then turned to Rowena. "You are right: this is a very complicated situation. But you must be given the chance to form your own opinion."

Even though she tried, Rowena could get no more from them. She was left with the certainty that information was being withheld from her, although she couldn't imagine what it might be.

*   *   *

The days passed swiftly for Rowena—too swiftly. Accustomed to the much slower, quieter pace of life in the valley, she was now thoroughly caught up in Paulena's very busy life.

There were numerous visits to various shops, all of them filled with wonders beyond Rowena's imagining. There were riding lessons where she struggled to learn the difficult art of riding sidesaddle. There were still more wardrobe fittings and further selections to be made.

She practiced curtsying under the watchful eye of her aunt and was taught court etiquette. And she learned to dance from a tutor hired for private lessons.

She also accompanied Paulena to several meetings of her suffrage group and discovered that nearly half of those present were her own people. At these meetings, the commander's name was regularly invoked. If he could be persuaded to support their cause, the parliament would surely give women the right to vote. Hopeful glances were cast her way, since by now it seemed that everyone knew of his interest in her.

She also went with Paulena and several other women, including Carlotta, to a settlement house, an experience that left her badly shaken and very angry. She saw haggard women and underfed children who had been abandoned by their husbands and fathers, either through death or desertion. When she asked Paulena why these women continued to bear children they couldn't feed, she learned that they had no choice.

"Birth control is regarded as an evil here," Paulena told her disgustedly. "Women are expected to bear as many children as they can."

Rowena was appalled. Among her own people, no woman bore children who were unwanted, the means of preventing them having been well-known for many centuries. Paulena explained that this stricture had come down from the Warrior clans, where it was necessary to replace those who died in great numbers in battle.

But Rowena also learned that here, too, the Dazhinn women disregarded the rule against using their magic. They had to be very careful, but since the few doctors willing to work among the poor were always harried, the women were able to deal with the lesser complaints without attracting their attention.

As they rode home, leaving behind the dirty, foul-smelling streets of the poor, Rowena's anger at the injustice in this land rose again. She would never understand these people, she thought disgustedly. Many of them seemed quite nice, and yet they tolerated conditions such as those she'd just witnessed. How could they do it, when there was clearly enough wealth to go around?

Paulena told her that things would improve in time, remarking that even Zach had expressed the opinion that something must be done to improve the lot of the poor.

"Of course," Paulena added with a grim twist to her mouth, "his concern seems not to be for the poor themselves, but for the cause of civil order. There were riots last year when some of their houses were pulled down to make way for new factories."

When they reached the house, Rowena was handed a letter. Paulena immediately recognized the crest on the seal and told her it was from Zach.

Rowena stared at the elaborate crest that showed a great bird clutching arrows in its talons. A falcon, she assumed, though she'd never seen one. She knew from her history that the Warriors had once used them for hunting. She frowned at the words surrounding the bird, but they were in a language she didn't know.

"It's the old language of his people," Paulena told her. "It means 'Victory or Death.' I asked Zach about it once."

Rowena opened the message and scanned it, then turned to the curious Paulena.

"He's asking me to join him for a ceremony at the garrison, to celebrate the king's birthday."

Paulena frowned. "That could be very difficult for you. I've never gone there; none of us has. We fear that the presence of all those Warriors would be very upsetting." She shuddered.

The presence of just one of them was quite enough for Rowena. "Then you think that I should decline the invitation?"

"You will have to decide that for yourself."

"I think that perhaps I should go," Rowena said. It seemed to her that she needed to be reminded of the importance of her mission—

and visiting the home of the Warriors would certainly do that.

Besides, there was the intriguing challenge of being the first of her people to enter the modern-day lair of the Warrior clan.

Chapter Six

Since she was riding in a carriage sent by the commander, Rowena had no opportunity to see the royal garrison, headquarters to the army, until she was inside it. And then the first thing she saw was the commander himself, resplendent once more in his gleaming white uniform with its ceremonial sword.

He opened the carriage door and extended a hand to her. She took it and felt even more strongly than before that uncanny awareness of him that seemed to vibrate deep within her.

"Welcome to Shemoth, Miss Sandor," he said with a slight bow.

Shemoth. The very name sent shudders through her. That had been the name of the ancient stronghold of the Warrior clans. This could not be the same place, but as she stared at her surroundings, she saw that it had probably been built to look the same as that old fortress high in the mountains beyond the valley.

This fortress, too, was built into the side of a mountain, with great battlements and high towers and soldiers scurrying to and fro. A large platform with chairs had been set up in the very middle of the huge courtyard.

But Rowena noticed all this only in passing. For a moment, she feared a return of her illness, because she felt that same light-headedness and strangeness she'd felt after her Descent. Then she knew it must be a reaction to the presence of so many Warriors.

The army was composed of ordinary men, but all the officers were of the Warrior clans, and she could tell easily from their uniforms and from their demeanor which ones they were: tall men with erect carriage and an arrogant way of striding about.

"The king will arrive presently, together with his entourage, but in the meantime, allow me to offer you some refreshment after your journey."

She nodded her thanks and he led her across the stone courtyard and through a wide arch. Inside, she was confronted by soaring walls of stone and carved wooden arches. The walls were decorated with a bewildering array of armaments, and one wall was completely covered by a gigantic mural. She stopped to stare at it.

"That was commissioned when the place was built," he told her. "There are no such murals in the original Shemoth, since my people weren't inclined toward such things."

Rowena thought that if his clan *had* had any artists, they would certainly have painted this way. The scenes were all of great battles, shown in hideously gory detail. She turned away without comment, and he led her up the wide staircase and then down a series of corridors, where old suits of armor stood in shadowy niches.

Then they emerged once again into a large room with still more armaments and walls lined with portraits, all of them formal portraits of men mounted on great black horses. She recalled the stories about the horses of the Warrior clans: huge animals who had carried the men into battle.

Finally, she noticed the large crest above the stone archway ahead of them: the same crest she'd seen on his letter. And she belatedly realized that the portraits must all be his own ancestors. She'd known, of course, that in ancient times, the clan chieftain had been a hereditary title, but she hadn't realized that that old tradition must still hold true.

She stopped before one time-darkened portrait and drew in a sharp breath. He stopped beside her.

"The resemblance is remarkable, isn't it?" he said as he, too, stared at it.

"Who is it?" she asked, although she thought she already knew the answer.

"That is Egan, the chief at the time of the final battle—or nonbattle—with the Dazhinn. Legend has it that that was painted by a Dazhinn artist who had been captured in an earlier battle."

Rowena had to suppress a shudder. It seemed likely that the artist had indeed been one of her people. The fine quality and great detail of the painting suggested that.

"Whatever else one can say about them, the Dazhinn did have talent in art," he remarked. "As you can see, this painting is of far superior quality to the others, excepting perhaps the more recent ones.

"Given the fact that my own people did not possess such talents, I've often wondered if that might have given rise to the stories about their magic. I have in my quarters some other items that are said to have come from Dazhinn artisans, as well."

She could not look at him and she dared not speak. Her mind was filled with the fate of her unlucky ancestors who'd been captured and enslaved by the Warriors.

But he seemed not to notice her silence as he went on. "At the time of Egan, there was a small colony of Dazhinn living and working in the old Shemoth. Egan, it seemed, had developed a taste for Dazhinn art of all kinds, so instead of killing those he captured, he set them up to create things for him. It was certainly a better fate than that suffered by Warriors who fell into the hands of the Dazhinn."

"Wh-what do you mean?" she asked.

"If the legends are true, the Dazhinn would rob the men they captured of their minds—and

151

then cast them out of their valley to wander about as helpless as babies."

"That can't be true!" she stated heatedly before she could stop herself. Her people would never have been that cruel.

He smiled at her. "Do you believe, then, that they were no more than gentle artisans or that the magic they practiced was only of a harmless nature?"

"Yes, of course. At least, that's what I was taught."

"Then you were taught wrong, Miss Sandor. The Dazhinn were as fierce and brutal in their own way as my own people—perhaps more so."

This time, she managed to control her tongue, but she was seething inside. How like a Warrior, she thought, to make up such stories in order to excuse their own behavior. Her people had never sought to conquer, only to defend themselves against the rapacious Warriors.

"If they did as you said, then they must have possessed magic," she told him pointedly.

"Not necessarily. There are plants that can produce such effects when chewed or brewed into tea. In their milder forms, they were used for many years—and are still being used—to take away pain."

He was right about that. Such plants grew in their valley and were used by her people, although they as often used their magic to accomplish the same ends. But she'd never considered the possibility that such plants could be employed to destroy a mind—and she certainly didn't believe her people to have been capable of such a thing.

"Have you decided to try to persuade me to believe in Dazhinn magic?" he asked in a teasing tone as he led her through the archway beneath his clan's crest.

Never had the temptation been greater to do just that, but Rowena merely smiled. "I don't know that I believe in it myself, Commander."

They entered what was obviously a formal reception room, filled with heavy, dark furniture in the highly ornate style that seemed to be so popular here. The art that adorned the walls was of quite good quality, and she recalled that he'd mentioned his wife had collected art.

"Are these your personal quarters?" she asked.

"Yes. I keep a small house in the city as well, but I've been staying here since those assassination attempts. When I stay in the city, I use an apartment at the palace that His Majesty has kindly put at my disposal."

He gestured to an open doorway. "There's a smaller sitting room through here."

She followed him through yet another doorway, then stopped abruptly, unable to prevent a small cry from escaping her lips. The room could have been in any of the larger homes in her village. All the golden wood furniture and virtually everything else in the room was obviously Dazhinn in origin.

Or so she thought at first. Upon closer inspection, she saw that several pieces, while quite well done, were of somewhat inferior quality.

"Do you like it?" he asked, watching her as she walked around the room, picking up various items to examine them. There were the etched silver and gold bowls and urns that were present in all Dazhinn homes, as well as several black-wood and gold boxes that were also a common item among her people.

"These are the Dazhinn items you spoke of?" she asked, trying very hard to keep her voice even.

"Yes. Everything here is Dazhinn—except for a few small items of furniture that were made more recently in that style." Then he repeated his question.

She nodded, unable for the moment to speak. At least he didn't have any tapestries. If she had seen evidence that any of her own ancestors had been enslaved by the Warriors, she knew she could not have maintained her outward calm. As it was, she saw what was clearly the work of people whose descendants she knew. As with Sandor tapestries, other crafts tended to be handed down over the centuries family by family.

"Why do you have it here," she asked, her voice harsher than she'd intended, "when you hate them so."

"I don't hate the Dazhinn," he replied, seemingly surprised at her words—or perhaps at her vehemence. "They're long gone and of no concern to me now. And I *do* admire their work."

An aide entered at that moment, bearing a

tray laden with food and drink. Rowena continued to look around the room as his words echoed through her brain. "Long gone." She felt like a ghost, a pitiable wraith that had somehow gotten lost in time.

As they ate, he began to talk about the day's events. She managed to nod and make appropriate comments, but her mind was still on his dismissive statement about her people.

He's right to dismiss us, even though we do still exist, she thought. There are too few of us and our magic is of no consequence in this world. Even if they were suddenly transported back to their original home, she doubted that he would consider them to be a threat.

"Are you feeling ill, Miss Sandor?" he asked with concern as she belatedly realized he had fallen silent. "If you'd care to rest for a while . . ."

"No, I'm fine," she assured him. "Forgive me. I was just woolgathering. I'm afraid I tend to do that."

She saw the glimmer of amusement in his eyes and realized that it was highly unlikely that any other woman had ever failed to pay the closest possible attention to him.

"Silence is a quality rarely appreciated by women in my experience," he observed.

She smiled, trying out the flirtatious smile she'd practiced before a mirror a few times. "Tell me, Commander, what would you do if the Dazhinn suddenly reappeared?"

For one mercifully brief moment, something flickered in his eyes. Then he laughed. "I'm not

155

sure. I suppose that would depend upon their intentions."

She laughed, too, but something in his words troubled her for reasons she didn't understand.

Another aide appeared, a young Warrior this time. There was no mistaking his pride of bearing. "His Majesty will be here within the half hour, Chief."

Zach thanked the man and dismissed him, then turned to her. "He will be reviewing the troops before we dine, and that may take a while, since he also will visit the armory and ask many tedious questions to show that he's interested. Are you certain that you wouldn't prefer to rest and join us later for dinner?"

"No, I'd like to join you if I may." She would have preferred to stay here, even though she wasn't tired. But she knew that she'd come here to see her people's enemy on display.

"You may indeed. The queen has not accompanied him, but others of the court will be bringing wives."

She wished that Paulena or Tabitha were coming—or even Duncan. But both Duncan and Tabitha's husband, although they were noblemen, were busy with preparations for the birthday celebration in the city.

They started to leave the room, but suddenly he stopped and laid his hand over hers that rested on his arm.

"I'm very glad that you accepted my invitation. To be quite honest with you, I didn't expect it."

"Why not?" she asked, surprised.

"There is already gossip at court, and I thought that might displease you," he replied, watching her intently as he spoke.

"If that is all the court has to talk about, then they should find themselves something more important to do."

"My thought exactly," he replied with a smile and a small bow.

Commander-in-Chief Zachary MacTavesh viewed the display before him with little interest, although he took care to disguise that fact. Parades and precision drills and displays of horsemanship did not make an army, but he had long since become resigned to the annual pageant for the king.

Instead, his thoughts strayed to the woman seated behind him, out of sight now but scarcely out of mind. In fact, she hadn't been out of his mind for long since he'd first met her on the beach.

Only those who knew him well were aware of the fact that Zach was a very astute observer of human behavior, and even then, they were often surprised when he noticed certain things. But it was an ancient trait of Warriors, harking back to a time when all combat was of necessity hand to hand. Divining an enemy's weakness or hesitation was an important ingredient of victory.

At the moment, he was puzzling over the uneasiness he'd noticed in Rowena Sandor from the moment she'd arrived here. It surprised him, because she was usually so self-possessed.

Was it him or this place? he wondered, then decided that perhaps it was both. After all, the two were inextricably linked, and she'd already expressed her feelings on the subject of war.

And yet she'd accepted his invitation and had seemed surprised when he'd told her that he thought she'd decline. But had she come merely out of curiosity about Shemoth, or because she enjoyed his company?

That, he decided, was the question that tormented him most. Furthermore, it was a question he'd never been confronted with in the past. Women were invariably drawn to him. But there were women—and then there was Rowena Sandor.

He found her fascination with the damned Dazhinn charming, if rather strange for a woman who seemed otherwise exceptionally rational. Her heated denial of their cruelty argued for a vivid imagination. But then she came from a family of artisans and was one herself, and such people were always given to flights of fancy.

He smiled, thinking that her defense of the Dazhinn might well spring from a feeling of kinship with them, since they, too, had been great artisans.

The king interrupted his thoughts with some questions and comments, and when at last he was able to retreat again into his mind, he turned to the problem she presented.

He must have her. Never in his life had he wanted a woman so much. The need gnawed at him incessantly, even when she wasn't around. Furthermore, it was a need that couldn't be satisfied with anyone else. He'd already tried that, and it hadn't worked.

He chafed under the restrictions of the times. His illustrious ancestors had had no such problems. If they wanted a woman, they took her. He felt himself hopelessly caught between urges far more suited to those times and the reality of his own life. And the result was that when he was with her, he found himself thinking too much about centuries past, when society imposed no such restrictions.

There was nothing for it but to marry her. An affair was simply out of the question. She was the niece-by-marriage of his oldest and best friend. Furthermore, she wasn't a widow or divorcée and was, in all likelihood, a virgin.

Zach wasn't sure why the thought of marrying her troubled him. After all, he knew he should marry again. She was young, but he'd also accepted the fact that he would have to marry someone younger, even though he preferred the company of women past their giddy youth. Unfortunately, such women were also past their safe childbearing years, and he needed heirs.

So why was he bothered by the idea? The reason eluded him, seeming to spring from some deep part of him that he couldn't quite reach.

Then he wondered if what might be troubling him was the possibility that she would refuse. She'd seemed quite adamant about not marrying, though he wasn't inclined to take that at face value—even from her. All women wanted husbands and children. Not even Rowena Sandor could be *that* different.

The parade ended and the king expressed his great interest in visiting the armory. Zach left off his thoughts gratefully and resumed his role of host.

Rowena, too, was glad that the interminable display was ended. Seated next to the king's eldest daughter, a sharp-faced young woman perhaps 15 or 16 years of age, she'd been forced to endure the girl's incessant chatter and questions. Raised in a society where no one set himself or herself above others, she was shocked at the princess's assumption that everything she said or did was acceptable, even welcome.

The king announced his intention of visiting the armory, and the women, it seemed, were to be ushered into the fortress to await them. Rowena was most unhappy at this turn of events, because she wanted to see just what weaponry they possessed. Knowing that she couldn't insist upon accompanying the men herself, she decided to let the annoying princess speak for her.

"Father, I would like to see the armory, too," the girl said eagerly, thanks to a gentle "push" from Rowena.

The king turned to her, surprised. "But my dear, you've never shown any interest in such things before. Wouldn't you rather join the ladies?"

The girl shook her head adamantly. "No, I

want to come with you. Uncle Zach won't mind, will you?" She smiled at the commander, then turned eagerly to Rowena.

"Miss Sandor will accompany me."

"Very well, then," the king said—and it was done. Rowena managed to look displeased when the commander's eyes met hers.

Rowena and the princess rode in a hastily summoned carriage, while the king and the commander and other men mounted their horses. The armory was a considerable distance away in the sprawling complex. Having accomplished her goal, Rowena was more kindly disposed toward the irritating princess and let her ramble on.

"What I've heard is true, isn't it, Miss Sandor? I've seen for myself now how Uncle Zach looks at you." She sighed, then went on without waiting for a response. "I wish I were older. Then I'd marry him myself."

Rowena thought about the commander's remark earlier. Even if she were older, she doubted that this noisy young woman would have a chance. Silence was not one of her virtues.

By the time they reached the armory, the princess was declaring Rowena to be her "good friend," and Rowena decided not to disabuse her of that belief. She was actually beginning to feel some sympathy for her, trapped as she must be in such a rigid life.

For the next hour, they trooped through the vast armory, where Rowena saw the true power of the barbarians. She hadn't been particularly impressed by the parade—but here she saw awesome sights.

There were rows upon rows of rifles with sharp knives affixed to their barrels. Rowena knew they were rifles only because she'd seen some in a glass-fronted case in Duncan's study and had asked Paulena what they were.

But it was the other weapons that truly horrified her, and she listened closely as the commander talked about range and accuracy, finding it necessary several times to silence the princess with her magic. There were huge guns mounted on wheels that fired exploding projectiles many times larger than the bullets she'd seen in Duncan's study. If a small bullet could kill a man easily, then how many could be killed with the foot-long versions she saw here? And the commander said that they were accurate within a few feet at a range of two miles!

She tried not to shudder as she imagined those guns being trained on her valley, raining death upon them all.

And there were other things, too. The commander seemed quite excited about something he called a "grenade," a device that a man could throw that would then explode in the midst of the enemy.

Finally, he began to talk about chemicals, a term Rowena had heard but didn't quite understand.

"We are very close to developing a gas that can be contained in a shell that will explode upon contact with the ground. All that remains is to develop masks for our own troops," he said proudly, "and we're making progress on that as well."

"And what does this gas do?" the king inquired, clearly impressed.

"It will kill all who breathe it within a matter of an hour, Your Majesty. With it, we can destroy far more of the enemy more quickly than with more conventional means."

Rowena was appalled. She felt quite literally sick thinking about it. He had spoken of a weapon so powerful that it would prevent war because no one would dare to use it. Surely this was what he'd meant.

"And the Atanians have nothing like this?" the king asked.

"No, although they're working on it. I'm confident that we're several years ahead of them on this."

"Well done, Zach!" the king said, clapping him on the shoulder and showing the most animation Rowena had yet seen. "Perhaps that will deter them—if they know about it, of course."

"Oh, they know about it," the commander replied. "I've made certain of that. But I think it will only spur them to war more quickly, before we have too much of it."

The king nodded soberly as Rowena stood there, horrified. He didn't even seem to notice that the commander had virtually ensured war would come quickly by giving the enemy this information.

"Yes," he said. "I begin to see the importance

of moving quickly. We must discuss this further in council."

Rowena saw the gleam of triumph in Zachary MacTavesh's pale eyes and averted her gaze quickly. She felt too ill to be angry with him at this point, and after all, he was simply playing the role assigned to him centuries ago.

Throughout the long dinner that followed, Rowena retreated into her thoughts as much as possible. Having now seen the power of the barbarians, she was convinced that if that power were brought to the valley, the spell would be destroyed. How could it not? The magic her people possessed was so small by comparison with what she'd seen. It might have taken them many centuries, but they had indeed found their own, far more potent, magic.

When the dinner was over, the royal party prepared to depart for the city. The carriage that had brought her here was the last in the long line that awaited them in the courtyard, and after saying her good-byes to the princess and several others, Rowena started toward it, still lost in her bleak thoughts and wanting nothing more at the moment than to be away from this place.

The commander was still in conversation with the king and several noblemen. She knew she should wait to thank him for the invitation, but went instead to the waiting carriage, deciding she could thank him later.

But just as the driver got down to assist her,

the commander suddenly appeared and the man quickly moved away. She managed a smile.

"Forgive me for not waiting to thank you, Commander, but I find that I'm very tired."

"I'm sorry you didn't have the opportunity to rest earlier," he said. "I don't know what got into Princess Melba and I'm sorry that she insisted upon dragging you along with her."

"She seems a very lonely young woman," Rowena remarked, for lack of anything else to say.

"She is, I think. Her two sisters are much younger and her mother is unwell."

"She seems quite fond of you."

He chuckled. "So she is, though her fondness has become something of a problem in recent years."

Rowena smiled. "Yes, she told me that if she were older, she'd marry you."

He rolled his eyes. "I thank the fates every day that they conspired to keep so many years between us."

In spite of her bleak mood, Rowena laughed. His occasional teasing and jokes had a strange effect upon her—perhaps because it happened so rarely.

The driver had already opened the carriage door, and he now assisted her inside, then stood there in the doorway.

"I must remain here tomorrow, but I will be coming into the city the day after. Would you do me the honor of dining with me then? I thought, given your interest in the Dazhinn, we might dine at Tralanna. Or have you been there with your aunt and uncle?"

"No, although Paulena told me about it." It was one of the elegant eating places in the city, and the name derived from her people's annual festival following the harvest.

"Thank you. I'd like that," she told him.

"If the weather permits, we could go riding in the royal park in the afternoon," he went on. "That is, if you enjoy riding."

"I do, but I've just barely managed to learn to ride sidesaddle," she said.

He smiled. "And you don't like it much. I don't blame you. At home, women always ride astride, as they must where you grew up. Sidesaddle looks charming, but like so many things women do, it must be a nuisance."

"You begin to sound like my aunt's group, Commander. I'm sure they'd be happy to know they have an ally in you."

This time, his chuckle became a laugh. "I might have guessed that Paulena has already introduced you to them and their cause."

"She has—and I support it."

"I would not have expected it to be otherwise," he said, his smile still in place. "We will talk about it sometime."

Indeed we will, she thought, recalling the women's interest in his position. If a Warrior could be persuaded of the rightness of their cause, then perhaps Paulena was correct when she said it would happen.

His eyes bored into her for a long, uncomfortable moment. She saw a hunger there that should have frightened her, but instead she felt a very unwelcome response deep inside, as though his gaze possessed the power to melt away her resistance.

Then he backed away from the open carriage door. "Good-bye, Miss Sandor."

He closed the door and vanished the moment she responded with her own good-bye. It seemed that he was now as eager to get away from her as she was to be gone from this place—and him.

"Yes, we are aware of their weapons—except for the gas. I hadn't heard about that, but some of the others probably have."

It was the day after her trip to Shemoth and the first opportunity Rowena had had to talk to Paulena without risking being overheard by the ever-present household staff. They were walking through the gardens, where the beauty and the fragrances that surrounded them seemed so incongruous with talk of weapons of death and destruction.

"But, Polly, you can't seriously believe that the spell would hold up against such terrible things." Her aunt had suggested several times that even if war came to their valley, they wouldn't be in any real danger.

"Who is to say if their weapons are more powerful than our magic?" Paulena asked, not really answering her question.

"But the spell is already weakening. You know that, because it began before you descended.

And it grows worse, year by year."

"Which means that one day we will be forced to return whether or not there is war." Paulena nodded solemnly. "That is why I think the risk you would be taking is not worth it."

She had a point—and one that had occurred to Rowena as well. In fact, she'd made that very point to the Council, and she now gave her aunt the answer they had given her.

"We need more time so that we can change things here."

Paulena said nothing, but her silence felt very heavy to Rowena. Even though her people had very serious strictures against prying into another person's thoughts, it was impossible—at least among family and close friends—not to pick up some things. And what Rowena sensed was that her aunt was holding something back. Furthermore, it wasn't the first time she'd sensed that.

"Polly, I don't know what to do," she said miserably. "I think he will very soon persuade the king to go to war." She related the conversation at the armory.

"He has virtually guaranteed that the Atanians will take some action by letting it be known that the gas exists, but is not yet fully ready. And the king did not protest his actions."

"The king never protests. I think even he regards Zach as being the true ruler. He is quite satisfied with having all the trappings and leaving Zach to rule the land. Throughout history, that has been the case more often than not.

"The kings have always feared the Warriors—

and the Warrior chieftain in particular. The present king's great-grandfather may well have died at the hands of the Warriors because he tried to prevent a war."

"I don't understand. If the Warriors are so powerful, then why don't they rule? Why bother with a king at all? There wasn't one when they tried to fight us."

"That's true, but several centuries later, an ancestor of the present king somehow managed to unite all the warring factions that made up this country at that time. He accomplished it through peaceful means. Then he persuaded the Warrior chieftain at that time to join with them.

"Like us, the Warriors have never been great in number, but as we made up for that with our magic, they always made up for it with their ferocity.

"So a deal was struck between them that has held to this day. The Warriors defend the country, while the king rules it. The Warrior chieftain is the one man who does not bow before the king, though he is sworn to defend the king as well as the country. And his officers, who are all Warriors themselves, of course, swear their allegiance to him, not to the king.

"I think that the truth is that the Warriors have no taste for the ceremonies and other duties of the king and they are quite content to let him have them. Certainly that is true of Zach."

Paulena had been gazing out over the gardens, but now she turned to Rowena. "I think Zach will ask you to marry him—and perhaps soon. He's not a patient man in any event, and he knows that he cannot have you unless he marries you. Your status as my niece prevents him from persuading you to be his mistress."

"I'm not so sure that he will—ask me to marry him, I mean. He senses something that troubles him about me."

Paulena nodded. "Yes, he finds me troubling as well—and probably for the same reason. I had once thought that he merely resented the control I have over Duncan, but now I'm inclined to think that something in him knows who we are. That's why I worry when you begin to talk about the Dazhinn."

Her mention of that prompted Rowena to tell her about his quarters at Shemoth and his revelation that the Warriors had once had a colony of Dazhinn artisans working at the original Shemoth.

Paulena nodded. "I have seen those things and he told me about the colony, too. He used to keep a house in the city and I saw them there. I remember thanking the gods that there were no Sandor tapestries."

"I kept thinking how terrible it must have been for them," Rowena shuddered, then recalled the absurd story the commander had told her about her own people.

"He said that when our people captured Warriors, they robbed them of their minds and then sent them from the valley as helpless as babies," she said scornfully.

"I hadn't heard about that," Paulena said,

but Rowena thought she didn't seem at all surprised.

"Surely you don't believe such a terrible tale?"

Paulena shrugged. "That happened in the distant past. The most difficult thing for all of us who descend is understanding that a period that is no more than ancient history to them is still quite close in time to us."

"But our people have never been cruel!" Rowena protested. "All we've ever wanted is to live in peace with our neighbors."

"So we've always been told," Paulena replied cryptically, then quickly changed the subject.

"There is a meeting tonight. We'll be having some speakers from the Parliament. Will you come with me?"

"Speakers from Parliament?" Rowena echoed. "Men?" The two meetings she'd attended had been all women.

Paulena nodded. "There are some good men in Parliament who support us, but until now, none of them has been willing to say so openly. The meeting will be very well attended, and there will undoubtedly be some hecklers. Duncan wanted to ask Zach's officer who is in charge of civil order in the city to provide protection for us, but I persuaded him not to make the request. The man would certainly go to Zach before agreeing, and I would prefer not to force his hand just yet."

Rowena was astonished at the number of people who filled the hall to overflowing. She had arrived early with Paulena and was seated in the front row, while Paulena, Carlotta, Tabitha, and several other women were up on the stage, together with the two members of Parliament. One of them was a slim, handsome man with dark hair and dark eyes that burned with intensity. The other was an older man who smiled and laughed a lot.

Rowena turned again to scan the audience and saw that every seat was now filled and many people were standing at the back of the large hall. Most were women, but to her surprise, there were a fair number of men as well, most of whom appeared to have accompanied wives. The women were of all ages, but the men in attendance were almost all young.

Her gaze fell on a small group of rather rough-looking men standing near the doors. Others were casting looks their way as well. Rowena hoped there wouldn't be trouble. Paulena had said that she thought they would do nothing worse than shout insults.

Duncan was not among the men present. Neither were the husbands of Carlotta or Tabitha. Paulena had told her that they'd decided not to use their powers to persuade them to come. All three men were powerful enough that their presence would not go unnoticed, and the women felt that they should wait until their support would be more important.

"Their support will be assumed by most people, in any event," Paulena had told her, "because otherwise, they wouldn't permit us to become involved."

People were still milling about, talking among themselves or going up to the stage to speak with the women there. Rowena glanced up at the stage and saw that Carlotta and Paulena were trying to attract her attention. She left her seat and approached them. They came to the edge of the stage and leaned toward her.

"We're worried about those men at the back," Paulena said. "Someone overheard them talking outside and thinks they may be here to do more than try to shout us down."

"Do you mind giving up your seat and going back there to keep an eye on them?" Carlotta asked.

Rowena nodded quickly. The words were not spoken, but she understood what she was to do. She made her way through the crowd and down the side aisle, going to the back of the hall where she was no more than 20 feet from the group of men, who were laughing among themselves.

Then Carlotta rapped sharply on the podium to quiet the crowd and the speeches began. Within moments, several of the men began to shout taunts and insults. From where she stood, Rowena could now see a large sack that sat on the floor in the midst of them. Obviously, it contained something they intended to throw at the stage.

Although she was already angry at their rudeness, she let them continue to heckle the speakers for a time. To have shut them up completely would be suspicious. Everyone knew they were here to cause trouble.

Then, as the first of the Parliament members began to speak, she saw several of the men looking down at the sack, and she decided it was time for them to cease their activities. She sent that message to them loud and clear, then watched with satisfaction as they stopped shouting and simply stood there passively. A few people turned to see why the heckling had stopped, but most ignored them as the impassioned younger member of Parliament began to talk about equality for women.

Rowena focused her attention on him, although she kept an eye on the troublemakers from time to time, in case she needed to reinforce her "message." He was a marvelous speaker and Rowena was quite impressed with his sincerity.

She looked over the nodding, clapping crowd and thought again that there were good people here. She could no longer think of all of them as barbarians.

When Paulena rose to thank everyone for attending, Rowena sent a "message" to the group of men to leave. One by one, they turned and filed out, leaving behind their sack. As soon as they were gone, she walked over to see what it contained. But when she drew close to it, there was no need to open it. She could smell the rotten fruit and vegetables. She picked it up and carried it out to leave it in a corner of the lobby, then returned smiling with grim satisfaction. Magic did have its uses, even here.

Everyone adjourned to an adjoining room where refreshments had been arranged. As

Rowena made her way through the crowd, she heard more than one exclamation of surprise that the men hadn't further disrupted the proceedings.

But most people seemed to be talking about David Weilor, the younger member of Parliament. Rowena wanted to meet him, and was pleased to find him standing with her aunt and Carlotta. But before she could reach them, Tabby laid a hand on her arm.

"Everyone is talking about how strange it was that those men just shut up and then left quietly. Perhaps we converted them." Her eyes gleamed with wicked amusement.

Rowena laughed. "Why didn't I think of that?"

Together with Tabby, she made her way to Paulena and Carlotta, and her aunt promptly introduced her to David Weilor. Rowena told him quite sincerely that she was very much impressed with his speech.

And as they talked, she found herself equally impressed with the man himself. There was a difference between the way he treated her and the manner in which she—and women in general—were treated by most other men. In fact, if she hadn't known better, she would have thought him one of them.

"Of course," he said after reviewing the situation in Parliament, "what happens depends largely upon the commander—as all things do."

Rowena, who had managed not to think about him for the entire evening, was unhappy to have his name arise now.

"Court gossip reaches down even to the most lowly members of Parliament," he told her, smiling. "And I am wondering if you can persuade him to our point of view."

"That remains to be seen," Rowena said carefully. "I claim no influence over Commander MacTavesh."

"He can be a nuisance," David Weilor went on. "But in the past, he has also been supportive of our efforts to increase the power of Parliament. He's a very hard man to figure. I'm told it was much easier to know where previous Warrior chiefs would stand on any issue."

She made no response, although she certainly agreed with him about the complexity of the commander. Instead, they talked of other things, and she found herself liking David Weilor very much. In fact, she was hard put to recall any man other than poor dead Lothar whom she'd liked this much. And it was clear that he found her company pleasurable as well, since they remained together for the rest of the evening, parting only when Paulena announced that it was time to leave.

"You seem quite taken with Mr. Weilor," her aunt remarked when they were in their carriage.

"I am. I truly like him, Polly. He seems so much like the men at home in the way he treats women."

Paulena nodded. "Yes, we've noticed that. And he isn't the only one. Things *are* changing here, though I'm not sure we can lay claim to any real part in it."

"But it is you and Carlotta and Tabby who are the leaders of the group," Rowena pointed out.

"True, but we couldn't be leaders if we didn't have followers. Do be careful about David Weilor, though. If word gets back to Zach about your interest in each other, it could be bad for him. His position in Parliament is already rather precarious."

"What do you mean?"

"He is too outspoken on too many issues, and he is beginning to attract a sizable following. He's spoken out recently on several occasions against going to war with the Atanians."

"But what could the commander do?" Rowena asked.

"He could do anything he chose to do," Paulena said flatly. "But what he will probably do is find someone to run for his seat in the next election and then see to it that that candidate wins."

"How can he do that?"

"The elections are not always honest, though everyone pretends that they are. Votes can be bought."

"Would he do that?" Rowena asked.

"He might. Zach talks about the people's right to govern themselves and I think he truly does believe that, but he is still a Warrior, and all his instincts push him to do what he believes is right for the people, even if they do not see it that way themselves.

"Besides"—Paulena smiled—"Something tells me that Zach could be a very jealous suitor, and woe to any man who caught your eye."

Chapter Seven

"I understand that you've met David Weilor."

Rowena turned to the commander sharply, unable to conceal her surprise. How could he know? Did the man have spies even here—in his own country?

"Yes. He spoke at the meeting last night. Am I being spied upon, Commander—or do you have your agents watching our group?"

"The latter." He smiled. "It's impossible for me to keep myself informed firsthand about everything."

Terror crawled along her spine as she wondered if the men she'd cast a spell on could have been *his* men. Then the fear was mixed with anger as she thought about their plans to disrupt the meeting.

"I'm told there were some men there who appeared to be planning to cause problems, but that for some reason, they failed to do so."

She nodded. "Yes, there were some men at the back who shouted insults for a time, but they did nothing else."

"What do you think of Mr. Weilor?"

She thought that he seemed curious and nothing more, but she still chose her words carefully. "He's quite a good speaker, and of course I agree with what he said."

"He is making enemies, though, and I'm afraid that he's the type who wouldn't even realize that."

"Are *you* one of those enemies?" she asked, staring at him.

He laughed. "Sometimes I forget how blunt-speaking you are. No, I'm not an enemy of his—not in the sense that I was referring to. I was speaking of the kind of enemy who might attempt to silence him—permanently."

"You mean *kill* him?" she asked, now finding this conversation ominous indeed.

He nodded. "We live in a time of great changes and great passions, and there are always those who might allow their passions to be carried too far. I had intended to speak to Paulena about him, but since you've met him, you'll do just as well. He should learn to be careful—if not about what he says, then about his person."

"Why don't you just tell him this yourself?"

"Because coming from me, it would sound too much like a threat. I would rather that he heard it from a supporter."

"I will ask Paulena to speak to him about it. But who would this enemy be?"

179

"That he must figure out for himself—and I'm sure that he can. There are those in Parliament and at court as well who believe that he wants too much change too quickly."

"I understand that he's spoken out several times against war. Doesn't that make him your enemy?"

"It makes him an adversary, but not one that overly concerns me. When it comes to issues of war, Parliament has very little power."

They rode on through the wooded park that made up a large portion of the grounds of the royal palace. Rowena wondered exactly what he'd been trying to tell her. Was he genuinely concerned for the safety of David Weilor—or was he using her as a messenger to warn Weilor of his own displeasure?

And just what had his agents at the meeting seen? There were several other men standing at the rear of the hall, in addition to the troublemakers—men who'd given up their seats to women in the overflowing crowd.

I am playing a very dangerous game, she thought with an inward shudder. He may not believe in sorcery, but if he sees or learns of too many incidents that are connected to me, he will surely become suspicious.

But what could he do about those suspicions? She couldn't envision him confronting her with accusations of sorcery. On the other hand, she certainly *could* see him sending someone to check into her nonexistent background.

Then she fought down her panic. It wasn't

very likely that he'd check on her background. To do so would mean that he doubted Paulena as well, and she was married to his best friend.

"Does your women's group plan to march during the king's birthday celebration?" he asked, breaking the long silence between them.

"No. It was discussed and some wanted to do that, but Paulena and Carlotta persuaded them that it would be inappropriate."

He nodded his approval; then his mouth twisted wryly. "They show signs of becoming experts at politics. No doubt they will want to sit in Parliament themselves one day."

"Would that be so terrible, Commander?"

"Not if it were those two. They are women of uncommon intelligence and good sense. Unfortunately, the same cannot be said for most women."

"Nor for many men," she challenged.

"That, unfortunately, is true. I have given this matter quite a bit of thought, and it seems to me that I could support the right of married women to vote."

"*Married* women?" she echoed angrily. "Why? Because you think their husbands would tell them how to vote?"

"Voting, as you know, is secret. They could easily agree to vote one way and then vote the other in the privacy of the booth."

"Then why restrict it to married women?"

"Because it has been my experience that women become more serious and thoughtful once they're married."

"I resent that!" She flared. "By implication, you are saying that *I'm* silly and thoughtless."

He chuckled. "There are exceptions, of course—but laws cannot be made on the exceptions."

"I fail to see why marriage should render a woman more acceptable, but not a man."

"Are you trying to provoke an argument, Miss Sandor? I thought you'd be pleased to know that I will support suffrage for women. I doubt that you expected it."

"No, I didn't expect it, Commander, but I find your attitude very annoying. It becomes a rather hollow victory."

"A hollow victory is still better than none at all," he pointed out with a smile.

"Coming from a Warrior, that is a dubious statement indeed. Do you think your ancestor felt that he'd earned a victory when the Dazhinn escaped?"

She had given the first example that came to mind, but she regretted it immediately. When would she learn to think before she spoke?

He was silent for a moment before replying. "No, he felt as though he'd been robbed of a victory that would surely have been his. I take your point, but those are my terms, nonetheless."

Your terms, she thought, but this time, she prudently held her tongue. There were times when she truly did enjoy his company, but there were also times like now when his arrogance reminded her of just what he was.

"There is a pleasant spot just over there. Let's

rest there before turning back."

Without waiting for her response, he dismounted and then came over to help her from the saddle. Dismounting from a sidesaddle without assistance was all but impossible, so she accepted his aid, thinking angrily that this was yet another way of making women appear to be helpless.

The few seconds they touched seemed like hours—or a lifetime. They avoided each other's eyes and he held her as though she were made of the most delicate glass. Her awareness of him drowned out all thought and left her feeling weak and heavy and almost unable to move.

And once again, she found herself being drawn back in time, transported by the raw, primitive nature of her feelings. Back to a time when Warriors and Dazhinn clashed in a younger and less civilized world, when men and women faced each other without the conventions of this carefully constructed life.

Does he, too, feel this? she wondered, knowing she could find the answer in his eyes, but unwilling to seek it there.

They seated themselves on the mossy bank of a small stream, surrounded by rich, damp, earthy smells, wrapped in the soft light of the thick woods. A discreet distance away, two soldiers waited with the horses. They had been following them at a distance for the entire ride. He'd explained that even here, in the far reaches of the royal forest, he felt it necessary to have protection now, and the irony was not lost upon her, since she herself now represented the only threat to him.

They talked easily, the words flowing effortlessly even as their true thoughts remained unspoken and became instead a silent current that flowed between them.

He spoke of his youth, of growing up in the distant mountain stronghold of the Warrior clan. Old traditions remained, he said, probably unchanged for centuries. It sounded grim to her: a schooling based on harsh discipline and self-denial and daunting physical tests combined with careful attention to other studies. Still, he told her, he would send his own son back there for such an education.

She thought of the contrasts with her own upbringing in a society that gave children the maximum possible freedom to explore their talents, overseen with gentle indulgence by adults. She told him something of this, taking care to prevent its sounding too different from what she assumed to be child-rearing practices here, at least among rural folk. She already knew about the strange distance parents seemed to keep from their children among the upper classes, turning them over to servants for most of their childhoods.

"The methods may be very different," he commented, "but both of us grew up in places where raising a child becomes the responsibility of the whole village or clan."

She was startled by this observation, because she had been dwelling on the differences. But she knew he was right. And why not? she thought. Both of us come from ancient traditions that have remained unchanged. He may be almost as much a stranger to this world as I am.

And somewhere during this time, this idyll in the midst of the turbulence surrounding them, Rowena came to the knowledge that had been there for some time now, its exact origins unknown to her: she could not kill this man.

She could not even hate him, though she knew that he might soon take actions that would almost certainly spell disaster for her people.

This revelation should have surprised her, but it didn't. She admitted now that it might well have been there from the beginning, from that moment on the beach when she'd opened her eyes to find him there. The Council and the astrologers had made a mistake.

But what, then, was she to do? If she communicated this to them through the 'paths here, they would almost certainly punish her by forcing her to remain here. And then they would find someone else to accomplish her mission.

If he noticed her lapse into silence, he made no mention of it. Instead, they remounted their horses. This time, it was one of the soldiers who assisted her into the saddle, and when she briefly met the commander's gaze as they set out again, she understood why. The astrologers hadn't been entirely wrong.

Back home, she wanted to tell her aunt of her decision—a decision she knew Polly would approve and one she thought might soothe away some of the conflicts she knew were tearing her aunt apart. But by the time she found Paulena, she'd thought better of it. Until she knew what she *would* do, as well as what she wouldn't do, she must keep her silence.

Instead, she told Polly what the commander—whom she had now begun to think of as Zach in her own mind even if etiquette dictated that she refer to him by his title—had said regarding his support for women's suffrage.

"I argued with him about it, but I do not believe he will change his mind," she finished.

"It is what I expected." Paulena nodded. "Though it's not going to sit well with Carlotta and some of the others. Nevertheless, it is a beginning—and more will follow."

"He must know that, don't you think?"

"Of course. Zach will give in inch by inch, when we want to leap miles at a single step. That is his way."

Rowena thought about his upbringing and saw that it could be no other way for him. Was that why he'd told her about it in the first place? Rather than merely making polite conversation, had he been trying to help her understand him?

She then went on to tell Paulena what Zach had said about David Weilor. "He truly seems to be concerned for him, though he must surely regard him as an enemy."

"Perhaps not. Mr. Weilor doesn't yet have enough power to pose any threat to Zach, even though he gains adherents daily. And Zach is quite right to be concerned for his safety. I've already spoken to Mr. Weilor about that, but he brushes off such concerns. Still, I will speak to him again."

Rowena had been prepared to dislike Tralanna, resentful as she was of these people's usurpation of Dazhinn traditions. But it was an elegant, beautiful place filled with happy, laughing people and delicious aromas, and she had to admit that in spirit at least, it wasn't far from the original meaning of the festival celebrated by her people after each harvest.

On the first floor, people dined at various-size tables in two large rooms, but they were led up the broad, curved stairs to the second story. There, to her surprise—and uneasiness—they were ushered into a small but luxurious room that contained only one table, set for two.

Her uneasiness sprang from the lush intimacy of the scene, where the predominant color was a deep, rich red, lit by the mellow glow of gaslights that reflected off heavy silver and intricately etched crystal and creamy, gold-banded dishes. A white-coated servant poured wine and then withdrew, closing the door behind him and shutting out the noises of other patrons.

Zach picked up the leather-bound menu that had been placed at his elbow. "Since you've not been here before, allow me to order for you."

She'd been well schooled by Paulena in such matters and knew that ladies were expected to

let their gentlemen companions order for them.
So she arched a pale brow.

"You would in any event, wouldn't you? Women aren't expected to know their own minds."

"I've no doubt whatsoever that you know your own mind, Miss Sandor. All I meant was that since you haven't been here before, you couldn't be expected to know which dishes are exceptionally well prepared here."

"Nor can you be expected to know my preferences, Commander."

He handed her the menu. "In order not to scandalize our waiter, would you at least allow me to give him your order?"

Having gained at least a small victory, she acquiesced—and that seemed to set the tone for the evening. Once again, she had the feeling that they were players upon a stage—a very elegant stage—while beneath the smiles and the polite conversation burned the fires of ancient times when Warriors swooped down from their mountains to confront Dazhinn magic.

It isn't fair, she thought. At least in part, he is able to play his ancient role, while I cannot. He is still a Warrior, but I am forced to conceal who I am.

One delectable course followed another as their conversation flowed smoothly, and all the while the whispers of long-ago times filled the gaps.

Something else could be heard in those silences as well: the sensual beat of desire. She could see it in his eyes, those pale, nearly colorless eyes that could so often seem hard and cold, but now were soft and warm, heated by the fires within. And try as she did, she could not prevent her body from responding, from edging ever closer to a curiosity about the ultimate act of desire.

The seduction had become mutual. They seemed to her to be circling each other warily, but the circle grew ever smaller, drawing them together even against their will.

And she was sure that he, too, had doubts. Somewhere inside this complex man was something that was warning him, but surely without making that warning clear. And of course, even if the warning had been clear, he would not have accepted it because the Dazhinn and magic belonged to the distant past.

"Would you think it improper of me to say that I very much enjoy your company, Miss Sandor?"

Her mouth curved in a wry smile. "Since you've just said it, the question is moot, is it not?"

He smiled, but his eyes remained serious. "Do I dare hope that you don't find my company too unpleasant, however you may feel about Warriors?"

She tried to meet his gaze with her own, but found it nearly impossible. In the carefully polite language of this society, they were edging close to an intimacy that sent fear rippling through her even as a very different emotion sent heat in its wake.

"I find your company very interesting, Commander. Otherwise I wouldn't be here."

Those solemn eyes remained on her. "Sometimes I think you might just vanish without a trace—much like the Dazhinn who seem to fascinate you. Perhaps that's just the result of our initial meeting."

It took considerable effort on her part not to show her shock at that statement. "I assure you that I won't just vanish," she said firmly.

But his mind seemed to be lingering on their meeting on the beach. "When I think of you—which I'll admit is often—I always see you as you were that day."

"Sick and nearly helpless, you mean?" she inquired archly.

But he shook his head. "No. You might have been sick, but you didn't strike me as being helpless. Nor have you since that time."

You knew, she thought. You knew even then what I am. You've always known—but you won't let yourself believe it. You may have felt it even more strongly then, because I hadn't yet been molded into a "proper lady."

As they finished their dinner, Zach was still trying to fathom his feelings about her. The matter had taken on a great urgency, because his hunger for her seemed to grow with every moment he spent in her company. He was not a man to be easily frightened, but he was very uncomfortable.

He thought he understood some of the caution he felt in the face of such overwhelming desire.

It was surely no more than the understandable concern of a man who feared the hold a woman might gain over him. He'd seen that often enough in other men—including Duncan—and he'd privately sneered at it, certain that such a thing couldn't happen to him. After all, he'd lived past the lusty years of his youth without its occurring even once.

But he wasn't completely satisfied with that explanation. There was something more here—a caution that sprang from some other source.

And she was cautious and wary, too. That was what made it even stranger. Zach was perfectly aware of the fact that he was certainly the most eligible man in the land. Any unmarried woman could be expected to use all her wiles to capture his attention. Furthermore, he'd discovered from their conversation this afternoon that she was older than he'd thought: well past the usual age at which women married.

It made him uneasy to think that he might have misjudged her. Perhaps she truly was serious about not marrying. In his experience, the only women who felt that way were those who had no hope of finding a husband. But she certainly didn't fit into that category. She was easily one of the most beautiful women he'd ever seen, and it was obvious that he wasn't alone in making that judgment. However off-putting her candor and her strength of will might be to some men, those "faults" were far outweighed by her beauty.

She'd told him that she had dedicated her life

to her work, and yet he knew she wasn't pursuing that now. But if she'd told him the truth, then she would probably return to her home soon, even though she'd been vague in her responses to his questions about the length of her stay.

He wondered if something might have happened at home to send her here—perhaps a love gone astray? It might be worth checking into. He knew several men who could undertake such a mission and be depended upon to act with discretion. Paulena had told him where she was from, but only the general area. Still, it was the most rural part of the land and her family would surely be well-known there.

Yes, he thought, I will send someone there to look into it. And he immediately felt better for taking some action to unravel the mystery of Rowena Sandor.

Duncan and Paulena had gone out for the evening, and so were not yet at home when they arrived. Thunder rumbled and lightning flashed in the distance, but the night had a sultry softness, and when Zach suggested a stroll through the gardens, she agreed, even though pleading tiredness would certainly have been the more prudent course.

They moved slowly through the aromatic gardens in a companionable silence into which the siren song of desire soon intruded. Inside the safety of the high-walled garden, he had dismissed his ever-present guards.

"I should think that you would be missing

your work," he commented after a rather lengthy silence.

She thought his statement rather curious, but responded honestly. "I do miss it, although I've been quite busy. In fact, I told Paulena only yesterday that I would like to find good wool and silk threads so that I can return to work. The greater problem may be finding the plants I use for dyes."

"Does that mean that you intend to stay here?" he inquired in a tone she thought seemed too carefully neutral.

"For a time. I still don't know how long."

"It seems to me, Miss Sandor, that such indecision is alien to your nature."

She slanted him a glance. "We all have our moments of indecision, Commander. I imagine that even you have had them from time to time."

He laughed. It was a sound she'd grown to like. "As usual, the arrows you send my way are right on target. Of course, I prefer to think of any indecisiveness as being mere caution."

She smiled, and what came from her lips next was totally unplanned, and had sprung directly from her thoughts without passing through the filters of caution or propriety.

"I find it very admirable that you are able to poke fun at yourself from time to time. But I warrant that very few people have seen that."

"You're right. Save for Duncan, no one else has seen it."

"Not even your wife?" she inquired curiously.

"My wife took herself very seriously, Miss

Sandor. She was born into the merchant class, and they tend to be that way."

"And Warriors are not that way?" she asked disbelievingly.

He was silent for so long she thought she might have offended him, but when he spoke, she realized that he'd simply been thinking about her question.

"We are and we aren't. Warriors, like the nobility, have existed for a very long time and our place in the scheme of things was established centuries ago. The merchant class, on the other hand, is relatively new, and its members have yet to find that sense of identity.

"They don't even know their power yet, because they're so busy trying to emulate the nobility. But they are the future."

"It seems to me that you spend quite a bit of time thinking about the future, Commander."

He gave her a surprised look. "Of course. Nothing is so foolish as living only for the present—or dwelling in the past."

He could not have intended it, but his words dealt her a blow that was nearly physical. The future was something her people had been determinedly avoiding for several generations now—ever since they'd discovered that the spell was weakening—and perhaps for all the centuries since they'd begun living under that enchantment.

She thought about how she—and most others—avoided looking at the telltale blurring at the horizon, knowing that it whispered menacingly of a future they could not control and had much reason to fear.

Yes, she thought sadly, we have been foolish indeed. But it still annoyed her to know that that error had been pointed out to her by no less than the leader of their ancient enemy.

We are truly doomed, she told herself—and perhaps we deserve it. Not even the efforts of the Descenders could change that. They were too few in numbers to bring about meaningful changes in this complicated world. Furthermore, if he was right about the future power of the merchant class, they'd been concentrating on gaining access to the wrong group.

"Why do you say that the merchant class is the future?" she asked as they reached the gazebo, where the gas lamps cast their mellow glow into the darkness. "Surely the nobility—and the Warriors—will not permit that."

"The power of the nobility has always been in their great landholdings, at a time when money as we know it didn't exist," he explained. "But power is increasingly being concentrated in the cities, in manufacturing and trade, which is where the merchant class came from. Many of the nobility are virtually penniless now, even though they still have their land."

"But surely Duncan—"

"Duncan is one of the few who saw the future and accommodated himself to it. When he began to invest in factories and ships, many of the nobility sneered at him. But he was right."

"And what about the Warriors?"

He heaved a sigh. "That is the question, isn't it? The Warrior clan has never been wealthy, but in recent years, many—including me—married into the merchant class.

"We will survive, Miss Sandor, because our skills will still be needed to protect all that the merchant class has acquired. War is a sad fact of human life, and as our country grows ever richer, its neighbors grow ever more envious. But if I were to guess what will one day be written about me in our histories, I would say that I will almost certainly be referred to as the last of the great Warrior chiefs. And it won't be because of who I am, but because of the time I happened to live in.

"When there are wars, the Warrior chief of the time may be seen as being great—if he's victorious, that is—but I think that the time when a Warrior chief can wield power such as I do is coming to an end."

She was stunned and, amazingly, saddened as well to hear his predictions. It occurred to her that he must view himself in much the same way she saw herself and her people: relics of a past that was slipping away.

"But you fight to hold on to that power," she pointed out.

He smiled. "Of course—and I will continue to do so because that's my nature. Perhaps I can help to shape the future, but those who come after me will play a lesser role in it regardless of what I do."

"You're a very complicated man, Zachary MacTavesh," she said, speaking her thoughts.

"As you are a very complicated woman, Rowena Sandor," he replied, smiling down at her.

Then his smile drained away slowly into that now familiar look of desire that caused her heart to skip a few beats and her breath to catch in her throat. The moments ticked away loudly as tension wrapped them both in its silken bonds. And then they were in each other's arms, with neither of them quite certain who had made the first move.

One moment they were apart, and the next, they were locked in an embrace, their bodies imprinted on each other, their lips too eager, too hungry, to be gentle. She arched to him and he surrounded her and both of them wanted much more. Her hands slipped around the corded muscles of his neck and his slid down to cup her bottom and draw her to him, forcing her against the unyielding hardness of his male desire.

Rowena wanted what she had never wanted before—and what she could never have imagined wanting from this man she'd been sent here to kill. Now, finally, she understood the need men and women had for each other, a need no other man could have awakened in her.

His lips and tongue plundered hers and she responded in kind, a wholly new chapter in the ancient battle between their people. And when at last he lifted his mouth from hers and stared at her, she thought she saw an understanding of that in his eyes, though of course it couldn't be there.

"I'm sorry," he said raggedly, even though he didn't let her go.

"There's no need for you to be sorry," she replied huskily.

He arched a brow. "Are you saying that neither of us is playing by the rules, Rowena?"

"No, we're not—and we never have." She stopped abruptly, before she could go on to say that his people and hers had always played by their own rules.

He seemed confused as he stared at her, and the uncharacteristic expression gave him the appearance of a much younger man, even a boy. She kept silent, but she wanted very badly to tell him the truth and take away what she knew must be the source of his confusion. If there'd been even the slightest chance that he would believe her, she might have done it and risked the consequences.

He reached out to gently brush a stray curl from her cheek, then kissed the spot softly. She turned her face and kissed the corner of his wide mouth. Then his lips were gliding over hers again, much gentler now as he covered her face and then her throat with kisses.

"Even in my youth, I never wanted a woman as I want you now," he said, his voice a hoarse rasp against her ear.

Rowena opened her eyes to look at him, but something else caught her attention and she stiffened. He raised his head and stared at her, then turned sharply to look behind him.

"Who's there?" he said, his voice harsh and his body rigid as he held her against him.

The shadows beyond the gaslights shifted—and then Abner stepped slowly into the light, bowing.

"Your pardon, Commander. I was merely out for a stroll and didn't know you were here."

Rowena felt Zach relax, but could not let go of her own fear as Abner's gaze fell on her. He murmured a quick good night and another apology and melted into the shadows.

Zach stood there with his arm around Rowena and realized that this was the second time he'd seen the man stare at her with barely contained hatred. But why should he hate her? She could have done nothing to him; they'd only recently met.

He glanced down at Rowena, who was still staring off into the darkness where the man had vanished. Yet another mystery. It seemed that Rowena Sandor was surrounded by mysteries.

She moved away from him, then suggested that they return to the house. As they walked back through the gardens, Zach reflected that perhaps he owed the servant a debt of gratitude. If he hadn't shown up like that, he might well have proposed to her on the spot.

Zach still didn't understand his reluctance to marry her—or even to admit that she had become indispensable to his happiness. What he did know was that he could ill afford such distractions right now. The latest news from his agents was very disturbing.

"Abner! I'd like to speak to you."

He stopped reluctantly, then looked around as though plotting his escape, but Rowena persisted.

"If it becomes necessary, I will ask Duncan to send you away from here," she challenged.

"Oh?" he jeered. "And what makes you think he'd pay any attention to your demands?"

"I believe he would. And it's only a matter of time before the commander notices your behavior toward me."

He laughed unpleasantly. "From what I saw, he's not likely to notice a cannon being aimed at him, let alone me."

"Abner, I don't understand you. It almost sounds as though you're willing to risk our people for the sake of your hatred for me."

"And what about you, Rowena? What are you willing to risk? Or have you forgotten why you're here?"

"I haven't forgotten," she assured him. "But if you succeed in making him suspicious of me in any way, you put my mission at risk."

"There are some of us who think you won't do it," he challenged. "We're making our own plans."

"How dare you? The Council—"

He made a dismissive sound. "The Council isn't here—and we are. Tell me something. What did the Council tell you about our purpose for being here?"

She frowned. "The same thing they told everyone. You're all here to try to change things, in case we must return."

He sneered. "Well, maybe I was wrong, then. Maybe they do intend to let you return."

"What are you talking about?" she asked, trying not to let her sudden fear show.

He leaned close to her and smiled nastily. "They told you the truth—but only part of it. If you don't believe me, ask Paulena. She knows the truth, even if she tries to ignore it."

Then, before she could ask anything more, he turned on his heel and strode away. Rowena stared after him. What was he talking about? What part of the truth didn't she know?

She hastened to find her aunt, determined to get to the bottom of this, and determined as well to get Abner out of here as quickly as possible.

What had he meant when he'd said that he and some others were making their own plans? Were they intending to try to kill Zach?

She thought about Abner's earlier statement that he wished *he'd* had the chance to kill Zach, and she didn't doubt for one minute that he would try it now—especially after seeing the two of them together last night. Abner certainly didn't love her. In fact, she thought he was too filled with anger and hatred to love anyone, but that wouldn't stop him from wanting to destroy any man he saw as being a rival.

She started off to find Paulena, her thoughts

unwillingly returning to last night. Without conscious intent on her part, her hand came up to touch her mouth and a shiver of pure pleasure went through her at the memory of his kisses.

And it's not just his kisses, she thought uneasily. The more time I spend with him, the more I get to know the man. How was it possible that she could actually like him? If Paulena was right, she could see herself becoming attracted to him—but how could she possibly *like* him?

On the other hand, she'd already met people she liked here: Duncan, David Weilor, several of the women in her aunt's group. But none of them were Warriors.

She finally found Paulena in her boudoir. The dressmaker was putting the final touches to her aunt's gown for the king's birthday ball tomorrow evening. Rowena admired it, thinking that despite the constricting undergarments she'd never accept, she had grown quite fond of the luxurious fabrics and designs of clothing here.

"Are any adjustments required for your gown, dear?" her aunt inquired.

Rowena shook her head. "No, it's fine. I tried it on earlier. Thank you."

"Then we must go through my jewelry and decide what you should wear with it."

Rowena nodded distractedly. The ball wasn't of great interest to her at the moment. She smiled, recalling Zach's observation that they would probably be the only two people there who would much rather be elsewhere.

As soon as the dressmaker and the maid had

gone, Paulena turned to her with a worried expression. "Did Zach say anything to you last night about problems?"

"What do you mean?" She now remembered that Zach and Duncan had withdrawn to Duncan's study the moment he returned last night, and they were still there when the women had gone off to bed. She hadn't given it much thought at the time, because she was still shaken by Abner's sudden appearance and what he had interrupted.

"Something has happened. I don't know what it is because I fell asleep before Duncan came up to bed, and he was already gone when I awoke this morning. But I know he went to the palace."

Rowena frowned. "Zach said nothing to me, and he seemed very much himself."

Paulena shrugged. "Well, I'll find out when he returns. Did you speak to Abner yet about last night?"

Rowena had told her aunt about the episode and her intention to speak to Abner about his behavior toward her. She nodded.

"Polly, he says that the Council has not told me the truth—that those of you who've descended know something I don't. Is that true?"

She'd been hoping desperately that her aunt would deny it, but no sooner were the words out of her mouth than she knew Abner had indeed spoken the truth. Polly turned away, pretending to fuss with her hair.

Saranne Dawson

"Polly? I must know the truth. You even said yourself that there were things I must decide for myself. Is that what you meant?"

Paulena's gaze met hers briefly, then slid away again. "We were told not to discuss it with you, Rowena, since you are to return."

Rowena stared at her. "Then there *is* something! Polly, you must tell me! Whether or not I'm going to return, I'm here now—and I deserve to know the truth."

But Paulena shook her head. "I know you want to return, and I will not be the one to prevent that. I'm going to insist that Duncan get rid of Abner, even if it means losing the opportunity to find a good placement for him. In the meantime, please stay away from him, Rowena."

She gave Rowena an imploring look. "Don't you see? Abner wants to guarantee that you can never return. It would be his revenge for your refusal to marry him."

Chapter Eight

Rowena didn't want to be impressed. She still harbored within her considerable guilt when she allowed herself to become entranced by anything in this world, even if she'd stopped thinking of its inhabitants as barbarians. But as she joined the throngs being presented to the king and queen, she could not help feeling that she had entered an enchanted world of a very different sort.

On her previous visit to the palace grounds to go riding with Zach, she hadn't been inside the palace itself. Now, with him beside her and Duncan and Paulena behind them in the line, she stared at her glittering surroundings in undisguised admiration.

The ceiling was higher than any she'd seen and gleamed brightly as hundreds of gaslights reflected off its gold-embossed design. The floor of the long hallway was covered with thick, ruby-red carpeting and the walls were hung with fine old paintings and the elaborate crystal and gold sconces that held the gas lamps. At the end of the hallway, she could see into the huge ballroom, where wood parquet floors gleamed. Off to one side, an equally large banquet hall was already set up for the 500 guests.

Around her, the guests themselves added to the opulence: the women in beautiful gowns and glittering jewels and the men in their formal black and white evening attire, enlivened by medals and sashes displaying the various honors bestowed upon them by their ruler.

Beside her, Zach was dressed in one of his white uniforms with its splendiferous gold braid and ribbons and medals and the ceremonial sword. Here and there in the crowd, she saw other Warriors in white uniforms: tall men of arrogant, erect bearing who would have stood out even in this crowd regardless of their attire.

Slowly, they made their way to the head of the crowd, where a formally clad servant announced their names in a sonorous voice.

"Commander-in-Chief Zachary MacTavesh and Miss Rowena Sandor."

Zach did not bow, but she curtsied as she'd been told, uncomfortably aware of many hundreds of eyes upon her. The king was friendly to her, explaining to his small mouse of a queen that he'd met her at Shemoth. Rowena thought that the woman looked far too timid to be in such a high public position. She might have been quite pretty if it weren't for the drawn, pale look on her face.

Beside her stood Princess Melba, together with the two younger princesses. Her smile grew when she saw Rowena and she immediately began to chatter animatedly, providing a sharp contrast with her quiet mother.

"How lovely you look, Miss Sandor. Uncle Zach tells me that you were here riding with him. Will you come to ride with me sometime? I adore horses, don't you? I have a lovely white mare who's about to give birth. I can hardly wait."

She might have gone on forever, but the line was moving forward and Duncan and Paulena were being presented. The princess looked at Rowena imploringly and repeated her invitation. Rowena had forgotten her initial irritation with the girl and assured her that she would indeed come to ride with her. As they moved from the line into the banquet hall, Zach leaned close to her.

"You seem to have won the heart of the princess with very little effort."

"I feel very sorry for her, and she is sweet, in spite of the chattering."

"She has a difficult life, as I believe I told you. And it isn't helped by the fact that she knows her father would have preferred a son."

"What will happen when the king dies?" Rowena asked curiously.

"Oh, he will undoubtedly choose a husband for her from among her distant cousins, and then set him on the throne."

"That's terrible!" she said angrily.

"I agree. There is no reason why she cannot become queen herself, since the throne has become less and less important."

She gave him a disgusted look and he raised a hand to ward off the angry words that were about to follow.

"What I meant was that a woman on the throne would not have been acceptable in the past, when the king exercised real power. But the duties are now largely ceremonial and Melba could handle them well enough. She's quite a bright young woman and has fought hard to see that she receives a good education."

His pale gaze swept the large banquet hall. "She's quite taken with my nephew, who's here somewhere. He will graduate from Ashwara next year and I intend to bring him onto my staff, so they'll have time to get to know each other better. Unless I have a son, Daken will be the next Warrior chief."

"And how does he feel about her?" Rowena asked, sensing a scheme here.

"Oh, he's fond of her, but at twenty-one, he's far too busy chasing everything in skirts." Then he gave her a chastened look.

"Your pardon, Miss Sandor. Sometimes I forget myself."

"Your honesty more than makes up for your lack of proper manners," she replied, smiling at his discomfort.

He flashed her an amused look as they moved to their places at the long table set on a dais at the head of the room. "Well, it's time for both of us to put on our best manners and try to survive this evening. I hope you're not too fond of dancing. Not that you'd lack for partners if you were here with anyone else."

The dinner was lengthy and made even longer by the many toasts to the king's good health. As she stared out over the crowd, Rowena thought she spotted Zach's nephew among a small group of Warriors. He bore a strong resemblance to Zach and she was pleased to see that he laughed often and easily. She'd begun to take an interest in the forlorn princess, and knowing Zach, if he'd decided this was a good match, it was likely to happen.

Finally, the dinner was over and they all moved into the ballroom, where an orchestra was tuning up for the dancing. She learned she was correct in her assumption that the laughing young man was Daken, when he suddenly appeared to be introduced to her. In his handsome face, she saw what Zach must have looked like before age and responsibility had hardened his features.

"The princess expressed the hope earlier that you might ask her to dance," Zach said to him after the introductions. "And Miss Sandor might enjoy having a skilled partner as well."

Daken grinned at her. "My pleasure. I'm afraid that my uncle believes dancing to be beneath his dignity."

Rowena saw Zach's eyes narrow and quickly thanked Daken, then pointed out that the princess wasn't far away and appeared to be looking in his direction. Undaunted by his uncle's wrath, Daken chuckled.

"She's not so bad—when she stops talking long enough to take a breath, that is."

Then he bowed to her and made a hasty exit, threading his way through the crowd to the eager princess.

"I wonder if I was that insufferable at his age," Zach said, watching him.

"No doubt you were. He's not insufferable. He seems quite typical of his age to me."

He glanced at her. "No doubt you're right. You're closer to that age than I am."

"Does that bother you?" she asked, having detected something in his voice that suggested it did.

She'd expected him to protest that it didn't, but to her surprise, he hesitated, then nodded.

"Yes, I think it does. When I'm with you, it's easy to forget the difference in our ages, but I think it must trouble you."

"Why should it? I haven't given it a thought, actually."

He stared at her intently for a long moment, and she couldn't decipher his thoughts. She wondered if she'd mistaken the reason for the hesitation and confusion she'd seen in him. Could it be that the difference in their ages really troubled him that greatly? Paulena had suggested that possibility, saying that she'd heard him make disparaging remarks about men his own age who had married younger women or chosen younger mistresses.

But she'd spoken the truth when she'd said that she hadn't given it a thought. Such alliances among her own people were unheard of, but she didn't think of him as being so much older than she was. Or perhaps she didn't think of herself as being so much younger than he. With all that was on her mind lately, she felt as though she'd aged years in just a few weeks.

The dancing began, and Rowena was surprised to hear some familiar melodies: music her people always played for their dances. But there was a very big difference. Not only were some of the instruments different, but the lighthearted gaiety of the tunes suffered from being played much more slowly.

In fact, it was difficult for her to think of the activity here as being dancing, since it bore little resemblance to the high-spirited movements of her people. Of course, she thought wryly, such dancing would be impossible in the elaborate gowns worn by all the women present—not to mention those stifling corsets.

Zach did indeed dance, and for a big man, he moved with a rather surprising grace, though it was clear that he wished he were elsewhere. When the music ended and they had exchanged the ritual bow and curtsy, he smiled at her.

"I believe you were having difficulty maintaining your decorum, Miss Sandor."

"What do you mean, Commander?" she inquired, having thought that she'd managed quite well, given the fact that she'd had so little practice.

"I believe that your feet wanted to move more

quickly than this music permitted."

She laughed. "That's true. I find this dancing to be scarcely more than walking."

"I've seen country dancing a few times, and I can understand how you must see it that way. But for me, this is quite enough."

"Well, for two misfits, we can at least congratulate ourselves on not having tripped over each other's feet."

She danced with both Duncan and Daken, while Zach danced with Paulena and the princess. But even as she moved about the floor with them, her eyes unconsciously sought out Zach to find his gaze meeting hers.

What will I do about him? she asked herself. Everything seems to be slipping beyond my control, and I need answers to questions not even formed.

She saw Carlotta and then Tabby and wondered if they would be willing to tell her what Polly wouldn't. It seemed unlikely; they were her aunt's friends and would almost certainly share her view. Still, she must find a time to talk with them.

As the evening wore on, Rowena found herself less and less able to join in the festive atmosphere. The melodies had brought back a sharp longing for the simplicity of her other life, and she was both shocked and saddened to realize how little she'd thought about it in recent days. Was that only because she was all but certain now that she would never see her old home again, despite her cousin's prediction?

"Would you be scandalized if I suggested that we leave?" Zach said, quietly breaking into her reverie.

She shook her head. "No, I'm tired. All that food and wine and the music. But do we dare leave?"

"Strictly speaking, no one leaves before His Majesty. However, if you could contrive to look a bit pale, I can always tell him tomorrow that I had to tend to you."

"That shouldn't be too difficult, since in truth I do feel the need for some fresh air."

He took her arm and led her through the crowd and then out of the ballroom and through a series of rooms until they finally emerged into an inner courtyard of the palace with a many-tiered fountain at its center. Silence surrounded them, broken only by the musical sounds from the fountain.

But they weren't alone. Even here in the safety of the palace, two soldiers followed them at a discreet distance. In view of her concern about Abner and his friends, Rowena was glad to see them there. It wasn't likely that Abner would be lurking about here, but she couldn't be sure. As Duncan's aide, he undoubtedly had access to the palace. It occurred to her as well that Polly had never said whether they'd managed to place any of their people inside the palace.

"My quarters are just over there," Zach said, indicating a set of stairs at the far side of the courtyard. "Will you go there with me for a while?"

She hesitated. The invitation sounded innocent enough, and she'd been in his quarters at Shemoth. But she knew it wasn't acceptable behavior for a lady, and she knew as well that the invitation could be far from innocent.

"I don't plan to seduce you, Rowena," he said gently. "I will admit to harboring such thoughts, but I promise not to act upon them."

She looked up at him, into those eyes that showed his thoughts all too clearly. No, she thought, he won't deliberately seduce me—but then he doesn't have to. We are both of us caught up in this thing, prisoners to the movements of distant stars.

"I trust you, Zach." And as she spoke the words, she knew she meant them. It was a measure of just how strange and complex her life had become that she could trust a Warrior—and not just any Warrior, but their chief.

Trailed by the two soldiers, they ascended the stairs and he unlocked the door to quarters that were both larger and far more elegant than those at Shemoth. But there was no evidence of her people here. These rooms were decorated with the same heavy fabrics and ornately carved furniture as the rest of the palace.

He offered her some wine, and then, when she declined, summoned a servant and requested that tea be brought for them. A chill lingered inside the thick walls of the palace even on this warm evening and he lit a small fire, then turned to her.

"I will be leaving the city tomorrow and will

214

probably be gone for several weeks."

"You're returning to Shemoth?" she asked, worrying now about what his departure meant as she remembered Paulena's statement only hours ago that something had happened.

He shook his head. "I will return there, but only briefly. Then I will be touring the northern garrisons. I tell you this because I would rather not be gone right now. If I had my choice, I would remain here and try to persuade you to marry me."

Since her mind was still on the possible reasons for this tour, Rowena was slow to react to his final words. Then she simply stared at him. He smiled.

"Surely this does not come as a shock to you, Rowena. I, ah, thought I'd made my feelings rather plain."

"Uh, yes, you have," she admitted, fighting down her panic.

"I cannot promise to be the best sort of husband," he went on, his speech now giving the impression of having been well rehearsed. "My work requires long hours and many absences from the city. Shemoth is no place for a woman and I would not want you to feel confined here, either. But I do have a house here in the city, and while I'm gone, I'm having steps taken to make it more secure.

"It's neither as large nor as grand as Duncan and Paulena's home. I'm not a wealthy man. But I think you would find it comfortable and of course you may furnish it as you wish."

"I . . . I don't know what to say, Zach." And that was the truth. She couldn't marry him; it was out of the question. But saying no wasn't as easy as she would have expected.

He took both her hands in his. "You could begin by saying that you . . . have feelings for me. And I won't press you for an answer now."

Then he seemed once again to revert to a prepared speech. "There is a small cottage on the grounds that you could use as a place to mix your dyes and work on your tapestries. And I promise not to try to interfere with your suffrage work."

Rowena was stunned to realize how much thought he'd given to her and her comfort and happiness. On the surface, Zachary MacTavesh seemed as insensitive as the husbands of Carlotta and Tabitha, and yet she'd already seen evidence that there were great depths to this man—many layers of thought and feeling that had broken through to the surface in the past for brief moments.

"I'm very flattered that you should have given so much thought to me," she said, rather more formally than she'd intended. But it was a formality belied by the huskiness in her voice.

He arched a brow. "Now you sound like any other woman—and not like yourself."

She laughed, although it was laughter with a nervous edge. "I do care for you, Zach. But this is a very difficult decision for me."

"Then I will say no more. But there is another reason I brought you here. Excuse me for a moment."

He left the room and Rowena took a deep breath to steady herself. She was finding it nearly impossible to cope with the myriad emotions now assailing her. Of course she couldn't marry him—but why did a part of her want to believe it possible? Could she actually be in love with this man—her enemy? The enemy of her people? Why else would the thought of spending her life with him seem so beguiling?

And as if that weren't enough, there was the question of his sudden decision to visit the northern garrisons: the very ones that bordered the land of the Atanians and included her people's valley.

She feared that war was coming—a war that would almost certainly break the spell that held her people safe. And the man who would start that war was asking her to marry him.

She was so lost in her thoughts that she'd paid scant attention to his statement that he had another reason for bringing her here. But she was reminded of that when he reappeared, carrying a small, narrow wooden box.

She recognized the intricately carved and polished blackwood box immediately. Blackwood trees grew only in the valley, and had been used for many centuries by her people for carving objects of great beauty.

He opened the box and carefully removed the contents as she stared, transfixed by the sight. The delicate necklace seemed even more fragile in his big hands: a necklace that bore the unmistakable mark of her father's family's craftsmanship.

217

Rowena's father had died when she was just a child, but he had plied the family's craft and she possessed several pieces of his work that had come to her through her mother. There was no doubt in her mind as she stared at the necklace that it had been made by one of her own ancestors!

The light gleamed off fine strands of gold chain, the links so tiny as to be nearly invisible. Scattered along the lengths of the delicate chains were precious stones, themselves intricately etched and then partially covered with very fine gold wire. Her father's sister had such a necklace, passed down through the centuries. It was no longer possible to make them, because the precious gems did not exist in the valley. Before the Dazhinn ascended into their spellbound world, the gems had been purchased from seafaring merchants who'd brought them from far corners of the world.

"It is Dazhinn, as you may have guessed," he said, apparently mistaking her silence for awe at the beauty of the necklace. "There is more, but this is one of my favorite pieces. I have no sisters, so these things were passed on to me when my mother died." He paused and lifted it, holding it carefully between his fingers.

"I would like you to have it, Rowena, whether or not you decide to marry me. As you know, I don't believe the Dazhinn were sorcerers, but in their work I have seen something akin to magic, and I often find myself thinking of you in that same way."

"M-me?" she stammered as panic skittered along her spine.

He nodded and laughed. "There is a quality to you, Rowena, that I suppose explains your fascination with them. I can define it no further because I lack the skills of a poet. Will you accept the gift?"

She could do no more than manage a nod, and then he was slipping it over her head and the chains were slithering over her bare throat, cool against her heated skin.

He reached out to smooth them, adjusting the fine chains and then admiring them before his gaze traveled slowly back up to her face.

"I can no longer imagine my life without you, Rowena, but if you choose not to accept my proposal, at least promise me that you will think of me when you take out this necklace."

It was, she knew, the closest this proud man would ever come to begging, and it was on the very tip of her tongue to tell him that she could not imagine a life without him, either. But she held back and merely nodded, then stretched up to kiss his cheek.

"Thank you, Zach. No one has ever given me such a beautiful gift, but I would not need it to be reminded of you."

He held her loosely and his lips met hers with great gentleness, a carefulness that was in its own way even more erotic than the impassioned kisses they'd shared before. It was a giving and a withholding, a sensual teasing of all her senses. The small space between them filled up with the promise of naked flesh meeting naked flesh, even as heated skin chafed beneath elegant fabrics.

"It is time I return you to your home," he said at long last, his voice low and husky. "And to safety. You would not be safe here for much longer."

She nodded, but a voice inside was begging her to tell him that she would stay, that the danger he warned about was a danger she would gladly accepted.

Rowena used every argument she could think of to persuade Paulena to tell her the truth, but her aunt continued to insist that her only hope of returning home lay in not knowing that truth. And when Rowena turned to Carlotta and Tabitha, she got the same response. It was clear that they felt they had to protect her from something—something that the Council would not risk having the others at home discover through her.

What *was* this secret? The more Rowena thought about it, the darker it became. And yet, except for the leader, they weren't bad people. Had they simply become bound to a decision made long ago—a course of action that might have been set in place at the time their ancestors had created the spell?

She considered and then rejected the notion of going to one of the 'paths who could reach across the barrier with their minds, and demanding that she be allowed to communicate with the Council.

She might get an answer, but she would almost certainly lose any hope she had of being permitted to return.

Time was running out for her. War seemed almost inevitable now, and with it, an end to the life her people had led all these centuries. Whatever action she was going to take—or try to take—she couldn't do it without knowing the truth.

As for Zach's proposal, she simply refused to let herself think about it now. She couldn't marry him, but accepting that became much easier after he'd gone. Even then, however, she would find herself thinking about how it felt to be in his arms—and how she had wanted more.

She finally decided that however unpleasant it was, her only hope of learning the secret Paulena and the others were hiding lay with Abner. Knowing that he could not be acting alone, she determined to seek out the others.

Abner had his living quarters above the large carriage house at the rear of Duncan and Paulena's property, and on several occasions, she'd happened to see him leaving just after dark. She knew he might be going anywhere, but her instincts told her that he was meeting the others. So she decided to follow him.

This undertaking was not as easy as it should have been, owing to the fact that ladies simply did not go about alone at night. Furthermore, she had to elude her aunt as well. So several days passed with increasing frustration until she finally found a way.

Duncan and Paulena had been invited to dinner at the home of friends, and although the invitation included Rowena, she managed to beg off by feigning a headache. Then the moment they left, she stripped off her fine clothes and put on the loose trousers and shirt she'd been wearing when she had arrived. They were not dissimilar to the clothing worn by servants and other workers in the city, and she added a cap she'd managed to steal from one of the gardeners, who'd left it lying about.

Most of the household staff were either off or retired for the night, so she stationed herself at a window that had a view of the carriage house. She could only hope that Abner would go out tonight as he did most nights.

By the time it was full dark, she'd nearly given up—but then she saw him, a dark-clad shadow moving along the road that led from the stables around to the front of the house. Quickly, she slipped out the kitchen door and began to follow him.

The streets in this part of the city were deserted and dark, and she rather belatedly began to worry about her safety. She'd heard Duncan complain about rising crime, but until now, she'd led such a sheltered life here that she hadn't given it much thought. At home, of course, crime was virtually nonexistent and she could go anywhere at any time in total safety.

Following along in Abner's wake, she soon

found herself entering a poorer part of the city she'd passed through many times before, but always in the safety of a carriage. There were some people about, although not many, and she hurried along, averting her face and hoping that the billed cap she'd pulled low on her brow would keep her from being recognized as a woman.

Then they were in a slightly better neighborhood of small houses that stood close to each other. Cooking smells and voices drifted out onto the narrow sidewalks. Several times, soldiers passed by, mounted on their handsome horses. She thought about Zach and felt a deep ache inside, a longing for something she knew she couldn't have.

Ahead of her, Abner made several turns on the narrow streets, and then suddenly turned in to one of the houses. Rowena stayed in the shadow of a large tree and watched as he knocked several times and then entered the house, even though she saw no one come to the door.

She recalled what Paulena had told her about the houses to which her people were generally taken after they had descended, and she wondered if this might be one of them.

Cautiously, she approached the house. On either side, neighboring houses stood less than ten feet away. The house to one side was lighted and she could hear people talking and laughing inside, but on the other side, all was darkness. So she crept between that house and the one where Abner had gone. There were lights in the downstairs windows, but even on this warm night, the windows themselves were closed and drapes had been drawn.

As she stood there in the darkness, she could hear the faint hum of voices, although she couldn't make out the words. Then, as she cast a glance back at the street, she saw two men approaching the house. They didn't notice her there, but she got a good look at them as they passed beneath a street lamp near the house. She recognized them both. One was the older brother of a friend. He'd descended several years earlier.

They, too, knocked, and she decided that it must be a signal of some sort: two raps, then three more after a brief pause. As soon as they disappeared inside, she went to the door herself. These were her people here, and however surprised they might be to see her, she knew they would do her no harm.

She knocked as she'd heard the others do, and was about to try the doorknob when the door was opened and she found herself facing a cousin who'd descended about five years ago. He stared at her warily, obviously not recognizing her as she stood there in the shadows. She pulled off the cap, letting her golden hair tumble about her shoulders.

"Gilbert, it's Rowena. I must speak with you."

"Rowena! What are you doing here?" His eyes darted behind her, scanning the street.

"I followed Abner," she said, at the same time advancing into the house and forcing him to back up.

She closed the door behind her, then turned to confront the group that had now gathered. Except for Abner, the eyes that met hers weren't hostile, but neither were they particularly friendly. Mostly, they seemed as shocked as Gilbert was.

"I came here because something has been kept from me," she stated, meeting their gazes one after the other. "Paulena and Carlotta and Tabby are concealing something from me because they fear that if I find it out, I won't be permitted to return."

Silence met her words, and then Gilbert spoke. "They're right, Rowena. Do what you were sent here to do and then go home. We can't help you."

"I have no intention of doing what I was sent here to do until I know the truth," she stated firmly.

"You're just seeking excuses," Abner sneered. "You won't kill him. I saw the two of you together."

She met his glare with an icy stare of her own. "I've had about all I intend to take from you, Abner. Your behavior is inexcusable. You hate me because I turned down your proposal of marriage."

There were a few gasps at those words, and ten pairs of eyes swiveled in his direction.

"At least I asked you to marry me. The almighty commander won't make that offer."

She smiled unpleasantly. "As a matter of fact, he already has. I'm to give him my answer when he returns."

"Where is he?" someone asked. "At Shemoth?"

She shook her head. "He's on a tour of the northern garrisons. He's making plans for war—and very soon, I think."

This was greeted by more silence, but she saw the fear in their eyes.

"You have to stop him, Rowena," Gilbert implored. "We need more time. If he dies, it will be a while before the next chief is able to persuade the king to go to war."

Rowena shook her head. "No, I think that things have already gone too far. His death might delay war for a time—but only for a very short time. I think the king has already been persuaded. I went riding yesterday with the Princess Melba and she says that her father is prepared to declare war."

"But we understood that the king was resisting," Gilbert said doubtfully.

Rowena shook her head. "I think it's the new weapon that made him change his mind."

"What new weapon?" several voices asked in unison.

"Something called chemicals—gases that can kill. I don't really understand it."

They all stared at her in horror—the same horror she felt when she thought about such deadly, terrible things.

"I know they exist," she went on, "because I was at Shemoth when the king came to visit and I saw the place where they make weapons."

"You were at Shemoth?" Gilbert asked, wide-eyed.

She nodded, shivering. "We cannot hope to defeat them with our magic. They have weapons that are far too powerful."

"We can't believe her," Abner said angrily. "She tells us just what *he* wants us to hear."

Rowena turned on him, her eyes flashing. "Do you think I would betray my people?" she challenged.

He seemed about to respond, but Gilbert cut him off. "Do you think war will come to the valley, Rowena?"

"Yes." She sighed. "I was there at Ashwara with Paulena and Duncan and the commander. I think he wants war to come, and especially there. He wants to avenge the loss his ancestor suffered there. And the Atanians want it as well."

"The spell will be destroyed," one of the women said. Rowena didn't know her by name.

"Yes. I think that will happen."

A long, heavy silence followed, until finally one of the men spoke up. He was older than the others, and Rowena didn't know him.

"We're not ready yet. We need more time."

"Time for what?" she asked.

"I think you must know, Rowena," Gilbert said. "It's true that the Council will never permit you to return if you know the truth, but there may be nothing to return to in any event."

He glanced at the others, who all nodded solemnly, with the exception of Abner, who had withdrawn to a corner of the room sullenly. When Gilbert saw that they agreed, he went on.

"The Council never actually lied to us, but they didn't really tell the truth, either. They said that they wanted only to put our people into positions of power in order to change things here in case we have to return. What they *didn't* say is that they have intended all along that we should rule this land—as we did centuries ago."

"Rule this land," Rowena echoed. "But we never ruled. We tried to keep to ourselves."

"That's not true, Rowena. I know it's what we were taught, but it isn't true. Our ancestors ruled here. They used their magic to control everything and everybody. They conquered everyone—except for the Warriors. You can read all about it in old books at Ashwara. I've seen them myself."

Rowena stared at him, remembering what Zach had said about the brutality of her people. "But those books were written by the Cassatans," she said, spitting out the hated word she hadn't used for some time now.

"Yes, but they merely confirm what we were told before we descended," Gilbert said. "And the Council wants that power for us again. Ever since the Gateway was discovered, they've been planning for the day when the Dazhinn will rule again."

"And we *will* rule," Abner shouted, returning to the group. "We will kill the king and MacTavesh and get rid of the Parliament."

"It won't happen, Abner," Gilbert said quietly. "There aren't enough of us, and the Council has never understood how much things have changed here. They live in the past."

"They make fun of us," Abner screeched, his face flushed. "They dare to make fun of us."

For the first time, Rowena felt a twinge of sympathy for Abner. In his outrage at the treatment of her people, she heard her own anger. But she could spare no time to be angry now. Instead, she was trying to accept what she'd been told.

Could it really be true that her people had been warriors themselves—warriors who had used magic as their weapon? She thought about her peaceful home and wanted to disbelieve it. But she was picturing old tapestries made by her own ancestors that had depicted battle scenes—tapestries she'd seen only once because her grandmother and mother had hidden them away, and after their deaths she hadn't looked at them again.

She remembered how disturbing they'd been—unlike the tapestries woven later. The magic in them had spoken of great valor and of bloody battles. Her grandmother had explained them away as being created to depict the ravages visited upon her people by the Warriors, but perhaps she'd known all along what they truly were, since she'd hidden them away in trunks.

An argument had broken out between Gilbert and Abner and people were choosing sides. Most seemed to agree with Gilbert that their cause was lost, but some sided with Abner, who was determined that, despite their small numbers, they could prevail.

"The commander says that the future belongs to the merchant class," she said into a brief silence as the two sides glared at each other. When all eyes turned to her, she continued, explaining what he'd told her.

"He says that he will probably be the last Warrior chief to wield great power," she finished quietly, recalling that poignant conversation.

"He said that?" Gilbert asked disbelievingly.

She nodded. "I think he believes that the Warriors belong to the past as much as we do."

"Don't believe her!" Abner shouted. "She's in love with him and can't be trusted!"

"I'm not in love with him," Rowena protested. "But I believe he speaks the truth. He is a man who thinks much about the future—as we haven't."

"I've had enough of this!" Abner sneered. "The rest of you can wait to be killed, but I'm going to save our people."

He turned and stormed out of the house, followed by three others. No one made a move to stop them, but Rowena saw the worried look on her cousin's face.

"What will he do?" she asked, thinking about his earlier statement about wanting to be the one to kill Zach.

Gilbert shrugged. "I don't know. He's mad, Rowena. We asked the Council through the 'path to take him back, but they refused."

"Have you spoken to Paulena about this?" she asked, certain that they couldn't have.

Gilbert's expression became closed. "No."

"Why not?"

"Because Paulena wants nothing to do with

us. She's gone over, along with Carlotta and Tabitha."

"What do you mean?" she asked, although she already thought she knew.

"They side with the Cassatans," he said, spitting out the word angrily. "Especially Paulena."

"She loves Duncan," Rowena said, feeling compelled to defend her aunt. "He's a good man."

"He has Warrior blood in him—did you know that?"

"Yes. Zach . . . the commander told me."

Gilbert's blue eyes flashed at her. "So you're on a first-name basis with him. What Abner said is true, isn't it? You're in love with him."

Rowena drew herself up stiffly. "Even if I am, I would never betray my people—and neither would Polly."

"You betray us merely by the fact of loving them," one of the women cried. "How could you love a *Warrior*?"

Rowena had no answer to that, so she ignored the question. "The Council must be made to understand that their plan will not work. I think it would never have worked, even if we had more time. But now there may be no time if war comes to the valley. They should be preparing our people to return to this world."

"How can you prepare people to die?" Gilbert asked coldly.

"They will only die if they try to fight the Warriors."

"They? You do not include yourself, Rowena?" Gilbert inquired unpleasantly.

231

"I was speaking of those at home, who know nothing of this."

"But you are safe, aren't you?" Gilbert persisted. "He will protect you."

"I have no idea what he would do if he learned the truth about me," she replied. But she was lying and Gilbert was right: Zach would protect her.

"How many others feel as Abner does?" she asked, far more concerned about them than about the group here, regardless of their taunts.

"There are about fifty of them," one of the men said. "A small group, to be sure, but they are in a position to cause a great deal of trouble."

"How?" Fifty seemed a very small number to her, regardless of their positions.

"Most likely through assassinations, perhaps combined with some display of their magic that could terrify people."

Rowena was appalled. "Would they really do that?"

Gilbert and the others nodded. "They've been threatening it. They believe that they could create havoc, especially if they timed it right."

"But what would they gain from havoc?"

"Power for our people. If the spell is broken and there is at the same time a display of our magic, we could still gain the upper hand, despite our small numbers."

Rowena felt terror pierce her spine and chill her to the core. Would it work? The legend of the Dazhinn was still very much alive here, even if people made light of it. If they suddenly reappeared in the valley and Abner and the others arranged a display of Dazhinn magic, it could work—especially if Zach were preoccupied with a war.

"Don't you see, Rowena? If we don't sieze power, we will be killed." Gilbert looked at her imploringly. "The Warriors would never let us live unless they fear us. I don't like Abner's methods, but it's the only way to save our people."

"There has to be another way," she stated, but with far more certainty than she felt.

Chapter Nine

"I had to know the truth, Polly."

Paulena nodded slowly, her eyes bright with unshed tears. "Yes. I should have told you, but I wanted to protect you."

She sighed as she got up to stare out through the windows into the rain. "It came as such a shock to me—to all of us, I suppose. But they didn't tell us until just before we descended, and by then it seemed that there was no turning back.

"Besides, at the time it didn't seem such a terrible thing for us to rule. We were convinced that the Cassatans were evil people who needed to be changed. And the Council impressed upon us the fact that we would simply be resuming our rightful place.

"What they didn't tell us, of course, is how much things had changed here, even though they must know that. They said only that the Warriors still controlled the people, and that was enough to make us agree.

"The difference for me was that I met Zach. I wanted to hate him, but I soon discovered that I couldn't. One day, he arrived here before Duncan had come home, and we had a long talk. He told me that he believes the time when the Warrior chief wields great power is coming to a close—and I knew he spoke the truth. It was then that I knew the Council was wrong."

"He told me that, too," Rowena acknowledged, not at all surprised that those words should have had such an effect upon her aunt since she, too, had been unable to forget them.

"I tried to convince the others of this, but only a few would listen. The others accused me of being under Duncan's influence. So I simply withdrew from any contact with them, except when it was necessary to pass on information through the 'path. And the truth is that I've done very little of that." She paused and flicked a glance at Rowena.

"I haven't once tried to influence Duncan, except through words. I think the others know that—and hate me for it, especially since I'm in a better position than any of them to make my influence felt. Or I was until *you* arrived, in any event. Now, between us, we hold the greatest power of any of our people."

"Then we must use it to help them," Rowena stated firmly. "But what can we do?"

"I don't know. The only thing I do know is that we can't change the others—especially Abner and his allies. I've talked to Abner many times. I know that he has used his powers to try to influence Duncan. He's accused me of countering with my own magic, but that isn't true. I've countered only with arguments—and I've won."

"We must get him out of this house, Polly—and away from Duncan. If they carry out their threatened assassinations, Duncan will surely be a target as much as Zach is."

Paulena nodded, her brows creased with worry. "I've spoken to Duncan about it, telling him that Abner has been very unpleasant toward both of us, but he's reluctant to get rid of him. Abner has done a very good job of insinuating himself into Duncan's affections."

"Then you must use your magic to change his mind. You can make it work, Polly, because you have love on your side."

"Yes, I know, but I fear for Duncan's sanity if he has both of us trying to control him for opposite purposes."

Rowena was silent. She hadn't thought about that. "I must go back," she said into the silence between them. "I must persuade the Council to give up their plans."

"They won't let you come back—especially once Abner reports to them about last night."

"Perhaps I can go back without their approval."

Paulena frowned. "What do you mean?"

"Think about it, Polly. We have only the Council's word for it that the Gatekeepers are necessary. And we already know that the Council has lied. They must have guessed that at least some Descenders would begin to feel as we do, and by telling us that only the Gatekeepers can guide us between the worlds, they were making certain that no one would try to come back on their own."

"But the danger . . ." Paulena gasped.

Rowena cut her off, her mind made up even as she spoke. "The danger is there; I agree. But the greater danger lies in doing nothing at all.

"If war comes to the valley and the spell is broken, and at the same time, Abner and the others carry out their plan, our people will die, Polly. Magic or no magic, we will die."

"But going back there will not prevent war from happening here—in the valley, I mean."

"No, I think that cannot be prevented—unless we return to the valley before there is war."

"I don't understand."

"If the Dazhinn were to suddenly reappear in the valley, it would surely give both sides pause. And perhaps our magic would be strong enough to hold them off."

"But those weapons you saw at Shemoth . . ."

"Yes, I know. I asked Zach once what he would do if the Dazhinn were to return to their valley, and he said that would depend upon their intentions. If we returned and he was convinced of our intention to remain peaceful, he would not attack the valley."

"I'm not so sure about that." Paulena frowned. "Zach has a powerful need to avenge his ancestor who was robbed of victory."

237

"Yes, but he loves me and has asked me to marry him. So if I convince him that we mean no harm—"

"You didn't tell me about his proposal. What did you say?"

"I more or less promised him an answer when he returns."

"Do you love him, Rowena?"

She sighed. "I don't know. When I'm with him, he makes me feel as though there's no other place I would want to be—not even back home."

"Then you love him. I knew I truly loved Duncan when I realized that I couldn't use my magic on him."

"I can't marry him unless he knows what I am and accepts that. And I don't think he will. But I have no time to think about that now. I want to go to Cliff House. Then from there, I will go on to Ashwara—and into the valley."

Paulena opened her mouth to protest, then closed it again and nodded. "We will go tomorrow."

"No. I want to go alone. You need to stay here to protect Duncan. We can't be sure when Abner and his allies might decide to strike. And Duncan is likely to be their first target—especially if Abner thinks he might be sent away from this household."

"You conducted a thorough search?"

"Yes, Chief. We checked every town and village in the region. No one has ever heard of the Sandor family—or of anyone who weaves tapestries."

"Could they have lied to you for some reason?" Zach asked, hating the desperation in his voice.

"I don't see why they would. We were posing as agents for a wealthy merchant who had heard about Sandor tapestries and wished to purchase one. We even bought various local crafts to prove our mission."

Zach thanked the men and dismissed them, then began to pace around his temporary quarters. What shocked him most was that somewhere deep inside, he wasn't shocked. Some part of him had known all along that Rowena was lying. But why?

And if she was lying, then Paulena must be lying as well. She'd claimed to have come from the same region.

His thoughts began to turn to those differences he'd sensed in both of them—and in a few others as well: Carlotta and Tabitha came quickly to mind. He wondered what backgrounds they claimed for themselves, then recalled that either Paulena or Carlotta had said once that they'd known each other as children.

He stared unseeing through the garrison window, where his men were engaged in arms practice. For the moment, thoughts of the impending war were far from his mind.

What were Rowena and the others hiding, and why did they find it necessary to hide anything? What could be so terrible in their backgrounds that they would go to such lengths?

An image of Rowena, never buried too deeply in his mind, swam up now. As always, he saw her as he'd seen her for the first time, on the beach that day. It was strange that that remained his image of her, despite all the changes since then.

And he thought about his powerful, primitive reaction to her—and the brief fear he'd felt, even though he could certainly have had nothing to fear from her. Or so he'd thought. He began to wonder now if what he'd really felt that day had been a sort of premonition of the type that had saved him and his men in battle several times.

He knew he had to get to the bottom of this. His tour was nearly completed. Tomorrow he would leave for Ashwara to issue orders that the university be evacuated. Already, forces from Shemoth and several other garrisons near the city were being mobilized to set out for Ashwara. The enemy was gathering its forces on the other side of the border.

He had so much to do, but somehow, he intended to find the time to confront Rowena with his knowledge of her lie.

When she saw the big house perched upon its cliff, Rowena felt tears springing to her eyes. The memory of the day when she'd first met Zach was etched into her brain with startling clarity, even though she'd rarely thought about it since then.

So it was for him, too, she thought, recalling

the times he'd mentioned it. It's as though our fates were sealed that day. But what, exactly, was their fate?

She accepted the driver's hand to alight from the carriage, then dismissed him after telling him that she would be needing him to take her to Ashwara the next morning.

When she entered the house, she was surprised at how different her impression of it had become. The first time she saw it, she had been awed by its luxury and size. Now, after living in the city, it seemed both smaller and far less opulent. What would she think when she got home?

She spent the remainder of the day wandering along the beach, until she reached the spot where she'd fallen asleep and Zach had found her. She tried to recapture her first thoughts about him, but found that what came instead were those moments in his arms and her increasing respect and admiration for him.

Paulena might have been right when she suggested that the star-crossed attraction could be mutual, but that didn't account for those other feelings. Those came from a different source altogether.

"I *do* love him," she whispered. And she knew that the stars had little to do with it. But she knew, too, that her love was doomed. She might be able to prove to him that she was Dazhinn, and he would accept that—but he would never accept *her* once he knew. Still, if she could persuade him not to harm her people . . .

241

She shook her head at the sad irony. She'd been sent here to save her people and she might yet accomplish that—but at a far higher cost to her than she'd ever dreamed of.

Early the next morning, Rowena set out for Ashwara. She hadn't yet figured out just how she was going to get down to the valley, but she'd brought along her old trousers and shirt and shoes, hiding them in a small valise she'd borrowed from Paulena. Paulena had given her directions to the old dirt road that led from the hilltop town of Ashwara into the valley: the route they'd taken the day she arrived.

The first thing she noticed as the carriage made its way through the crowded streets was the presence of soldiers—far more of them than she'd seen at the time of her other visit here. But there were many students as well, so she assumed that Zach hadn't yet carried out his threat to the dean to evacuate the university.

She had told the driver to take her up to the old fortress that was now the university. The dirt road that led down to the valley ran quite near there, and her hope was to make her way from the fortress into the valley on foot, after finding someplace to change clothes.

But as soon as she'd dismissed the driver, telling him not to return for her until late in the afternoon, she recalled the old books that had been mentioned several times: books that told the story of her people. She had time, she decided, to read what had been written about the

Dazhinn by their contemporaries.

She made her way to the great library, only to be told that the ancient volumes she was requesting were available only to scholars, owing to their great age and value.

"I met the dean when I was here with Commander MacTavesh," she told the officious librarian. "Perhaps you could obtain permission from him."

She was about to accompany her request with a slight mental push, but it quickly became apparent that that wasn't necessary. The mention of Zach's name propelled the man into action. He hailed a young aide and sent him to find the dean, and that gentleman appeared in short order.

"Miss Sandor," he said with a smile of welcome. "How nice to see you again. I see that our little talk when you visited before has whetted your appetite for more information about my favorite subject."

"Yes, it has," Rowena acknowledged. "I'm staying for a few days at my aunt's home down the coast and I would very much appreciate being allowed to study those books. I assure you that I will treat them gently."

"Of course. Allow me to escort you to a place where you can study them free from distractions. Then I will have them brought to you."

He led her through the maze of hallways and ushered her into a small room furnished as a study. Moments later, an aide appeared, carrying a large, leather-bound volume.

"This doesn't look as old as I'd expected," she

commented as the young man set down the book on a table.

"It was written nearly four hundred years ago by the greatest historian of the time, and he collected in the book the writings of earlier historians. I think you will enjoy it, although I warn you that it is sometimes difficult to read. Perhaps when you are finished, we can talk a bit."

He opened the heavy volume and paged through it carefully until he found the section he wanted. "You are welcome to read as much as you like, of course, but you will find most of the information about the Dazhinn contained in this section."

She thanked him and he sighed heavily. "It's fortunate that you've come when you have, Miss Sandor, since I fear that we are about to be closed down."

"Oh?" she asked in alarm. "I saw that there seemed to be many more soldiers about this time."

He nodded sadly. "The garrison is being reinforced and I've been told to expect Commander MacTavesh very soon."

"Yes, I knew that he was touring the northern garrisons," she said, echoing in her own thoughts the dean's words about the fortunate timing of her visit. If she had arrived to find him here, her plans would certainly become more difficult.

"It's strange, isn't it, that after all these centuries, the Valley of the Dazhinn still holds such significance to both sides. It is, after all, a valley of no consequence to anyone anymore."

He bowed and wished her a pleasant day, then left. His final words echoed in her ears. "A valley of no consequence to anyone anymore" -except, of course, to those for whom it was named.

The book proved difficult indeed, but she made her way slowly through the pages, feeling as though she'd slipped through time itself. All that she'd heard was there—and more. Her people had indeed ruled all those around them—except for the Warriors. The battles between these ancient foes had been responsible for an almost perpetual state of war, with the resultant heavy loss of life.

According to the historian, the Dazhinn had conscripted armies by robbing them of their free will and sending them into battle on their behalf, then augmenting those armies with their magic.

The accounts were very detailed and Rowena felt sick reading about men sent to certain death by her ancestors who were determined to defeat the Warriors at any cost. How could they have done such a thing?

And as she forced herself to read on, she began to wonder if such a thing could happen again. Surely none of her people now possessed the powers of their ancestors. It was generally acknowledged by them all that their magic had diminished over the centuries as they lived within the grand spell created by those powerful sorcerers. But what if some of them did still possess those powers?

Then she read several accounts of Warriors

who'd been captured by her people and later released with their minds forever gone: the story that Zach had told her. It was said to be the favorite form of revenge taken by the Dazhinn against their enemies, since they considered it to be more terrible than merely killing them.

Rowena wanted to close the book and leave this place, but she forced herself to read the account of that final battle. The writer had obtained it from the personal diary of Zach's ancestor. She wondered if the original diary still existed. Even if it didn't, Zach must certainly have read this account. Why, then, did he refuse to believe it?

Perhaps, deep inside, he does believe it, she thought, and that is why he wants a victory here. If war comes to the valley, he won't just be fighting the Atanians, but the ghosts of his ancient enemies, the Dazhinn.

What had he felt down there in the valley when he visited it as a student? She was certain that he must have felt something. No Warrior could approach the most powerful sorcery her people had ever created without feeling its power.

She closed the book, filled with a great urgency to leave this place, even though she feared what lay ahead. The dean hadn't returned, and that was just as well. She had no desire to talk to him now.

There were toilet facilities just off the study and she picked up her valise and went in there, then struggled out of her unwieldy clothing and into the pants and shirt and soft leather shoes. If the dean showed up at this inopportune moment, she would simply tell him the truth: that she intended to walk down into the valley. He would certainly think it odd behavior, but he wasn't likely to stop her.

But no one was about as she came back out into the study and then into the hallway. At the far end of the long corridor, she saw a door that almost certainly led outside, and when she opened it, she saw that she was on the far side of the fortress, with only two small buildings between her and the stretch of woods that would take her to the road into the valley.

No one saw her as she hurried past the buildings and plunged into the woods. From there, it was no more than a 15-minute walk to the narrow dirt road. She left the valise hidden behind a tree and started down into the valley.

Zach paced back and forth on the roof of the fortress, staring at the distant mountains where he'd grown up, then shifting his gaze down into the valley. Beyond the hills to his left, at the far end of the valley, the enemy was massing along the borders. They would choose that spot for their invasion, rather than risk intruding upon his clan's ancient home. There was only a small garrison now at the old fortress of Shemoth, but the Atanians were flatland warriors and would not attempt to fight in the mountains.

That end of the valley was always shrouded in mists and would provide good cover for the enemy. But it could provide cover for his men as well. He thought about the steep cliffs there and knew it would take only a small contingent with heavy artillery to wreak unacceptable losses upon them. Within a few days, the artillery would be arriving at Ashwara, after taking a circuitous route from Shemoth that should have kept them from the spying eyes of the enemy.

So war would come again, after 500 years, to the Valley of the Dazhinn. As he stared down into the dense forest below, Zach felt a chill. Then, before he could dismiss it, he saw something moving down there and took out his glasses.

Someone was walking down there, a solitary figure in white, moving along the old dirt road that twisted through the forest. He adjusted the glasses, then drew in his breath sharply. It couldn't be! But the sunlight caught that familiar golden hair and made a mockery of his denial.

He hurried from the rooftop and ordered an aide to find the dean forthwith, at the same time ordering his horse to be brought from the stable.

Rowena felt the power of the spell the moment she began her journey down into the valley on the steep, twisting road. The feeling was disturbing for a time, but gradually subsided into a low hum of energy that made her hurry along the road even faster than her normal walking speed.

Once she'd reached the floor of the valley, the road became all but invisible, overgrown with weeds, some of which were as tall as she was.

But she didn't hesitate. From somewhere deep inside her came a certainty of the direction she was taking. It was, after all, the twin of the main road that ran through the other valley in her enchanted home.

Here and there as she walked along, she saw familiar landmarks: a huge boulder, a glimpse of the stream where the road came close to it, even the slight rise and fall of the road itself as it followed the contours of the valley.

She was home—and not home. It was a very strange sensation. And she felt the presence of her ancestors so much more strongly here than she'd ever felt them before.

She shuddered, thinking about the descriptions of her people in the book. Even allowing for the fact that some things could have been exaggerated or even outright lies, the picture that had emerged was the opposite of what she'd been taught.

When, she wondered, was the decision made to rewrite their history? Had it been made by those who'd lifted the valley to its present place of enchantment? Were they ashamed of the things they'd done—or had there been some other reason?

She thought about her mother's oft-expressed distrust of the Council, even though various friends and relatives had served on it. Had she known something? Others had from time to time alluded to secrets known only to the Council, but Rowena had always ignored them, reasoning that it had little to do with her.

Whatever my people may have been or done in the past, they are different now, she told herself, then abruptly remembered Abner and his allies.

What was it her grandmother had said once? "Evil things can happen only when good people do nothing." Yes, that was it. She could no longer recall what had prompted that statement, but for the first time, she began to grasp the truth of it. Most of her people were good; she remained certain of that. But were they prepared to stop those among them who had evil intentions?

She paused to rest for a moment and turned around to stare at the fortress perched upon its hill. An image of Zach came into her mind, and she felt again the sharp pain of loss. Regardless of what the future held, it didn't include him. If it became necessary, he would protect her as best he could, but he would never accept who and what she was. The fierce conflict between their ancestors lay far too heavily on them both.

She set off again. Even walking as swiftly as she could, she knew that she wouldn't reach the Gateway until dusk. Not that it much mattered. The ever-present mists there created an artificial dusk even at noon.

Strangely, though, her fears about what could happen to her if she attempted to cross on her own had dwindled away. Perhaps, she thought sadly, it's because I have nothing to lose now.

Then she suddenly became aware of a change in the power that surrounded her here. Something was disturbing it, sending out small jolts that broke the low hum she could feel within her. She stopped, confused, and looked around her.

Fear prickled her spine and tingled along her nerve endings: a fear made all the worse because she couldn't identify its source. All she knew was that something had changed.

She scanned the area but saw nothing, and she was still too far from the Gateway to be feeling anything emanating from there. Besides, she'd felt nothing like this when she'd approached it before.

She started walking again, but the feeling persisted and seemed to be growing ever stronger. Did they know, somehow, that she was coming? Was this an attempt to stop her? Once she would have said that she understood all the powers of her people, even the ones she didn't possess herself, but she was no longer so sure of that. And neither could she be certain that they wouldn't attempt to harm her.

That thought left her feeling more alone than she'd ever felt in her life, and she felt tears stinging her eyes. But she kept going, more determined than ever to go back through the Gateway and bring the truth to her people.

The sense of alarm grew into near panic—and then she heard her name being called.

A deep sense of foreboding came over Zach as he began his descent into the valley, and by the time he reached the bottom, it had grown so powerful that his hands were trembling as he held the reins. Either his horse felt it as well, or his fear was communicating itself to the animal, because it shied nervously and snorted.

Zach had faced death many times in battle, but never had he felt such fear. He could taste it in his dry mouth: harsh and bitter. It was far worse than the other time he'd come down here, perhaps because he was a sober man now and not a half-drunk youth.

He cursed himself silently for the absurdity of such fear. It was no more than a valley, empty now, and even when the Dazhinn had lived here, they'd been no more than people. His primitive ancestor might have believed in Dazhinn sorcery, but he didn't. Everything had an explanation—even what he felt now.

He urged his horse along the nearly invisible road, where his sharp gaze picked out small signs that a cart or carriage had passed through here, and fairly recently, to judge from the tracks and the bent grasses and weeds.

Why would anyone have been down here with a vehicle? he wondered. He knew that the students still came into the valley, just as they had in his day. But it made no sense that anyone would have brought a cart or carriage down here.

At least he knew why Rowena had come down here. The dean had told him about her arrival this morning and her interest in the old history book. After reading about the Dazhinn, she'd apparently decided to visit their ancient home.

No other woman he knew would have done such a thing—but she would.

Then, through the trees and beyond a bend in the road, he saw a flash of white. He thought about the information he'd gained from his agents and wondered how to go about confronting her with her lies. For a man who didn't suffer fools or liars, he was strangely reluctant to face her.

Despite his efforts to hold his fear at bay, his hands were still trembling and sweat had broken out beneath his uniform. He fought it for all it was worth because he couldn't let her see it. Then, when he had her in view at last, he called her name.

Rowena turned, recognizing the voice and knowing instantly why she'd felt that difference in the spell that held the valley in its thrall.

When she saw him approaching on his huge black stallion, she was, for one brief moment, held prisoner by a powerful mixture of fear and rage. And she knew that what she felt was what her ancestors must have felt toward their eternal enemy.

It's Zach, she told herself, and he is not my enemy, even if his presence here does present a big problem.

She stood there waiting for him, willing the fear and anger to go away. She would not be able to get to the Gateway now, but as he drew closer, she found that she didn't mind. In fact, as he brought the horse to a halt and dismounted,

253

she had all she could do not to run to him and fling herself into his arms.

"How did you find me?" she asked as he approached her rather uncertainly.

But even as she spoke, that low hum inside her and around her increased in volume until it was roaring in her ears. And she could see now the rigidity in him, even as he smiled at her.

Then his smile faded as he stopped and began to look around them, and she knew that he, too, felt or heard something. It would be worse for him—far worse.

She moved toward him out of pure instinct, out of a deep certainty that touching him would free them from the spell that grew ever more powerful. But it seemed as though she were walking through water, barely able to put one foot before the other. And he was moving just as slowly.

The roar in her ears was deafening and now it seemed as though the light was fading, even though several hours of daylight remained and the sky above the valley had been cloudless. He was nearly invisible to her now, even though they were less than 20 feet apart. She kept moving, forcing herself toward him, thinking only about how good it felt to be in his arms.

The gap between them closed and she reached out to him, grasping the hand he extended to her. His pale eyes were fixed upon her, and for one brief moment, she knew the thrill of Dazhinn power as she saw fear in this strongest and most powerful of men.

Then the roaring was gone and the light returned, and all she felt was that thrumming within her. He drew her roughly into his arms and the mouth that sought hers was hard and demanding, as though his need to claim possession of her had overwhelmed his better instincts.

Pressed against his hard body, Rowena was keenly aware of the unnaturalness of this meeting and of the wrath of all her ancestors. She could feel their disapproval, but she ignored it and returned his kisses hungrily. They had no future, but they had now, and she would not let her bloodthirsty forebears take that from her.

"I love you, Rowena," he said, his voice a harsh rasp against her ear.

She drew back within the circle of his arms and stared at him. Suddenly, it seemed all-important to say it—not just to him, but to the ghosts of her ancestors that haunted this place.

"I love you, too, Zach."

For a brief moment, it seemed as though the valley itself had gasped, sucking the air from them. Did she just imagine it, or was the steady rhythm of the spell broken for one instant?

"Let's get out of this place," he said, seizing her hand and leading her quickly to his horse.

He mounted the stallion, then pulled her up in front of him. The animal responded with alacrity, as though it, too, wanted to be away from here. Neither of them spoke until they had reached the top of the hill above the valley, and then both turned to stare back at it. She waited for him to say something, but he remained silent.

What did you see? she asked in her mind. What did you feel down there and how are you settling it in your mind?

"Are you staying at Cliff House?" he asked as they paused at the top of the hill.

She nodded, already anticipating his next question with a heated eagerness.

"I had thought to spend a day or two there myself," he said carefully. "Is Paulena with you?"

"No, I came alone." Yes, she said silently to the question he had yet to ask.

"May I join you there?"

"Yes, I'd like that."

He urged the horse forward as he asked about her carriage. She told him that it should be waiting for her and they rode back into the fortress, where he dismounted and helped her down, then led her across the great parklike courtyard to the entrance, where the carriage was indeed waiting.

She had thought he would join her in the carriage, but he chose instead to ride behind them, followed as always by his guards. She was belatedly surprised that he hadn't brought them with him into the valley and wondered if he had chosen to go alone because he didn't want them to feel his own dread of the place. They were both Warriors themselves.

During the long ride back to Cliff House, Rowena thought about this small, precious time they would have together. There was no doubt in her mind that they would be sharing more than the house. Was it wrong for her to want this man? Would she be betraying her people?

No, she decided. It can't be wrong for me to love him. But I will not betray my people. I will get through the Gateway and try to convince them that their scheme is wrong. But if I cannot convince them, I will stay with them, even if it means going to my death.

How she would manage to get back to the valley and to the Gateway she didn't yet know. But neither did she give it much thought. She would find a way. But for now, she would follow her heart.

They reached Cliff House, and he surprised her by sending his Warrior guards back to Ashwara. For a moment, she thought they were going to protest their dismissal, but being men who were accustomed to following the orders of their chief, they departed into the night.

When they entered the house, Zach asked the servants to bring them some supper, since neither of them had eaten. Then he dismissed them as well, leaving the two of them alone in the house.

They ate at a small table set up in front of the open doors that led to the terrace. The breeze carried the scent and sounds of the sea, and the incessant rhythms of the waves pounding the shore provided a sensual background to a scene that needed no more eroticism.

He asked about her readings at the library,

and she told him of her shock at learning about the brutality of the Dazhinn. It was difficult for her to talk about it even now, but she struggled to maintain the detachment he would expect, since he could not know that these were her own ancestors.

"Life itself was brutal in those days," he said. "We cannot judge the actions or the beliefs of our ancestors on the basis of our own behaviors and beliefs."

For one terrifying moment, she was sure that he knew the truth about her, but then she quickly realized that he was merely speaking in generalities.

"You would excuse what they did?" she asked in surprise.

"The Dazhinn were merely using the weapons at their disposal—as my people used what they had."

"But you don't believe in their magic," she protested.

His gaze met hers, then slid away to a distant point, as though he were lost in memory. How she wanted to ask what he'd felt in the valley. But she didn't dare.

"I don't believe in magic," he stated finally. "But as I said before, I think they may well have used certain herbs and plants that could have created that impression.

"In war, as in other things, perception becomes reality. If people believe something is true, then it *is* true, at least for them. And in those days, when we knew so much less about the world, it was far easier to believe in magic."

He paused, then went on in what she knew to be a falsely casual tone, despite the teasing note in his voice. "Tell me, did you feel any Dazhinn magic in the valley?"

She hesitated only a moment before nodding. Admitting at least some of what she'd felt might encourage him to talk about it, too.

"I felt *something*. I can't describe it. It felt like . . . an enchanted place. Or how I imagine such a place would feel."

He studied her face intently as she spoke, whether to gauge the truth of her words or to determine what he should say, she didn't know.

"It's a matter of expectations," he said finally. "If that had been any other valley, you would have felt nothing. But given its history, you expected to feel something—and so you did."

"But what about you? Given the Dazhinn's importance to your own people's history, you must have had such expectations, too?"

He chuckled. "So I did—and I, too, felt something. Myths have great power—even when we know they're no more than that."

He has dismissed it, she thought. He felt it and he's denied it. If I were to tell him the truth, he would merely think me mad. But it did present a way for her to make him see the impossibility of their love. He would certainly not want to marry a madwoman.

"The valley presents something of a problem to me," he went on, his tone now indicating that he'd moved away from ancient myths. "I am fairly certain that the Atanians will launch their first attack on Ashwara, and that they will cross the border at the far end of the valley, in a place with steep cliffs and an ever-present mist.

"What troubles me is how my men will react to fighting there. They're brave men, but even they are subject to the power of that myth. For that reason, I've decided not to send any of my clan down there. Instead, I will use other officers."

But Rowena had barely heard his final words. He was talking about the Gateway! "Wh-when will this happen?"

"Soon, I think. Perhaps only a matter of a week. We are following the progress of the Atanian army and at the same time moving our artillery to Ashwara. The cliffs I spoke of will provide the perfect place for us to defend the valley."

And it is surely the most vulnerable place for my own people, she thought with horror. What will happen if war comes to the very spot that provides the link between the two worlds? Would they be cut off forever—or would the spell break and send them all into the very middle of the fighting?

Then she started nervously as he reached out to take her hand. He withdrew quickly with an apology. "I'm sorry, Rowena. None of this is of importance to you. It's only that I've already become accustomed to speaking my mind freely with you."

Not of importance to her? She wanted to shout

at him that nothing could be more important to her. But she managed a smile instead.

"Please don't apologize. It's only that I'm tired after such a long day." For once, she was glad that in this society, women were viewed as being frail creatures.

"Then I will not press you to give me an answer just yet, although I wish you would do so."

She met his gaze and saw the desire in his eyes—and saw beyond that as well. He truly did love her; she was certain of that. The stars might have ordained that he would want her, but the love sprang from a different source. She understood that because she felt it, too. Drawn together by sources far beyond this world, they had found something else, too.

"I would be happy to marry you, Zach," she said huskily. And she could meet his eyes and know she spoke the truth. She *would* be happy to marry him, even though it was a happiness she would never know.

He drew in a sharp breath, clearly not expecting that answer. Then he smiled and took her hand again, bringing it to his lips.

"I had thought you would refuse. I wish that our marriage could take place now—right here and now. But it must wait until this matter of war is settled."

She knew what he was really saying, and she smiled at him. "A wedding is for everyone else to see. But if we believe we are married, then we are. You said yourself that perception is reality."

His wide mouth curved into a slow smile as he searched her face. "Are you saying what I think you're saying?"

"Yes, I am."

Chapter Ten

Her bedroom was softly lit by a gas lamp, and the bedcovers had been turned back by the servants. Zach carried her into the room and set her on her feet, holding her loosely within the strong circle of his arms.

Rowena felt a sudden stab of fear that threatened to become outright panic. The fear caught her by surprise. After all, she was prepared to risk her very life to carry the truth to her people. But fear it certainly was: the fear of intimacy. To risk her life suddenly seemed far less terrifying than to risk her body and her very soul.

"I won't hurt you, Rowena," he said huskily. "Surely you must know that."

She nodded mutely. She did know that, but it didn't lessen the fear.

He bent his head toward her and his lips touched hers softly as he drew her close. His kiss felt different this time, perhaps because she knew it was only a beginning, and not an end in itself. Now she could feel the full force of his need and his careful control, and she could feel, too, that melting response of her own body that paid no attention at all to her fears.

His lips drew a quivering, ever more powerful response from her as she arched to him, keenly aware of the barriers of their clothing. Time seemed to stop, until one moment was filled up and spilled over into the next. She felt both weak and powerful at the same time: unable to control the heat that was spreading through her, but still very much aware of his waiting for some signal from her.

His lips traced slow, warm lines across her cheek, along the sensitive rim of her ear, and down along the soft skin of her neck to the wildly pulsing spot on her throat. She arched backward to give him greater access, supported now wholly by his arms. A soft cry welled up in her and spilled out, drawing a deep groan from him.

He lifted her off her feet and carried her to the bed, then lowered himself down beside her, his pale eyes alight with desire that would soon surely snap that taut leash. The urgency in his big, hard body was something she could actually feel, a palpable presence in the room as though it existed outside both of them.

And yet he did not hurry. They lay there, arms and legs entwined and bodies tangled by their clothing, caught on the pleasurable edge of passion as lips and tongues and hands began, tentatively at first, to learn each other.

She had not changed from her trousers and shirt—had in fact forgotten all about the valise still hidden behind a tree at the hilltop overlooking the valley. But even those soft, worn garments were becoming unacceptable, confining a body that seemed to be swelling with a voluptuous ripeness.

He lifted the shirt and the soft clingy garment she wore beneath it and kissed the heated flesh beneath, sending tremors through her as he raised it higher still, until she gasped as his tongue glided along the soft, full undersides of her breasts.

She shivered in the cool air when he freed her from both shirt and chemisette, then sat up to rid himself of his stiff military shirt. She saw that his fingers trembled as he fumbled with the buttons and felt strangely reassured. He was certainly no innocent like her. He'd been married and had probably had many mistresses, and yet those tremors told her that he too felt the importance of this moment.

Then he was back on the bed that sagged slightly beneath his weight, and his hard, hair-roughened body was covering hers, pressing her down.

Passion burst forth from her as he drew first one and then the other of her hardened nipples into his mouth. The waves of sensation engulfed her until she was sure she could take no more, only to find that she did in fact hunger for more.

Rowena had lost all thought. She became instead a creature of sensations, her senses filled with him, her body wanting and then demanding more. She heard herself cry out, felt her fingers fumbling with his trousers and touching the hardness that lay beneath.

Their remaining clothes seemed to melt away, and then he was above her, moving cautiously now as his eyes devoured her nakedness. She arched to him, wanting him beyond all reason, and he slid into her, filling her, moving with a slow, careful rhythm.

The small twinge of pain was barely noticeable as she welcomed him and surrounded him. That sensation of ripeness about to burst was back again, even more powerful this time, frightening her with its intensity.

The tremors began there where they were joined and spread through her with the heat of a wildfire. The rhythms of their bodies were increasing, growing ever wilder, pounding, driving, out of control.

Then suddenly they had broken through, crested the waves of passion to reach that final ecstasy where her startled cry was met by his deep, satisfied groan.

He moved off her and held her close, his hands stroking her still-quaking body, his mouth covering hers in a soft sweetness as she clung to him, no longer finding his big, hard body alien, but instead feeling it as an extension of herself.

"I love you, Rowena," he muttered hoarsely. But she heard more in his voice, felt more in the arms that held her, saw more in the pale eyes that swept over her.

She saw a Warrior chief, a man of fierce pride and great determination, who would never give up what he'd won.

"I love you, too, Zach," she murmured as she began to slip away into an uneasy sleep, secure for now in his arms but dreading what was to come.

Zach watched her as she walked slowly along the water's edge, her feet bare and her full skirt caught in one hand to hold it away from the lapping water. She was looking for seashells, but his own eyes could see nothing but her.

They'd awakened early this morning and she'd immediately leapt from the bed to open the drapes and then the window, totally unconscious of her nakedness until she turned and saw him staring at her, his eyes roaming slowly over the gentle curves and swells of her body. For one brief instant, a flush had crept through her fair skin, but then she'd smiled. It was the smile of a woman who knows her power and revels in it—a smile that on the face of any other woman would have disturbed him.

She had taken her time returning to the bed, even after he'd thrown back the covers and revealed his naked eagerness to her. And when they made love, there was a difference. Already, she knew how to tease him, as though the knowledge had been there all the while, but buried beneath maidenly propriety.

He'd intended to initiate her slowly into the art of lovemaking, but suddenly he found himself the student, learning not only her but himself. She was sometimes shy and occasionally brazen, sometimes carefully controlled and other times wildly free.

Watching her now, he felt just a bit frightened, as though last night had loosened something in him, allowed a part of him to slip forever beyond his control. All his instincts cried out for total possession of this woman, and yet, deep inside, he knew somehow that he would never truly possess her.

Those unsettling thoughts reminded him of her lies and his need to know the truth. Whatever it was, it could no longer make any difference, but he had to know.

She bent and picked up something, then walked toward him, carrying a sand-covered shell to add to the collection at his feet.

Rowena prodded the delicate shell loose from the sand and turned toward him as he sat on the sand next to the pile of shells she'd been gathering. The sun was high in the sky. They hadn't left their bed until an hour ago—and even then only because a need for food had begun to compete with their hunger for each other.

She wished they could be naked again now, freed from the clothing that hid their bodies from each other and turned the sight of warm flesh into nothing more than a memory. As she bent to drop the shell onto the pile beside him, she felt his eyes on the low neckline of her blouse, beneath which she was brazenly naked.

"Can we swim?" she asked, uncertain as to whether one actually swam in the ocean.

"It will be too cold for you," he protested.

"Would you swim if you were here alone?"

He nodded, a smile teasing his wide mouth.

"Then we will swim. The servants can't see us here." They were some distance from the house, in fact at the same spot where they'd met.

"Ladies don't swim," he said, smiling. "Where did you learn?"

"At home, of course. Life isn't so . . . confining there. There's a lake—just a small one. It's rather shallow, so the water is warm, except for the middle where it's deep."

Her words brought back to her an image of her home and a shadow passed across her, briefly chilling the beautiful day. But she was determined to have this time, and she pushed the image from her mind.

"Swimming in the ocean is different," he warned her as he got to his feet. "You must stay close to shore."

They stripped off their clothes and walked into the water hand in hand until a wave caught them and spilled over them, pulling them apart. She cried out in surprise and he was there almost before the sound had left her throat, his powerful arms around her as yet another wave washed over them.

At first frightened by the rise and fall of the water, Rowena quickly learned to move with it, swimming when she could and letting the waves carry her along. He stayed close, obviously not willing to accept her word that she could swim. The water *was* cold, but the sun was very warm, and the combination was exhilarating.

Finally, they stumbled to shore and collapsed onto the hard, wet sand, bodies entwined as the water lapped gently around them. They made love again, taking their time and fighting the need that drove them both. Rowena wanted to hold the moment forever, the feel of his big, hard body pressed to hers, the knowledge that he would soon be deep inside her, driving them both over the edge into that incomparable oblivion.

Zach, too, wanted to stop time in its tracks. Nothing of his life beyond this place, apart from this woman, mattered now. Had he possessed the sorcery attributed to the Dazhinn, he would have kept them both here forever.

He had stopped wondering what it was about Rowena Sandor that so entranced him, that made him want her again when his body was still cooling from the heat of their last coupling. It no longer mattered.

He ached for her and reached for her again, covering her naked flesh with kisses, gently persuading her to let him give her that most intimate of kisses. Her resistance melted away quickly into shudders and moans. Incredibly, he felt himself begin to grow hard again.

"You speak little of your past," he said, watching her in the firelight, his eyes devouring her as though he hadn't seen her naked before.

Rowena turned to him, half-fearing that he'd caught her thoughts. She knew she had to tell him the truth, but she didn't know how. She could convince him. That would take only a few minor tricks they all knew. But how would he react? She didn't think she could stand it if that light left his eyes.

"There is little to say," she replied. "I think that my life didn't truly begin until I came here—until I met you."

"Do you trust me, Rowena?"

His voice was soft, but she heard and felt the importance of the words. And then, suddenly, she knew. He had made inquiries. He knew she'd lied about her background.

"Yes, I trust you," she said, forcing herself to meet his gaze. "Why would you think otherwise?"

He reached for her hand and drew it to his lips. "Then tell me the truth. I know you've been lying about your background. There must have been a reason—but it can't matter now."

"You're wrong, Zach. It does matter now—more than ever."

"There is nothing you could tell me that would change how I feel about you."

She stared at him. A wry smile played across her lips. "And what if I were to tell you that I'm Dazhinn? Would *that* change the way you feel?"

Her voice was light and teasing, belying the tight knot in her stomach. He released her hand and laughed.

271

"And I suppose you've worked your magic on me. That's why I can think of nothing else."

She shook her head. "You've forgotten your history, Zach. Dazhinn magic doesn't work against Warriors."

He chuckled. "That's a relief. I'd hate to think that I fell in love with you against my will." He arched a brow questioningly.

"Tell me, my Dazhinn sorceress, just where have you been hiding since your people were driven from the valley?"

"They—my ancestors, I mean—cast a spell. I can't really say where we went, except that we left—and took the valley with us."

"I see." He smiled, clearly willing to play along with her "game." "So how did you manage to return? We were in the valley only two days ago and it was still deserted."

"Was it?" she asked, watching him closely. "Did you not feel something, Zach?"

His smile drained away into uncertainty, but he said nothing.

"The power of the spell is there," she went on. "And a Warrior would certainly feel it. There is a Gateway between the two worlds: the valley where we once lived and the place we live now. That's how I returned."

"Rowena," he said, his voice filled with concern.

"I'm not mad, Zach—and I have told you the truth—or some of it, anyway. But you're not ready to believe it. I could show you the proof. There are small tricks we can all do, but you

272

would not believe them, either. We will talk again tomorrow, after you've had time to think about how you felt in the valley. I think a part of you has always known that we exist, but the rest of you continues to deny it."

He stared at her in silence as she got up and walked toward the bed. She turned to see his brows knitted and something close to fear on his rugged face. But he got up and followed her to the bed.

"You said that you came back. Why?"

She hesitated, then thought about Abner and his allies. She had to warn him. He might not truly believe her, but she had to try.

They were in bed. His arms were wrapped loosely around her as they lay side by side, their faces scant inches apart on the pillow.

"I was sent here to kill you. But their plan didn't work, so now someone else might try. You must be careful, Zach. They are desperate."

He released her and sat up, and she regretted her words when she saw the harshness return to his face. No longer was he the gentle lover. Now he was the Warrior Chief.

"Who are these others who might try?" he demanded.

"I cannot tell you. That would be betraying my people."

"You say that you love me, and yet you would let me be killed?"

"No, I will not let you be killed," she stated firmly. "But you must be careful until . . . until

I can persuade them." She knew that the one thing she dared not tell him was about her plan to return. He could prevent that, and might well do so.

"You will be safe if you keep your Warrior guards with you."

He stared at her, studying her face as though he were seeing her for the first time. "This is madness, Rowena. You have let your imagination get away from you."

"All of it is madness, Zach, but that doesn't make it any less real. Please promise me that you'll be careful."

He lay down beside her again, then propped himself up on one elbow. "I suppose that the Dazhinn were responsible for those two attempts on my life?"

"Yes. When they failed, I was sent. The astrologers said that our stars are crossed and you would not be able to resist me." She laughed.

"What they didn't say was that I would not be able to resist you, either."

He dropped down again and drew her close, pressing his lips to the top of her head. "Rowena, this game has gone too far. You're tired and you've had too much wine. We will talk in the morning."

She awoke to the sounds of men's voices: angry, demanding voices. By the time she had pushed away the last of her uneasy dreams, he was out of bed and pulling on his clothes. Then she heard footsteps in the hallway and someone was pounding on the outer door.

"Chief! We must talk to you!"

Zach turned to her briefly. Their eyes met, and his gaze softened. Then he turned away and strode through to the sitting room. The outer door opened and closed again and footsteps retreated into the distance, together with men's voices.

Rowena sat up and shuddered. She was still half-caught in her dreams and uncertain just what she had told him last night. But it didn't matter now. What did matter was the reason his men had come here. Something must have happened.

He was back within moments, his expression cold and harsh. "The Atanian army is on the move. I must return immediately to Ashwara. And you must get back to the city."

Panic welled up in her, rendering her speechless. What she had to do was to get to the Gateway before the war began. She was filled with self-loathing for having wasted time here.

Then she looked at him and said silently: No, I did not waste this time. It may be all we will ever have. It *is* all we will ever have.

He sat down on the edge of the bed and drew her into his arms almost roughly. "I love you, Rowena—and nothing will change that."

"I love you, too, Zach—and I'm glad we had this time together."

He kissed her then—a hard, demanding kiss even though there was no time for such demands. And then he was gone, his footsteps echoing down the hallway. She listened until she heard the front door open and close, then wrapped the bedcovers around her and went to the window.

He swung up into the saddle, then paused for one brief moment to look up at the window before riding off. She wondered if he had seen her there. And then she choked back a sob, wondering if they would ever see each other again. If they did, it would surely be as enemies because he would no longer be able to deny who she was.

She'd made a mistake last night. She'd let him believe that she was teasing—or that she was mad. It was a cowardly thing to do, although at the time she couldn't have known that it would be her last opportunity. How foolish she'd been, to believe that they could hold back time, when all the while, outside the love-space they'd created for themselves, the world was moving ever closer to disaster for them both.

Rowena sat astride the best horse from the stable, watching the carriage disappear down the road that led back to the city. Then she kicked her mount and rode on toward Ashwara.

It was fortunate that there hadn't been a large staff at Cliff House. Casting multiple spells was hard work for one unaccustomed to such things. But she'd accomplished it. If the household staff was questioned later about her, they would say that she had returned to the city in the carriage. The stable boy would have no recollection of handing over to her their best horse. And the carriage driver would recall only that he had taken her back to the city, where she'd suddenly decided to visit a street market instead of going directly to Paulena's.

After several warm, sun-filled days, the weather had abruptly turned cool and damp, as though the heavens themselves were acknowledging the end of a precious time carved out for two lovers.

Still, she thought as she urged the horse on toward Ashwara, the change in the weather was to her benefit. Thanks to the coolness and the damp mist, she could disguise herself better. She had taken from one of the staff a long cape of oiled cloth with a capacious hood that fell forward to all but cover her face. The narrow road here was deserted, but she knew that she would need the disguise when she reached Ashwara. The town would probably be crawling with soldiers by now, but they would see only a slender youth obviously bent on some errand for his master or mistress.

The closer she came to Ashwara, the more her mind was tormented by the danger that lay ahead. If she could not reach the Gateway before soldiers flooded the valley, all would be lost. And even if she did reach the Gateway, there was always the chance that she would not be able to get through on her own.

And what if she did succeed in getting through? Rowena had faith in the inherent goodness of her people—but what if she was wrong? After all, until she'd descended, she had believed these people to be barbarians. And many of those who'd descended still believed that.

It has to end, she thought. There has to be a way to stop a hatred that has persisted down the ages.

Onward she rode, as the mist now became heavier, turning into a driving rain by the time she reached the widely scattered houses on the edge of Ashwara. She hoped that the rain would slow down the armies on both sides that were now aiming themselves at her valley.

As she'd expected, the town itself was full of soldiers. No students were to be seen. They'd apparently scattered to their distant homes. Even some of the many shops were closed and shuttered. But at least there were some townspeople about, making her a bit less obvious as she guided the horse through the narrow streets.

She lifted her face into the rain and stared up at the great fortress high on its hill. He would be up there now, making his war plans. Had he banished her from his mind, relegated her to a dim corner?

She suspected that he had. However much he might have been a tender and gentle lover, Zachary MacTavesh was first and foremost a Warrior. And now he was about to right an ancient wrong by winning a battle here, where victory had been denied to his ancestor.

And yet she loved him, as she'd believed she could never love any man. Her body still ached for him. Her ears still strained to hear again his soft words of love. Her eyes wanted to look into his and see that love.

She moved on, cold and damp and frightened, threading her way through the narrow, cobbled streets. Once she left the center of the town, she saw with relief that there were no more soldiers around.

Rowena knew that she could not hope to enter the valley by means of the road she'd used previously. The soldiers would be using that road, and even if they weren't yet advancing into the valley, they would almost certainly be guarding it.

But there was another road—or there had once been a road. Even in the enchanted place where her people now lived, that road hadn't been used for many years. Once, in her grandmother's time, her people had often taken that road into the hills that formed the boundary of their spellbound existence.

Her grandmother had told her about it, about how, as children, they would dare each other to go as far into the hills as possible, until the powerful forces that existed along the boundaries of the spell would drive them back.

But by Rowena's time—and even her mother's time—that had ceased. They knew then that the spell was weakening, and it was deemed to be far too dangerous to test its limits.

She knew it could be difficult, if not impossible, to find that other road. But she had to try, using her memory of the main road as a guide. So she continued to head east, skirting the boundaries of the town of Ashwara. The homes were more scattered here: big, handsome homes belonging to the professors at the university and to wealthy local merchants. They sat back behind trees or tall hedges, and it wasn't likely that anyone inside would notice a rider out there on a rainy day.

One after another, the streets led her to dead ends at the high cliffs above the valley, with no sign of a road. She backtracked yet again, scanning the tops of the trees for the familiar bulk of the fortress in the distance, trying to use it as a guide to judge the distance, since the road she couldn't use lay close to it.

Then finally, she rode down yet another street and reached the end. But unlike the other streets, this one had a stone wall at its terminus, stretching across a slight declivity, with steep, forested hills rising on each side of its 30-foot length.

Even from her perch atop the horse, Rowena could not see beyond the wall, but she felt a surge of excitement. The wall surely had a purpose, and the fact that the land dipped to meet it suggested a road.

She dismounted and led the horse over to a nearby tree, where she tethered it to a branch. Then she made her way around the end of the stone wall, trying not to slip in the slick mud.

"Yes," she said aloud when she saw it. It wasn't much of a road, but it was there, shrunk now to a narrow passage through the ancient trees.

Filled now with an eagerness that shunted

aside her fears, Rowena returned to the horse and untied it. She sent thoughts to it of a dry stable and food and turned it to face the town, then slapped its flank and sent it away. Someone would soon find it and see to it that it was cared for. It was better to abandon it here than to take it down into the valley.

The narrow path was steep and slippery and on this gloomy day, at times nearly invisible. But Rowena was already filled with the unique energy of the spell cast by her ancestors and her mind had flown ahead to the Gateway—and beyond.

When she reached the valley floor at last, she soon came upon a spot where she could see that other road—and the fortress looming above it. She stopped and scanned it carefully, but saw no sign of soldiers. Perhaps they were waiting for the rain to let up. Zach had mentioned something about bringing heavy artillery from Shemoth, and she guessed that moving those huge weapons on wheels would be difficult in such weather. So, inconvenient though the rain might be for her journey, she was nonetheless grateful for it.

She moved more quickly now on the better road through the bottom of the valley. But before she'd gone far, she noticed the hoofprints. She stopped, peering ahead into the gray day. There weren't many of them, but it was obvious that a small contingent of men had come down here this day. The prints were too clear to have been made more than an hour or so ago.

An advance party, she thought; sent to scout out the best places for their troops and the artillery. They could even now be at the Gateway. But at least she would have the advantage of the ever-present mists there, and on a day such as this, it would be even darker.

Zach urged his horse up the steep hill, waiting impatiently for it to pick its way up the slippery slope as he cursed the rain. These damned mists were bad enough on a good day, but today there was barely enough light to see the men with him, and if it continued to rain, it would be impossible to get the artillery into position.

On the other hand, the enemy wasn't likely to be moving now, either, because they would be just as burdened by the weather.

He wanted to be out of this accursed place. In fact, he'd almost decided not to come. But if he'd sent any of his senior officers, they would have been subjected to that same prickly fear that now assailed him. He'd actually seen the relief on several of their faces when he'd said that he would go himself. They'd all been students at Ashwara as he had, and he knew they must have come down here. It was never talked about among them, but Zach didn't doubt for one minute that they'd felt what he was feeling.

And it seemed to grow worse as they'd approached this place, as though the damned mists somehow concentrated whatever it was. Zach slanted a glance at his young aide, a Warrior himself and a distant relative. The youth's jaw was set firmly and his posture seemed too rigid even for a Warrior.

His horse continued its slow climb up the slope and Zach's thoughts drifted back to the night just past. His brows furrowed in concern. That nonsense she'd spoken last night probably wasn't helping his state of mind, either.

"I think a part of you has always known that we exist, but the rest of you continues to deny it."

Zach drew in a sharp breath. He could hear her words as though she were here with him now, and for one irrational moment, he let himself consider the possibility that she had told him the truth.

No, dammit, he wasn't going to fall prey to her fantasies. When this was over, when they had time for themselves, he would help her give up such absurd notions. Marriage and the responsibilities she would assume would help, too, as would the children he hoped they would have.

And yet he knew there would always be something different about her, just as there was about Paulena. But he didn't mind that. In fact, that difference was part of what he loved about her.

He hadn't yet decided whether to tell Duncan of his discovery. If Rowena had lied, then her aunt was lying, too—as were several others who'd claimed to have come from the same region.

That thought made him very uneasy, even though he wasn't the kind of man who was inclined to see conspiracies in everything. But why were they lying? What were they hiding?

They finally reached the top of the hill and rode along its edge, surveying the narrow, completely enclosed valley below. Enclosed, that is, except for a narrow gap through which the enemy would come. He could see nothing down there. The accursed mist made it seem that nothing even existed.

Then he felt her presence again, so strongly that he found himself swerving in the saddle to look about. His aide turned to him questioningly, a hand already on the gun he carried in a holster.

Zach shook his head. "I don't like this place."

The youth nodded solemnly. "Neither do I, Chief. And neither do the others, although no one ever admits it."

Then, apparently emboldened by Zach's admission, the young man stared down into the mist. "Sometimes I wonder if maybe they really did exist: the Dazhinn and their magic."

Zach said nothing. In his mind, he was seeing her as he'd first encountered her on the beach. And he was hearing her again, telling him that he'd always believed in the Dazhinn.

Rowena heard the soldiers before she saw them. Sounds echoed weirdly in this part of the valley, so she couldn't be sure how far away they were, but she was sure that she was now close to the narrow opening in the cliffs that led to the Gateway.

She left the road, such as it was, and moved into the thick forest. Her cloak was dark in col-

284

or, and in the rain and mist, they weren't likely to see her if she was careful. But she had to get through that narrow opening.

She moved forward carefully, crouching low among the bushes and tall weeds, feeling the blackberry thorns scrape against her cape. The voices were clearer now, and she realized that they must be up on the cliffs. Yes, she thought, of course that's where they'd be. They're looking for a place to put their guns.

Then suddenly she felt something familiar: that break in the steady rhythm of the forces she'd felt before when Zach had found her in the valley. Could he be here?

No, she decided quickly. He would be back at Ashwara, planning the battle. What she felt must be the presence of other Warriors. And yet the sense that he was close by continued to plague her.

She ignored it and edged ever closer to the narrow gap in the sheer rock walls, moving more confidently now that the mists were even thicker. She could see very little and yet she knew she was moving in the right direction. The Gateway was beckoning. Did that mean she would be able to get through?

Minutes passed and she walked on, her steps faster now. Then suddenly the dark rock walls loomed just ahead. The voices floated eerily above her and for one moment before she ran through the gap, she thought she heard Zach's voice among them.

Once through the gap, it seemed that her feet

knew exactly where to go. Within moments, she felt the smooth stones beneath her feet. She was sure now that she would make it through. She'd been right, after all. The Gatekeepers weren't necessary.

She moved more swiftly along the path this time, waiting for that moment when her feet would no longer touch stone, eagerly anticipating now what had heretofore been the worst experience of her life.

And then it happened! She was floating, suspended in the thick, damp mist. She rolled herself into a tight ball as she'd done before, waiting for it to be over. But this time, she felt no fear. She was going home.

And just as her knees once again struck stone, she remembered her cousin's prediction: that she would return—but it would be different. Now she understood. The difference was within her.

Chapter Eleven

Rowena staggered along the stone path toward the Gateway. That weakness was back again, although not quite so bad this time. Or perhaps she was fighting it more than she had before, because she needed her strength and her wits.

The very fact that I have returned without the aid of the Gatekeepers will be to my advantage, she thought. People will know that the Council has deceived them, and they might be more willing to believe they have been deceived about other things as well.

The mists thinned and she saw the tall cliffs that marked the entrance to the Gateway. She paused and stared up at them, remembering how she'd thought she heard Zach's voice up there. In that other world, he was already planning the placement of the big guns that could spell the end of their existence here.

Suddenly, she was overcome with a sense of

the impossibility of her mission. How could she stop the war that would destroy their enchanted existence? Why had she ever believed that she could? And what, exactly, was she to persuade her people to do?

It came to her now that at some subconscious level, she'd believed that the Dazhinn were all-powerful. Even though she'd seen the powerful weaponry of their ancient enemies, some part of her had continued to believe that Dazhinn magic was even more powerful.

How arrogant we are, she thought, living in our safe, timeless world and pretending that we still possess the great powers of our ancestors. And yet we know that there is not one among us who could accomplish what they did when they brought us here.

But she had set herself upon this course and she would see it through. She had no choice. There were certainly those among her people whose magic was far more powerful than hers, and perhaps they could find a way to prevent the devastation that was to come.

She passed beneath the dark cliffs and stepped into the valley. The rain had stopped, but gray clouds lingered, moving sluggishly across the sky. She stared at the broad valley, where the crops that had been newly planted the last time she'd gazed upon it were now growing lush and full: corn, wheat, oats, and, in a wetland area, the bright green spikes of rice.

Beyond them, the town was a faint blur—and beyond that, hidden behind a hill, lay her cottage. How tiny and crude it would seem now, after the splendors of Paulena's homes.

Paulena. The though of her aunt brought a sharp twinge of guilt. Paulena knew what she'd planned to do, but unless she could persuade the 'paths to send a message back to her, her aunt would fear that she'd died in the attempt.

She regretted placing such a burden on Polly, who was already fearing for Duncan's life. There was no telling what Abner and his allies might do—especially if they learned that war was truly imminent.

And of course there was Zach. How long would it be before he learned that she was missing? It could be quite a while, depending on whether he remained at Ashwara or returned to the city. And what would he do? If he knew that she had lied about her background, then he must know that Polly had lied as well.

She began to walk toward the village, fighting the weakness that threatened to overwhelm her. With the crops long since planted, no one was working in the fields and it would be miles before she could hope to meet anyone who could provide a horse for her.

Then she saw them: a trio of figures riding toward her. They were still too distant for her to see them clearly, but she knew they must be the Gatekeepers. Something had alerted them to her presence.

There was no place for her to hide, and in any event, if she had seen them, they had surely spotted her by now as well. She wondered if they would be shocked to discover that she'd come through without their assistance. Perhaps they believed themselves to be indispensable; people often had a tendency to think that way.

She sat down alongside the road to wait for them, wishing that she could have some time to rest and prepare her speech before she was hauled before the Council. But that was not to be. The Council would demand her immediate presence the moment they learned she had returned.

The Gatekeepers slowed their horses as they drew near, and from the looks of consternation on their faces, she knew they had never guessed that anyone could pass through the Gateway without their spells.

They dismounted and the eldest of them—a kindly old man—spoke for them all.

"Rowena! How did you return? We felt something, but . . ."

She shrugged wearily. "I simply returned. I have to speak to the Council. Do they know I've come back?"

"No, of course not, since we did not know ourselves. I told Alma that we sensed something wrong at the Gateway, but that was all."

Rowena grimaced. "I've little doubt that she's guessed what has happened. May I borrow one of your horses?"

The youngest of them offered his mount, saying he would wait until a replacement could be sent. Rowena climbed onto the horse and set out for the town, followed by the other two Gatekeepers.

Her procession into the town was greeted by shock from many and welcome from others. Even though she saw relatives and friends among the crowds, Rowena kept moving toward Council Hall. She was no less weary than before, but a cold, hard determination kept her going.

She slid off the horse in front of Council Hall, where a crowd was already gathering. But they made way for her as she walked up to the open doors. How small it seemed now, when before it had been the largest building she'd ever seen.

"Rowena!" A Council aide appeared, apparently drawn by the sounds of the crowd outside. "How . . . ?"

"Take me to them!" she commanded, cutting him off sharply. "I must speak to them now!" Before I collapse, she added silently.

He gaped at her for another moment, then led her to a smaller chamber where the Council met on private business. All eyes were upon her even before the aide announced her presence.

Rowena met Alma's eyes, and then the eyes of each man and woman there. They were wary—but they were not surprised. So she was right: the Gatekeepers had been lied to as well. The Council knew it was possible to come through without their spells. No doubt that was why all Descenders were ordered to stay away from the valley. The Council didn't want to risk their being tempted to try to return.

They were seated at a large round table and the aide brought a chair for her. Rowena wanted

291

badly to sit down, but she remained standing.

"War will come to the valley within a matter of days," she said into the silence. "Even as I left, their weapons were being brought there."

"And why did you not stop them?" Alma challenged angrily.

Rowena met her gaze and held it. "If you are asking why I did not kill Zachary MacTavesh, it is because I love him."

There were a few gasps and many incredulous looks. Rowena smiled. "The astrologers either lied or they made a mistake. Or perhaps you knew I would fall in love with him, but believed I would still carry out my mission out of loyalty to my people."

"You betrayed us for a *Warrior?*" one of them asked in shock.

"I did not betray you. It is you who have betrayed all of us. You have let us believe that they are evil—and they are not. You said that your intentions were only to change their barbaric ways in case we had to return. But your real plan was to rule there one day. I know the true history of our people now—and I intend to tell everyone."

Alma rose up from her seat, her face contorted in rage. "You will do as you're told, Rowena Sandor!"

"Oh?" Rowena smiled at her unpleasantly. "And just how do you plan to force me to do anything? Do you plan to take away my mind—as our ancestors once did to their enemies?"

The looks on their faces told her that they

had known the brutal history of their people. Rowena was growing more tired by the moment—but she was also becoming angrier and angrier.

"How dare you lie to our people?" she asked, glaring at them.

"We have simply followed the traditions of the Council, Rowena," said one of them: her mother's cousin and a woman who'd been close to her mother all her life.

"Then it is time to stop! The spell will be broken, because war will come to the valley within a matter of days. You must prepare our people for this. And you also must put a stop to the plans of Abner and his allies—plans you must have instigated in the first place."

Once again, she did a slow sweep of the room, trying to guess how each member felt. And what she saw gave her at least some hope. Even Alma looked uncertain now. Clearly, they'd believed that their plans would work and war would be prevented. She pushed her advantage.

"Time has run out. Your plans might have worked if you'd had the time to put more of our people into high positions. Zach . . . Commander MacTavesh told me that the power of the Warrior chief will wane. He believes that he will be the last Warrior chief to wield great power, that in the future, the power will belong to the people—especially the new merchant class. And if a Warrior understands that his time is past, the Dazhinn should, too."

There was absolute silence as they gaped at

Saranne Dawson

her in astonishment. Then Alma made a dismissive sound. "No Warrior would say such a thing."

"But he did say it, Alma. He thinks about the future—unlike us."

"You haven't told him who you are?" asked one member.

She smiled. "Yes, I told him—but he doesn't believe me. He thinks I am caught up in some mad fantasy." She paused and sighed.

"It is not easy for anyone in their world to believe in old magic. They have made their own magic. They call it 'science.'" She went on to talk about the weapons she'd seen and about the terrible gas that could kill thousands who breathed it.

"But there are good things that have come from their science, too: medicines, inventions that make life so much better than it is here. They are things we could have as well, because for all their love of science, they still revere art and music and crafts.

"I asked the commander once what he would do if the Dazhinn were suddenly to return to their valley, and he said that would depend on their intentions. If we renounce this foolish belief that we can rule, I think we will be allowed to live in peace.

"And if we are correct and war breaks the spell, our sudden return to the valley might well spare thousands of lives. They will surely stop making war, if only because they will be so shocked by our return."

No one said anything, and Rowena now felt so weak that she could say nothing more, either. So she turned and walked out of the room, then staggered outside where it seemed the entire population had gathered.

Everyone began to pelt her with questions, but she shook her head and asked someone to help her home. Her cousin Seitha pushed her way through the crowd, leading a horse. She helped Rowena to mount, then climbed up behind her. The crowd parted for them, then surged toward the entrance to Council Hall. Rowena wanted to shout to them that they should demand the truth, but she was too tired.

Mercifully, Seitha asked her no questions. But when they finally reached Rowena's cottage, Rowena climbed wearily down from the horse, then looked up at her cousin.

"You were right, Seitha, when you said that I would return, but it would be different. What I didn't realize was that *I* would be the one who was different."

Seitha's dark blue eyes bored into her as she nodded. "You love him, Rowena—and he loves you. Rest now. I will return later."

Rowena nodded and dragged herself into her tiny cottage. Then she turned to stare at the departing Seitha. They loved each other—but would they ever see each other again? She wished she had asked her cousin that.

"Most people aren't angry as much as they are shocked," Seitha said as she poured some tea for Rowena. "And of course they're frightened as well."

Rowena stifled a yawn. She'd slept nearly 12 hours and still felt groggy, but at least she wasn't dizzy. The passage through the Gateway had obviously been easier this time.

"The Council has a lot to answer for," Seitha continued. "Although from what I've heard, a lot of people already suspected they weren't being told the truth."

"Then why didn't they speak up before?" Rowena demanded, thinking about her mother, who'd often hinted at such things.

"We've all become too good at deceiving ourselves over the centuries. We were safe here, so nothing else mattered."

"What will happen? Do you know—or have you had any visions?"

Seitha shook her head. "I don't know, and I've had no visions since a few days ago, when I saw you with the commander."

"You saw us?" Rowena asked in astonishment. A few days ago, they'd been at Cliff House.

Seitha nodded. "It was a very brief vision, but I knew it must be him. You were walking along the water's edge, holding hands. And I could feel the love coming from you both."

Rowena smiled. "Were we clothed at the time?"

Seitha stared at her, then burst out laughing. "Yes, and I won't ask why you asked that."

"Then you don't know if we'll see each other again?"

Seitha sighed heavily. "No, and I don't know what will happen, either. None of us have had any visions. We've lost our talent, just when it might have been most helpful."

She paused and stared into her mug of tea, then continued in a quiet tone. "There may be no more visions because we have no future. Some of the others believe that. We've never really been sure what would happen to us if the spell was broken. Everyone has just assumed that we would return to the other world."

"What do Egon and Dora say?" They were the leading scholars of Dazhinn history.

"They don't know, either. They say that our ancestors probably didn't stop to think about it. They were too busy trying to find a way to save us." She shuddered. "It's terrible to think that they did such awful things."

"So did the Warriors," Rowena reminded her. "Zach seems able to accept what his ancestors did, and he's not a barbaric man. I think we must accept that, too. We've spent all these centuries dwelling on the past. That's why it's so hard to accept."

"Tell me about Polly," Seitha asked her. Paulena was her aunt as well.

So Rowena told her: about Paulena and Duncan and about her life there. How distant it seemed now, how strange to talk about that world as she sat in her tiny cottage.

Seitha laughed as Rowena described the horrible corsets women wore, then became irate over Rowena's descriptions of the situation of women. But it was clear that she was thoroughly fascinated by that other world, and Rowena knew that everyone else would share that fascination.

If we do go back, she thought, we will not remain as we are now, even if the Warriors do leave us alone. It will be only a matter of time until our people will want to live as they do. That thought saddened her—until she realized that she was guilty of doing just what she'd been accusing them of doing: living in the past.

"Has the Council reached no decision, then?" Rowena asked after she had answered Seitha's many questions. This respite from her problems had been welcome, but it was time to think of the future.

"No. Members of the Council are meeting with groups of people, seeking their advice. But the truth is that no one knows what to do—or even if we can do anything.

"And the 'paths have been unable to reach the 'paths among the Descenders. They don't know why."

Rowena felt a chill at that piece of news. Could it mean that the Gateway had closed—that they might be drifting even farther from the other world?

Seitha looked at her solemnly. "There is one thing I should tell you. I spoke with Dora and Egon, and they are convinced that if the spell breaks and we are sent back, any Warriors in the valley will die."

Rowena stared at her in horror as a chill ran

through her. Zach would be in the valley!

"They said that everything they have read about the spell that brought us here convinces them of that. The valley was always protected against them."

"But Zach and other Warriors have gone into the valley," Rowena protested. "I'm sure they felt something, but—"

"Yes, but we weren't there. If we return . . ." She shrugged eloquently.

"I must go back and warn Zach."

"But you said that he doesn't believe you're Dazhinn, so why would he listen to you?"

"Then I must convince him. I have to see Katya—now!"

Seitha nodded. Katya was the one among them who knew the most about certain forms of their magic: spells they hadn't needed since they came here, ways of defending themselves against enemies. Rowena knew next to nothing about such things, but she was sure that there must be something she could do that even Zach could not rationalize away.

"Let me bring her here," Seitha suggested. "If you go out, people will delay you with their questions. I can tell them that you are still resting, and bring Katya here."

Rowena thanked her and she left. Katya's home wasn't far, and if she was there, she should be back quickly. But would it matter? What if she couldn't get through the Gateway again? Or what if she did get through the Gateway, only to find herself in the middle of a battle?

*　　*　　*

"Rowena, look!"

Rowena turned in her saddle to follow Seitha's pointing arm. She blinked a few times as she stared at the distant mountains. But no amount of blinking could change what she saw. For years now, their world had been blurry at its edges, but now the blurring was worse— and there was a strange, shimmering quality to the mountains and the sky above them.

"Did you hear that?" Seitha asked, raising her head to stare at the cloudless blue sky above them. "It sounded like thunder."

"Or like the big guns I saw at Shemoth," Rowena said, urging her horse on toward the Gateway. "The battle must have started."

It was early morning, and they'd left her cottage and skirted the town, riding through the woods and fields to avoid being seen. Rowena wasn't at all certain that she wouldn't be held captive if the Council knew of her intention to leave again.

"Rowena!" Seitha cried, catching up to her. "If the battle has started, you can't risk going through the Gateway!"

But Rowena ignored her as her mount thundered toward the cliffs that guarded the Gateway. When she reached it, she vaulted off the mare's back even before the animal had come to a complete stop. Seitha was still shouting at her as she ran through the gap in the rock cliffs to be enveloped immediately in the mists.

Blinded by the thick fog, she still didn't slow down. Then her feet touched the now familiar stones, and she ran even faster. Somewhere in the distance, she could hear dull booms: the thunderous sounds of the artillery. And for just a moment, she thought she heard men's shouts and cries.

She continued to run along the stone path, waiting for that moment when her feet could no longer feel them. But it didn't happen! The sounds of gunfire and shouting soldiers grew still louder, though she could see nothing in the thick mist. She knew that she should have reached that point where one world merged into the other— the place where she had drifted through the ether that marked the boundary. But her running feet continued to slap against the stones.

Then there was a moment of disorientation, when it felt as though something unseen had pushed her, and she fell. But the arms she put out to stop her fall encountered the wet stones. And now she was surrounded by noise!

She stopped, breathing raggedly, and tried to guess where the sounds were coming from. It was impossible to tell, but she was suddenly sure that she'd made it through. There was a thunderous noise—the artillery again— and this time, it seemed to be coming from somewhere ahead of her and above her. If the artillery was on the cliffs that guarded the Gateway, the sound should be behind her. Or had she somehow been spun about in that brief moment?

She was still considering what to do when there was an explosion behind her, and for one brief moment, she saw a brilliant flash of light. Her ears rang from the terrible noise, but even so, she could hear the shouts and screams of men and horses.

I'm right in the middle of it, she thought with horror before willing herself to calm. It might not be as close as it sounded. The fog twisted sounds, and the cliffs could cause echoes.

She started to move again, but more cautiously this time. She had to assume that Zach's army lay ahead of her, just beyond the cliffs, and that the artillery mounted up there was his.

Then she saw the dark cliffs rising just ahead of her, and at the same moment, two of the big guns fired simultaneously, the sound so close that she was certain they would hit her.

No, she told herself, they won't hit me because I'm beneath them. She recalled from the demonstration she'd seen at Shemoth that the shells they fired traveled a great distance. She didn't need to fear the guns, but she was sure that she would encounter Zach's soldiers soon. They must be surrounding the base of the cliffs in case any of the enemy made it through.

She stopped as the dark rocks loomed above her, ignoring the shouts that came down clearly from their tops. Now it was time to practice what Katya had taught her—and hope it worked. There'd been so little time to practice, but Katya had said she had more talent for it than most.

Rowena murmured the ancient incantations and sent her mind out to every part of her body, consciously "feeling" for her fingertips, her toes, the top of her head, until everything tingled as it had when she'd practiced under Katya's guidance. Then she walked through the narrow gap in the walls—and out into the sunshine.

She saw them immediately—scores of heavily armed men filling the valley, every one of them staring at her. She stopped, drawing in a ragged breath. If they saw her, there was no way she could cast a spell that would ensnare them all. There were just too many of them.

Katya had told her that she would be invisible to them, but she'd had no way to be certain of that, since the spell didn't affect her own people.

The soldiers continued to face her, their guns at the ready. But as she forced herself to walk toward them, no weapon was fired, and before long, she could see that they were looking beyond her, *through* her. The spell had worked!

Behind her now, up on the cliffs, the guns boomed again. She paused and turned to look up, and now she could see men and artillery lined up along the top of the cliffs. Then she heard the thud of horses' hooves behind her, and the soldiers in front of her swarmed forward on a shouted order from a mounted officer.

Rowena ran out of their path, scrambling for the steep, forested bank just beyond the cliffs that guarded the Gateway. Men were running down the hillside as well, and she positioned herself against a thick tree. She might be invisible to them, but she could still be crushed or shot if she didn't stay out of their way.

She stayed there for a long time, watching the battle being fought all around her. Bodies flew into the air as the things called grenades were hurled into their midst. The sound of gunfire was incessant. But the big guns on the cliffs had fallen silent.

And then she felt something else, something that might have been there all along, but was now growing stronger: that deep, almost painful humming sound she associated with the spell. For a time, the fighting men seemed not to have noticed it, but then here and there, she saw men pause and look about them with strange expressions.

The spell was breaking. She could feel it within her as the humming sound grew ever louder. Then, as she watched the men, she saw that it was affecting a few far more than most. The Warriors! Zach! She had to find him and get him out of the valley now!

Deciding that he would probably be up on the cliffs, she began to climb, paying no heed to the gunfire around her. But before she had gotten even halfway up the steep hill, she became aware of the darkness that was growing like a living thing. Even as she stood there blinking with disbelief, still more light drained away. Within a matter of moments, the day had turned to an eerie twilight.

She turned to look behind her, and could barely see the battle now. The sounds of gunfire and the explosions of the grenades and the shouts of soldiers all lessened, draining away slowly into no more than sporadic noises in the gathering dark.

Rowena had no idea what was happening. Did the darkness signal the return of her people to the valley—or was there some other reason for it, something in the protective spell of which they had no knowledge?

That deep humming sound continued, but seemed, to her ears at least, to be remaining steady now. She resumed her climb up the hill, wanting only to get Zach to safety. But as she climbed, she thought that she might not need the other tricks Katya had taught her so that she could convince him that Dazhinn magic was real. If darkness at midday wasn't enough, her pitiful little tricks certainly would have no effect upon him.

Finally, she reached the top of the hill. It was full dark now, and there were only faint sounds from the valley below: isolated shouts and gunfire. But not far away, she could hear men's voices, so she headed in that direction, praying that Zach would be among them.

Then, just as she began to make out shadowy figures ahead, she felt that tingling sensation that signaled the weakening of the spell she'd cast over herself. Katya had said that it wouldn't last long, though she'd been uncertain about the exact amount of time.

Rowena stopped and cast the spell again, knowing that she might have to pass many men before she could find Zach. Then she moved forward again, walking directly toward the soldiers.

She passed clusters of men around the big guns; some of them completely silent and others talking in low, frightened tones. And she heard the word "Dazhinn" many times. A smile curved her lips despite the horrors she'd witnessed. These were men who possessed mighty weapons, who were trained to fight to their deaths—but they were afraid now.

No fires had been lit, presumably because they didn't want to draw the attention—and the fire—of the enemy. So Rowena was forced to roam through the darkness, searching for him among the groups of men gathered along the cliff's edge. She had hoped that some break in the spell-sound might lead her to him, but it didn't happen.

And then she began to worry that something might already have happened to him. Even before she'd started up here, the spell had begun to affect the Warrior officers in the valley. They might well be dead by now. But surely he would be less affected up here on the cliffs.

She moved closer to the men she passed, staring at them. She was sure that some of them were Warriors. She could see a rigidity to their stances, and on the faces of a few, she saw both fear and pain. But none of them had fallen.

She stumbled on through the crowds of men, growing more desperate by the moment—and then she heard his voice!

" . . . out of the valley! Send half the troops back to Ashwara, and keep the other half at the top of the road into the valley. I want as many officers back at Ashwara as possible—and that includes most of you."

"What's happening, Chief? Is it the Da—" an anxious voice asked.

Zach cut him off sharply. "I don't know, but I'm not taking any chances. See that the artillery at Ashwara is well manned and trained on the valley."

Rowena had stopped barely 30 feet from him, close to the small group of Warrior officers surrounding him. She could feel the tension in the air and almost smell their fear. But this time, she didn't glory in the power of her people. One look at Zach was sufficient to send those thoughts away.

The men scattered to do his bidding and Zach began to pace along the edge of the cliff, barely visible to her in his dark battle uniform. Then suddenly he stopped and turned in her direction, a puzzled look on his rugged face.

Commander-in-Chief Zachary MacTavesh was caught in his worst nightmare. They had stopped the advance of the enemy into the valley. Only a few had persisted after the artillery barrage, and his troops down in the valley had been busy dispatching them when the darkness came.

But even before the light began—impossibly—to dim, Zach had felt that deep, terrifying vibration. All the Warriors felt it—and none of the others did. With an army composed mostly of Warrior officers, he knew he was now at a distinct disadvantage. The troops were good men and valiant fighters, but without leaders they could not prevail. If the enemy poured more men into the valley now . . .

He left off those thoughts. They wouldn't do that. The sudden darkness would have frightened them as well. He smiled grimly, wondering if the Atanians could be crediting *him* with this strangeness. He knew they feared the legendary Warrior clan and he'd done his best to spread rumors of "secret" weapons.

"A part of you has always known that we exist, but the rest of you denies it."

Zach came to a stop as her words whispered through his mind once more. He felt a knot of dread in the pit of his stomach. Where was she? He knew that she hadn't returned to the city—or not to Duncan's house, in any event. Duncan's note had said that Paulena was half-mad with worry about her and had no idea where she might be.

He stared into the darkness below. She couldn't be down there. She might be suffering from delusions, but she wasn't mad. She wouldn't walk into a battle.

His head throbbed. His whole body ached from the relentless tension that had gripped him. And it was far worse down there. Several of his officers had had to be carried out of the valley in a state of collapse. And yet he stubbornly refused to believe that it could have anything to do with the accursed Dazhinn. It was something else, something as yet undiscovered. When this was over, he intended to send scientists down into that damned valley with orders to find the source of the problem.

Rowena. He couldn't get her out of his mind, despite his many other problems. It almost seemed as though she were here, somewhere close by. He found himself turning, peering into the darkness as though he expected her to materialize before him.

"Chief!"

Zach saw not Rowena, but one of his officers, a non-Warrior who'd been down in the valley, hurrying toward him. He braced himself for more bad news.

"There's another division coming! They'll reach the entrance to the valley by daybreak." The man's voice broke on the final word as he looked around him at the blackness. "If there *is* a daybreak. Chief, I don't know how to tell you this, but according to my scouts, it's still daylight out there." He gestured toward the hills that surrounded the valley.

Zach nodded. The news didn't surprise him. The darkness was here and here alone. And he'd known there was an enemy division unaccounted for, though he'd been hoping it was guarding the western borders. That was why he'd sent a small scouting party into enemy territory to keep an eye out for more troops.

Zach thanked the man and dismissed him, then stared disgustedly at the silent artillery. It would be useless as long as this darkness persisted. And he'd been unwilling to position too many of his own troops here because despite the fact that the enemy had been gathering on the other side of the valley, Zach had doubted that they would concentrate too much of their resources in this easily defended place. Obviously, he'd underestimated their desire to seize the valley—or else he'd overestimated their intelligence.

But there was another possibility—one he didn't want to consider. If the Dazhinn were real, if they'd returned, wouldn't it make sense that they'd throw in their lot with the Atanians? It would be proof of that old saying that the "enemy of my enemy is my friend." The Warriors were their most ancient enemy.

Several of his officers appeared, and their worried looks told him that they'd heard about the second division—and probably about the daylight beyond the hills as well.

"We can't hope to keep them out of the valley now," he told them. "At least until we can see again. As soon as we know they've come into the valley, we'll resume firing even if we can't see them. Just be sure that none of our own troops are at that end of the valley. And get some artillery on the hillsides near the fortress. If the accursed Dazhinn *have* come back, not even their magic can stop the shells."

"Do you think that maybe they never really left, Chief—that they've been here all this time and we just couldn't see them?"

Zach stared at the man. His mouth opened to deny it, but no words came out. Instead, he was thinking about what Rowena had said: that the Dazhinn had taken themselves away, that they were there but not there.

"I don't know," he admitted, thus breaking an important rule for an officer, and especially for a chief. Indecisiveness was weakness. "But if they *are* there, they'll soon find out that they're facing an enemy far different from the one they faced in the last battle."

"Are you coming back to Ashwara, Chief?" another man asked. "I've heard that it's better there. The men who were carried out of the valley have recovered. They were fine as soon as they left the valley."

Zach nodded. He didn't want to leave, but he needed his wits about him, and right now, he felt himself on the edge of collapse as well.

Rowena had stood there listening to all these exchanges, watching Zach with concern. She was greatly relieved to hear him agree to return to Ashwara. He would be safe there. But then, as he walked off with his officers, she heard him say that he intended to lead the men himself when they went into the valley in the morning.

No! she cried silently. I must stop him! He will go to his death!

The spell over the valley was crumbling slowly. She was sure that was the way it was happening. She could feel it. And by morning—a morning that might or might not bring back the

311

light—it would be gone. If he was there then, he would die.

And many of her people would die as well. If they suddenly reappeared now, Zach would order his troops to slaughter them. And he was right. In the old-style hand-to-hand combat, Dazhinn magic could prevail. But they possessed no magic that could stop the guns and the grenades. The victory denied to his ancestors would be his—but he would die in claiming it.

She followed him and his men back along the hillside to the road that led to Ashwara. They had horses and were soon far ahead of her, but she knew the way.

She had just reached the spot where she'd left her clothing that first time she'd come into the valley, when she felt the spell that rendered her invisible weakening yet again. So she stopped and cast it one more time, then walked on toward Ashwara.

The entrance she'd used that other time was locked now, so she circled the great fortress and then passed unseen through the main gates, suddenly realizing that she had no way of knowing where he would be in the vast fortress.

She looked around the huge courtyard and saw that what had been total darkness in the valley and along the overhanging cliffs was in fact more like dusk here. Probably in the town itself it was still daylight.

For more than an hour, she roamed unseen through the fortress, searching for him. She was growing tired, probably from the effort required to cast and recast the spells, and she was very hungry.

Delicious aromas drew her to the kitchens, where she found the staff, augmented by young soldiers, preparing food for the troops. She moved among them, picking up a loaf of bread, some cheese, and a small chicken when a cook's back was turned. And then she realized that some of the people present were casting nervous looks in her direction.

She retreated quickly through the door into the kitchen garden, carrying her stolen food. The spell must be weakening! Obviously they couldn't actually see her, but they were somehow sensing her presence. If she didn't find Zach soon, she could be in real danger.

She wolfed down the food and set out again, garnering more strange looks from some of the men—particularly the Warriors she encountered. But still she couldn't find him.

"Chief, there's something you should, uh, know."

Zach whirled around to face the officer who was approaching him on the fortress's roof. What now? he thought as the man stopped uncertainly.

"Some of us think that there could be Dazhinn here in the fortress."

"What?" Zach frowned at him. If he hadn't known this man to be reliable, he'd have decided he was mad.

"We felt a presence, Chief. Remember the old stories, about how we could always sense their presence? Well, some of us have. It comes and goes, but we haven't seen anyone."

"Then conduct a search of the whole place. Check the kitchen staff as well. They're the only civilians here now. If you find anything, report to me. I'll be up here."

Madness, he thought when the man had gone. We are all going mad. And he shuddered, thinking about those old stories of Warriors robbed of their minds by the Dazhinn.

He stared out into the blackness of the valley. Even here, he could feel something. It wasn't nearly as strong, but it was still there.

His thoughts turned to Rowena. Where was she, and what role might she be playing in all this? Had she spoken the truth that night?

She said she'd been sent to kill him. He'd been trying to ignore those words because he knew she wasn't capable of doing such a thing. But what if she had no choice? She'd said that she couldn't betray her people.

Zach felt himself teetering on the brink of madness, leaning far out over that abyss. And then suddenly he felt her presence!

He turned and stared in disbelief as she came into focus: barely visible at first, then more clearly. One moment, he could see her only as a wisp of fog—and in the next moment, he was staring at a flesh-and-blood woman!

Chapter Twelve

Rowena hadn't intended that he should see her materialize before him. She had come up here in desperation, having searched for him throughout the fortress. And when she saw the stunned look on his face, she knew that despite all that had happened and despite the fact that she had told him she was Dazhinn, he still hadn't accepted the existence of her people.

So she stood where she was, wanting desperately to run into his arms but fearful that he would reject her.

"H-how did you get here?" he asked finally, his voice hoarse with disbelief.

"That doesn't matter," she replied in an impatient tone that was actually her attempt to hide her pain. "What matters is that you must trust me, Zach. Your life and the lives of many others may depend on that."

As she spoke, she took a few steps toward

him, still foolishly hoping that he would welcome her. But he didn't move, and she could read nothing in his expression save the shock she didn't want to see.

"You cannot go into the valley tomorrow. The spell is breaking, and when it does, any Warrior in the valley will die. Those who have studied the history of my people are very sure of that."

"The spell," he said, merely repeating her words.

"I told you the truth, Zach. When your ancestors were about to invade the valley, my ancestors cast a spell that lifted us to . . . another place. I don't understand exactly what they did; none of us does. And the spell has held all these years, but we knew that it was beginning to weaken. That's why our Council ordered that you should be assassinated. They knew that if war came to the valley, it could destroy the spell completely."

She paused, shifting her gaze from him into the darkness beyond the wall. "It's too late to stop it now. Even if you withdraw completely from the valley, the spell will break. But at least no one will die."

That is, unless you kill them, she thought, but didn't say yet.

His expression softened—but into pity, not love. "Rowena, I know that strange things have happened, but—"

"Your science will never explain it, Zach!" she interrupted angrily. Then she quickly traced into the air the rune that Katya had taught her.

316

Immediately, an eerie greenish light arced from her fingers toward him, not touching him, but rather hovering there in midair. He stumbled back a few steps, then stopped. She drew it back until it was no more than a halo surrounding her still-raised hand.

"You must recognize this from your histories," she told him. "This is how my people used to fight. Our spells do not work against Warriors—except for this one. Your people killed with bows and arrows and swords. The Dazhinn killed with their magic."

She slowly closed her fist and the light vanished. "I learned to do this only to prove to you that I speak the truth. We've had no need of such things for five hundred years."

She lowered her hand to her side and his wary gaze followed the movement. Then she told him about returning to her people to try to find some way to prevent this disaster, only to realize that it was too late, and there was nothing to be done.

"So I came back again to try to persuade you to stay out of the valley, and to let my people return in peace."

He stared hard at her, and she saw his shock give way to the cold calculations of a Warrior chief.

"But will they return in peace—or have they cast their lot in with the Atanians?"

His question caught her by surprise. "Why would they do that?"

317

"Because they might believe that the combination of their magic and the Atanians' weapons could destroy their ancient enemy once and for all."

She shook her head. "No. They've had no contact with the Atanians. You don't understand, Zach. My people have been locked in the past. They believe *all* of you to be barbarians. For years now, the Council has been sending some of our people here to insinuate themselves into positions of power—but not among the Atanians. They were considered to be too weak to bother with."

She hesitated, uncertain as to whether she should tell him the whole truth. But she owed him that.

"Those who came back were called Descenders. The rest of us believed that their mission was to change your society, so that if we were one day forced to return, we could live in peace. But I discovered that the Council was lying to us. What they really intended was for the Descenders to take over here so that we could return to rule. If there'd been more time, and if they'd gone about it differently, it might have worked. But it's too late now."

"So you admit that your people never intended to return in peace?" he challenged, still every inch the Warrior chief.

"I never knew of this plan. Only the Council and the Descenders knew about it, and some of the Descenders were unwilling to go along with it. Now everyone knows—and they all agree that it was wrong."

Rowena knew that wasn't really true. Alma and a few others, both there and here, would still try to cause trouble, but she was confident that they could be dealt with.

"Is Paulena one of those who refused to go along with the plan?"

"Why do you ask?" His question caught her by surprise.

"Because Duncan is my friend and I fear for his life."

"Duncan is safe," she replied, hoping it was true. "Paulena truly loves him and would never allow harm to come to him. She is quite capable of protecting him.

"They aren't our problem right now, Zach. You must stop this battle."

"It takes both sides to stop a battle, Rowena. And the Atanians outnumber us at the moment. What you are asking is for me to surrender—and that I cannot do."

"But surely you can stop them from coming into the valley?" she protested.

"Perhaps we could if we could use the artillery, but we can't use it effectively in the dark."

"Oh." She frowned. "Then I must speak to them and try to persuade them to stay out of the valley."

He shook his head, and for the first time, a smile hovered about his lips. "You might have magic, Rowena, but you don't understand war. If we retreat, they will pour into the valley. We will still defeat them eventually, but not before many lives are lost and whole towns are laid waste."

She remained silent, thinking. "Could you arrange a truce, so that we could speak to them together? If they believe that they will face not only your army but my people as well, they may retreat."

He stared at her for a moment, then turned away and walked to the low wall that surrounded the roof. Bracing his arms against it, he stared out into the dark valley. After several very long moments, he turned back to her.

"What will happen when this spell breaks—and when will it happen?"

"I don't know. None of us does. It will be soon, I think."

"But the darkness will remain until then—until the Dazhinn return?"

"I don't know that, either, though I think it probably will."

"I want to speak to this Council of yours."

"But that's impossible, until the spell is broken."

"You went there and returned," he pointed out.

"Yes, but you're a Warrior. You could never pass through the Gateway."

"Nevertheless, those are my terms."

"Zach, you could die if you try to get through!"

"If I get a guarantee from your Council that they will not make trouble when they return, and that, if necessary, the Dazhinn will fight alongside us, then I will arrange a truce and we will speak to the Atanians. Otherwise, the battle will be fought in the valley to avoid shedding the blood of innocent people in the neighboring towns."

"I refuse to take you to your death," she said stubbornly.

"This Gateway lies in that small valley with the mists?"

"Yes, but you cannot go there alone. You'll be dead even before you reach it. The spell is at its strongest there. You saw how it affected the Warriors who were down there—and it even affected you up on the cliffs."

He touched her for the first time, reaching out to take her hand. "Take me there. You told me that our stars were crossed. I've never believed in such nonsense—but then I never believed in the Dazhinn, either." His lips curved in a wry smile.

"Now it seems that I have little choice but to believe. Perhaps our stars were crossed in more ways than one, Rowena. It may be that we are destined to end the hatred between our peoples."

"But if you're wrong . . ."

"It's worth the risk. I know you think that as a Warrior, I cannot be a man of peace. But I have no desire to see people die: your people or mine."

She stared down at their clasped hands, then finally nodded. "I will take you."

*   *   *

"We will have to leave the horses here," she told him as the cliffs loomed above them in the darkness. The animals had become increasingly difficult to control as they rode toward the Gateway.

Zach nodded and dismounted, then came over to lift her from the saddle before turning to the soldiers who'd accompanied him.

"Wait for us here," he instructed them. "But only as long as you can do so safely."

Then he followed her through the narrow opening in the cliffs. She took a few steps, then turned to see how he was. She knew that the spell must be wreaking havoc upon him. She put out a hand to grasp his and started forward again before she could lose her courage.

But he took her hand and brought her to a halt, then drew her into his arms. "I love you, Rowena," he murmured against her ear. "The fact that you are Dazhinn doesn't change that. Nothing could change my feelings."

Then he hooked a finger beneath her chin and lifted her face to meet his. A smile curved his mouth and his pale eyes were lit by the love she had thought never to see there again.

"Perhaps I love you *because* you are Dazhinn. Always I have known that there was something different about you, and that it was that difference that drew me to you. If you have used sorcery on me, I hope you never stop using it."

"There's been no sorcery," she replied huskily

as she stretched up to kiss him.

Their lips met softly, almost tentatively, as though each feared this might be the last time. And then they parted just as uncertainly, as though in silent mutual acknowledgment that they would not allow themselves to believe such a thing.

The stone path was narrow, wide enough only for one person—but they continued to hold hands as they walked along it, with Rowena leading the way.

It happened as it had the last time. Rowena felt something, a sort of gentle shove, and began to pitch forward, still clinging to Zach's hand. They both fell to the stones, and he immediately surrounded her protectively as they stared into the impenetrable mist.

For a long, frightening moment, they were both held there. When they tried to get to their feet, some unseen force kept them pinned to the stones. Zach drew her closer still, and she could feel his frustration at not being able to combat the powers that held them in thrall.

"Let us go!" he shouted into the mist. "It is time for this to end!"

And then, to their joint amazement, it was over. They felt the forces withdraw, retreating to that low hum they'd felt before. They scrambled to their feet and walked on as before—but with Zach now in the lead. Neither of them knew if they'd gotten through until they saw once again the dark cliffs they'd left behind now looming in the thinning mist ahead of them.

When they walked through the gap in the sheer walls, they found a twilight world awaiting them. But in that eerie half-light, they could see the valley that had been her home: the fields and the faint lights of the village far ahead.

She immediately started forward, stopping only when she saw that he wasn't beside her. She turned to see him staring at the valley and the expression on his face told her that he'd clung to his disbelief until this moment. But she couldn't really blame him for that. He'd just stepped back 500 years in time.

"It is true, Zach. There are some things that not even your science can explain," she said softly, taking his hand.

He merely nodded as they started out again. Rowena could feel the tension in him, the unwillingness even now to let go of his certainty that such a thing could not be. He was still struggling to hold on to the present, just as her own people clung so tenaciously to the past.

"Where *is* this place?" he asked, his pale gaze roaming over the broad valley that was spread before them.

"I don't know. None of us really knows. We lack the great powers of our ancestors—and their writings indicate that even they didn't know what they'd accomplished.

"Some people believe that this valley and the other valley exist in the same place. Others speak of our existence in a separate plane, a space within a space." She smiled at him.

"Mostly, we don't think about it because it gives us headaches."

She pointed toward the distant mountains that bordered the valley. "See how the horizon is blurred? In my lifetime, it has always been that way, though it has grown worse in the past few days. But once it was sharp and clear. That's how we know that the spell has been weakening. But we don't know what will happen when it breaks."

They had both turned toward the mountains, but when they returned their attention to the road ahead of them, they saw a small group of figures on horseback riding toward them, their speed obvious from the cloud of dust around them. Zach continued to hold her hand, but his other hand went to the pistol holstered at his side.

"Who are they?"

Rowena squinted to see better. "I can't tell yet, but I imagine it's the Gatekeepers and perhaps some members of the Council."

They stopped walking and waited for the riders. In a few moments, Rowena confirmed that it was indeed the three Gatekeepers, who'd undoubtedly picked up signals of their arrival.

"The tall gray-haired woman in the center is Alma, the current leader of the Council, and the others are Council members," she told him, wishing that his first confrontation with her people here could have been with someone other than that unpleasant woman. Furthermore, the two Council members with her were her strongest allies.

"A *woman* leads your people?" he asked in astonishment.

"For now, yes. But sometimes the leader is a man. You've forgotten your history, Zach. Our people have always believed that men and women are equal. In fact, according to the history I read at Ashwara, that was one of the things that the Warriors held against us. Since we made war with magic and both men and women possessed that magic in equal measure, it gave us an edge against the superior numbers of our enemies, who were always male."

"Tell me about this Alma," he said, staring fixedly at the approaching riders.

"I don't like her and I don't trust her," Rowena said succinctly, knowing even as she spoke that she shouldn't have told him such a thing. So she hurried on.

"Her power isn't absolute. She's not like the king—or like you. She is merely elected to serve a three-year term."

Rowena stared at Alma, whose arrogant face was now quite clear. It was true that her powers weren't normally that great—but would that be different now? People were frightened and confused, and as a result, they might well be willing to follow her lead as they wouldn't have otherwise.

The group came to a halt some 20 feet away. All of them dismounted, but the Gatekeepers hung back, staying with the horses as the Council members advanced with Alma in the lead.

"Why have you brought him here, Rowena?" Alma demanded. "This is our valley, and Warriors do not belong here."

Rowena drew herself up and met Alma's glare with one of her own. "I would think that the very fact that he is here should tell you that he is welcome, Alma. Otherwise, he would have been struck dead."

Alma's gaze shifted to the silent man beside her. "You are not welcome here, Warrior chief. We have nothing to say to you."

"I came to make you an offer," Zach replied, his voice more pleasant than Rowena would have expected. "If your people will ally yourselves with us against the Atanians, I promise that you can return to your valley in peace."

"We make no alliances, Warrior—and if we did, it wouldn't be with those who forced us to come here."

Zach inclined his head slightly. "Very well. But you condemn your people—and many others as well—to death. You may have magic, but we have weapons that can reduce that magic to mere parlor tricks. I'm sure that Rowena has already told you about them."

"He speaks the truth, Alma," Rowena put in hastily. "And I don't believe that you speak for all our people."

Alma drew herself up haughtily. "The people have granted special powers to the Council to proceed as we see fit. We will do what we must

327

to save ourselves and our valley." Her lips curved in an unpleasant smile.

"And since you have seen fit to betray your people by taking a Warrior as your lover, Rowena, you are no longer one of us. But neither can we afford to let the two of you return through the Gateway."

Even as she spoke, Rowena had a sudden premonition of Alma's intention. She moved quickly, putting herself between Alma and Zach, and at the same time raised her hand and called upon the ancient forces.

Her sudden movement caught Alma by surprise, but she, too, raised a hand. Jagged bolts of green arced from each of them, colliding in a brilliant light that all but blinded everyone present. The very air around them vibrated, sending tremors through them all and causing everyone but Alma and Rowena to fall to the ground. Zach had drawn his pistol, but it flew beyond his reach as he crumpled heavily to the hard-packed dirt.

The tremors affected Rowena, too, but she stood her ground, holding on to the magic she'd called upon. In this moment, she understood the bloodlust of her ancestors as she never had before. A hot fierceness flowed through her as she countered Alma's magic with her own—and finally won as Alma's face, barely visible beyond the blinding haze, twisted with agony and hatred. Then the older woman fell to the ground and only Rowena's hand glowed with the magical green light.

She closed her fist and let the light fade, then fell to her knees beside Zach, who was struggling to get to his feet. The others remained inert, but she could see that they were still alive. The Gatekeepers had retreated, trying to control the frightened horses.

"We have to go back through the Gateway," she told him, reaching out to take his hand.

He hesitated for one brief moment before accepting it, and Rowena felt a sharp pain of regret that he had witnessed the extent of her power—a power she herself hadn't known she possessed until that moment. She had learned it and had demonstrated it to him, but not until she was forced to use it against Alma did she realize its full potential.

"I had to do it," she said softly, her voice a plea for understanding. "She would have killed you—and perhaps me as well."

Zach drew her into his arms, and she could feel the slight tremors that still coursed through his body. "I know," he said soothingly as he caressed her. "But she has forced you to make a terrible choice."

"I will go with you," she told him. "Maybe there is yet something we can do to stop the war."

He gave her a quick kiss, but his silence was eloquent. There was nothing that could be done now. Alma had called her a traitor to her people—and then had forced her to become just that.

They hurried back to the Gateway, pausing

for one last look at the valley before plunging into the thick mists. Alma and the others were beginning to stir and the Gatekeepers were moving toward them.

Hand in hand, they ran along the nearly invisible stone path. Rowena wondered if the Gateway would indeed open for them. The Gatekeepers might be able to stop them even now.

Abruptly, the stone path beneath their hurrying feet vanished. They both cried out, but their hands remained linked. Terror knifed through Rowena. This hadn't happened when they'd crossed through earlier. What could it mean?

They were floating in darkness, their bodies entwined. Winds howled around them, filling the void with an eerie keening sound. Zach tried to draw her still closer and she sought the comfort of his arms eagerly. But the winds seemed to be pulling them apart with unseen fingers, driving a wedge between them until only their hands were linked. And then their grip on each other began to loosen as she was pulled one way and he was dragged another until their fingers slipped apart.

"Rowena!"

His voice seemed to echo from a long distance away in the all-encompassing darkness. She shouted his name, but the wind howled still more, snatching the sound from her lips and carrying it off. She thought she heard him call her one last time, but the sound was very faint and very far away. And then there was nothing.

Zach swore as his knees struck the stones. He

groped about him in the darkness and felt the path. Then he got to his feet and began to call her again.

But there was no response, and he knew—without understanding *how* he knew—that there would be none. Her accursed ancestors had separated them with their damnable magic. Either that or the woman, Alma, had accomplished it with the help of her minions.

He stood there in the silent darkness, hoping against hope to get her back and feeling more helpless now than he'd felt even when she'd saved his life by using her magic against one of her own people.

Then the wind began to pick up again, this time pushing at his back, urging him onward. He fought it for a time, but it became even stronger, until he had no choice but to stumble forward along the stone path as he blinked back the tears of frustration that filled his eyes.

He had no idea how long he walked along the path, his heart heavy with the fear that he would never see her again. Silently, he implored the god he'd never really believed in and the ancient gods of her people to return her to him, offering up all the earthly powers he possessed in return.

Finally, a soft gray light began to replace the blackness and the wind at his back subsided. He stumbled to a halt as he saw figures in the twilight riding toward him. For one very brief moment, he let his hopes soar—but in the next, that hope gave way to shock.

Riding toward him was a group of Warriors—not his own men, but Warriors of an age long past. They moved slowly through the gray light, and it seemed that their horses' hooves struck nothing but air, because there was no sound. As he strained to see them more clearly, they stopped just a short distance away.

Zach stared with shock into a familiar face that could have been his own. But it was instead the face of his ancestor: Egan, the Warrior chief who'd led his people against the Dazhinn 500 years ago.

Was this a Dazhinn trick? Zach wondered. Or was it some sort of warning? He waited, his gaze never leaving the face of his mirror image.

For a moment that seemed to stretch out to touch eternity, the two men stared at each other in silence. Then Egan inclined his head slightly, and a moment later, he and his fellow Warriors had vanished into the mists.

Zach continued along the path. It felt to him as though his ancestor had given him his blessing—but for what? Was he indicating that he accepted Zach's love for a Dazhinn sorceress—or had he nodded his approval at their forced parting?

Ahead of him, he could see the tall, dark cliffs that marked the entrance to the Gateway and he knew he was back in his own world—but a world he would have given up gladly for her.

Rowena awoke to silence and a dim gray light. "Zach," she whispered—and then shouted. But there was no answer and then she knew there could not be one. He was gone. But where was he? Had he gotten through the Gateway, or had her ancestors exacted a revenge for her betrayal?

She was lying on the stone path and when she hauled herself into a sitting position, she could see the dark cliffs that framed the entrance to the Gateway only a short distance away. But would she walk out into the real valley or the enchanted one she'd just left?

She got to her feet, her thoughts focused only on Zach. Perhaps they'd both gotten through, after all. But if so, surely he would have returned for her. Or had her battle with Alma so unnerved him that he wanted nothing more to do with her?

With each slow step she took toward the cliffs, Rowena became more and more convinced that she was still in the enchanted valley, that the Gateway had been closed to her. Still, when she finally reached the narrow opening and saw her old home spread before her, enough hope remained that she sobbed at this undeniable proof that she had been turned back at the Gateway.

Was it possible that Zach, too, had been turned back—that he was also trapped here? No, she knew somehow that he wasn't. Either he had made it through, or he had been killed by her ancestors for daring to love a Dazhinn and follow her to the valley.

Clouds gathered overhead, blotting out the last

of the day's sunlight. The village was just barely visible in the distance, and the mountains that bordered the valley were lost in mist. Rowena began to trudge down the dirt road, giving no thought to where she would go or what she would do. It didn't seem to matter now. They had failed to persuade her people, and now Zach was gone.

She nearly missed the object that lay just off to one side of the road, half-buried in the weeds. In fact, she had actually passed it by before it belatedly registered on her tormented brain. Then she stopped and turned back.

It was Zach's pistol. She remembered now that he'd drawn it to defend them against Alma, then dropped it when the forces created by her battle with Alma had knocked him off his feet.

She picked up the weapon carefully, half-fearing that it would explode in her hand, but wanting it because it had belonged to him. She'd never seen one of them being fired, but she had seen the soldiers at Shemoth fire their rifles, and so she knew how it must work. And as she cradled the weapon in her hand, she began to consider what she should do.

Alma and the others must have assumed that she'd gone through the Gateway; otherwise, they would surely be here, waiting for her. Waiting to kill her, she reminded herself with a shiver.

She knew she dared not return to her cottage. It was isolated, but if they had any reason to suspect that she had come back, they would surely post someone there.

She stared around her in the fading light. The valley that had once seemed so large now became instead a very tiny prison. With night coming on, she'd have no problem finding a hiding place, but that was only a temporary solution.

What she needed to learn, she decided, was whether Alma and the others who'd met them had been acting on their own, or whether everyone else, too, regarded her as a traitor. Now that she thought about it, she realized that only Alma had raised the magic fire against her. But was that because she alone among them knew how—or because Alma alone had pronounced a death sentence on her and Zach? She wished that she'd paid attention to the others, but she'd been too busy protecting herself and Zach. It might well be that they were as horrified as she'd been that Alma would do such a thing.

Carrying the pistol with her, Rowena resumed her long walk toward the village. The only person she knew she could trust was Seitha, her cousin. No matter what the others might have said about her, Seitha would not betray her. Besides, Seitha had no affection for Alma, either.

Fortunately, Seitha lived on the very edge of the village, which meant that she should be able to get to her cottage without much risk. And Seitha, too, was unmarried and lived alone.

It was full dark by the time Rowena approached the village, where lights shone in every cottage. She left the main road and slipped through the shadows, passing by homes whose inhabitants she knew well, but who might now be her enemies. She was horrified to think that she was now an outcast among her own people.

She breathed a sigh of relief when she saw that Seitha's cottage was lit, but instead of going up to the front door, where a welcoming lantern hung over the carved and polished wooden door, Rowena hurried into the shadows and went to the back door, where she paused to listen for any sounds that might indicate that Seitha was not alone. Then, hearing nothing, she knocked softly.

She was about to tap again when the door was opened cautiously at first, and then flung wide. Before Rowena could say anything, her cousin had grabbed her arm and pulled her inside.

Seitha closed the door quickly, then stared at the pistol Rowena still carried. "What is that?"

Rowena lifted it. She'd nearly forgotten that she still held it. "It's called a pistol. It belonged to Zach. It's a weapon—what they use now instead of knives."

Seitha looked stricken. "Then what I heard is true? He *did* come here and try to kill Alma?"

Anger flashed through Rowena. "He did no such thing. We came here to try to persuade the Council to form an alliance in order to defeat the Atanians. Alma refused to consider it, and then she raised the magic fire to kill us both. Zach drew his pistol, but I fought Alma with my own fire."

She forced herself to calm down and told her cousin the rest of it. "I brought it with me because it's all I have left of him," she finished with a sob. "Except for this, that is."

With her free hand, Rowena lifted the gold chain that was hidden beneath her shirt and showed Seitha the necklace Zach had given her.

"It's Dazhinn!" Seitha gasped as she examined it.

Rowena nodded and explained how it had come into Zach's possession. Seitha was still staring at it. "It looks like the workmanship of your father's family: the kind of thing they used to make when they could still get precious stones."

"It is," Rowena acknowledged.

"But how can you love a man whose ancestors must have kept them imprisoned?" Seitha cried.

"That was five hundred years ago, Seitha, and there was cruelty on both sides."

Seitha looked doubtful, but finally nodded. "You're right. We must let go of the past."

"Tell me what Alma and the others are saying. Does everyone believe me to be a traitor?"

Seitha sighed. "Everyone is so frightened and so confused. I suppose that some probably believe her, but most people are more concerned about themselves, and Alma and her allies have used their fears to gain more power."

"Alma has told them that she knew of your betrayal through Abner, and that you proved it further by bringing the Warrior chief here." She paused, frowning.

"But what no one understands is how you managed that. He should not have survived to get through the Gateway."

"He may *not* have survived," Rowena reminded her in a choked voice.

"But he did come through," Seitha pointed out gently. "And that surely must mean that he was able to do it again."

"I got through as well, but I couldn't go back."

"I think maybe there is a reason for that," Seitha said. "You may have been prevented from leaving because you are needed here."

"But what can I do?" Rowena protested. "If I show my face, Alma will try to have me killed. I held her off with the fire, but I couldn't hold off more than one person."

"No one would countenance your being killed," Seitha stated firmly. "Even if they truly believed you guilty of treachery, they would never go along with that. Alma said nothing about attempting to kill you. She made it sound as though you did nothing, while Zach tried to kill her and the others. I doubt that anyone realizes you know how to wield the fire. After all, the rest of us have only learned in the past few days—and you weren't here then."

"Didn't anyone protest her lies?" Rowena asked. "They all saw what happened."

"Her allies on the Council would go along with whatever she said, but the Gatekeepers may be a different matter—especially Seth. He's a man of great integrity, and he must have been horrified at what Alma did. He's probably kept silent only because it didn't seem to matter. Both you and Zach were gone."

"Then we must speak to him as soon as possible."

"I'm afraid it will have to wait until morning. I was there when they returned, and he seemed quite ill. Someone said that the forces at the Gateway had affected him."

"Do you think the people can be persuaded to go against Alma and her allies?"

"I don't know. There is still so much hatred and distrust of the Warriors here. As you said, we are still living in the past." Seitha hesitated, then went on.

"There is a rumor going around that Alma contacted Abner before the 'paths stopped communicating. What I heard is that she ordered him and several others to make contact with the Atanians and offer them our assistance to defeat the Warriors."

Chapter Thirteen

Rowena lay on the sleeping mat Seitha had provided for her and stared into the dying embers of the cooking fire. She wasn't even trying to go to sleep, knowing that if it came to her at all this night, it wouldn't be for a long time.

She felt an odd combination of comfort and disorientation at being back here, in a tiny, primitive cottage much like her own. The aromas of the meal Seitha had prepared for them hung in the air, and she realized that it had been a long time since she'd smelled such things. In all her time at Paulena's homes, she'd been in the kitchens only twice, and then simply out of curiosity.

She made a disgusted sound, knowing that she was dwelling on such unimportant matters because, for a time at least, they could hold at bay the rest of it. She'd never been one given to such self-deception, but then she'd never before faced such terrible problems, either.

First and foremost in her mind was Zach. How she wanted to believe that he had returned to his own land, even if that would put him forever beyond her reach. She believed him when he'd said that he didn't want war, and she wondered if he would yet find a way to prevent it.

But she also believed his statement that if war was unavoidable, he would fight in the valley rather than let the Atanians wreak devastation on his own people. It would be far more difficult for him to do that now that he'd seen proof of the existence of her people in this enchanted place. But he would still risk breaking the spell to guarantee the safety of his own land and its people. She could not blame him for that.

What must be going through his mind now? she wondered. He would probably assume that she was here, that she'd somehow been prevented from returning with him. Or perhaps he thought she'd changed her mind at the last moment and abandoned him.

Or perhaps he thinks nothing at all because he's dead, whispered her darker side. Perhaps the creators of the spell let him through the first time only to take their revenge when he tried to return.

No! She could not let herself think like that. She must believe that somewhere, somehow, they would be together again.

Resolutely, she turned to thoughts of her present situation and what she should do. If the rumors Seitha had heard were true and Abner was trying to ally her people with the

Atanians, the situation was even worse than she'd expected. Furthermore, even if she could persuade the Council and the people that this was a mistake, there was no way to change it. Seitha had said that the 'paths were still unable to communicate with their counterparts on the far side of the Gateway.

As she examined and reexamined her options, Rowena came to the sad conclusion that there was very little she could do. Everything depended upon what happened beyond the Gateway, and if or when the spell would break. Seitha had told her that the scholars were now no longer so certain what would happen if the spell broke. They might drift forever in their enchanted space, cut off from the other valley and the world beyond— or they might simply cease to exist.

No one knew, so everyone waited, their gazes drawn now more than ever to the mountains that ringed the valley and grew ever more indistinct.

When Rowena opened her eyes to the gray morning light, she was surprised to discover that she'd slept, after all—and even more surprised to realize that her sleep hadn't been haunted by dark dreams.

Seitha was already awake and as they breakfasted on tea and bread with jam, they resumed their discussion about what, if anything, they could do.

They decided that Seitha would go to see Seth, the eldest of the Gatekeepers. If he had recovered sufficiently from his ordeal, he would surely speak up and put an end to Alma's lies.

After she had gone, Rowena paced restlessly about the tiny cottage, hoping that Seth would indeed speak out, but still unable to see how it would affect their current situation. Still, when the truth became known, at least she would no longer be considered a traitor.

When Seitha returned, Rowena knew instantly that something had gone wrong. Her cousin's normally high color had drained away to a sickly paleness and her mouth was set in a grim line.

"Seth died during the night."

"Oh no! Did he . . . ? Could Alma have . . . ?" Rowena stumbled over the questions. Surely Alma hadn't killed him! But she'd tried to kill *her!*

But Seitha shook her head. "He died peacefully in his sleep. He was an old man—older than I'd realized—and the strain from the forces at the Gateway yesterday was just too much for him."

She saw the stricken look on Rowena's face and shook her head firmly. "You are not to blame, though I don't doubt that Alma will try to make it appear that you are. Seth's heart was faltering and his daughter had begged him to stay away from the Gateway."

"What about the others?" Rowena asked, trying to convince herself that what Seitha said was true.

"They are not well, either, from what I heard. But they will recover. I wouldn't put much hope in either of them speaking out, though. Don't forget that one of them is Alma's cousin and the other received his appointment as Gatekeeper through her."

"What can we do?"

Seitha was standing at the window, her back to Rowena. She turned slowly, then gestured to the window. "It's too late to do anything now," she said in a quiet, sad voice. "Look outside. It is nearly midday, and yet it looks like dusk."

Rowena followed her gesturing arm and drew in a sharp breath. She hadn't paid any attention to the light, or if she had, had simply assumed that it was a gray, misty day. She suggested that now, but Seitha shook her head.

"There is a difference to the quality of the light. Everyone is remarking on it. Those who set out earlier to work in the fields have returned, saying that they heard distant sounds like thunder, but saw no lightning."

"The artillery," Rowena whispered, then explained about the big guns. Was that proof that Zach had indeed made it through the Gateway—or would the battle take place even without him?

Even as she stood there considering that, the light seemed to dim still more.

Every part of him ached with the need to get away from this place, but Zach continued his pacing along the tops of the cliffs, now and again raising the glasses to his eyes to survey the scene in the valley.

It was becoming more and more difficult to see anything down there, and he called a halt to the artillery fire. He could no longer be certain that the big guns wouldn't accidentally hit his own men in the accursed gloom.

"It's only midday," his aide said as he followed alongside.

Zach merely nodded, listening to the sounds of rifle fire and the explosion of grenades far below. He felt certain that the battle wasn't going their way. They weren't outnumbered by all that much, but since he couldn't send any Warriors into the valley, his men were being led by inexperienced and inferior junior officers.

Early this morning, after a nearly sleepless night of being haunted by the loss of Rowena, Zach had called together his senior officers, all of them Warriors, and had issued orders forbidding any of them to set foot into the valley.

He knew that he was risking being thought mad, but he'd told them where he'd been and what he'd seen. Rather to his surprise, no one had doubted him. It came to him as they talked that all of them had known—as Rowena had once said—that the Dazhinn and their magic were real. For 500 years, his clan had denied their existence—and yet they'd always believed.

Zach stared now into the face of his young Warrior aide and then into the faces of the officers who'd accompanied him. He could just barely see those faces now, as still more light drained away. But what he saw mirrored his own agony. The spell of the Dazhinn had reached into their

Saranne Dawson

very souls, sapping their strength and wreaking havoc upon their minds.

Down in the valley, the sounds of gunfire became more sporadic and the sharp booms of the grenades had ceased altogether. It seemed even darker down there. He could only hope that his men were following orders to retreat from the valley if darkness fell or if any other strangeness came upon them. They weren't Warriors, but he still wanted them out of that accursed place before the Dazhinn returned—*if* they returned.

Zach closed his eyes briefly and saw again that magic fire arcing from Rowena's fingertips and those of the woman, Alma. He had to suppress a shudder as he felt again the force of it, even though it hadn't been directed at him.

The Warrior in him wanted to know the power and range of such an unnatural weapon, but the man thought only of its use by the woman he loved: a Dazhinn sorceress.

Would he ever see her again? He had to believe that he would because the alternative was too terrible to contemplate. For a man who'd had only limited use for women, Zach had been transformed into something he barely recognized—and still couldn't quite accept.

He turned to his aide and requested that his horse be brought to him, then informed his officers that they would be returning to Ashwara. The relief on the men's faces was undisguised. Even at the fortress, they would still not be entirely free of the spell's influences, but at least it was bearable there.

The reports began to filter in shortly after they reached the fortress. The enemy hadn't yet succeeded in taking the valley, but it was clear that that would happen, unless the additional troops Zach had ordered from other garrisons arrived quickly. He'd been counting on their superiority in artillery to carry the day—but that was before Dazhinn sorcery had turned day into night.

The only good news he received was that his troops had managed to capture several enemy officers. Zach had ordered that to be given high priority, since he wanted to know what the Atanians were making of the unholy trickery.

What he learned was that his worst nightmare might well be coming true. The Dazhinn had offered an alliance with the enemy. The men they'd captured didn't know if the alliance had actually been formed, because their leaders were suspicious of a Dazhinn trick.

It will happen, Zach thought as he stood later on the roof of the fortress, staring into the darkness of the valley. No matter how much the Atanians distrusted the Dazhinn, they would accept their help, knowing that however they might feel about the Atanians, their true enemy was the Warriors.

Tears sprang to his eyes and he was glad to be alone. If the Dazhinn had allied themselves with the Atanians, it could only mean that Rowena was dead. He clenched his fists in helpless frustration. He would still win; there was no doubt of that, although the victory would be costly. And when it was over, he would put an end to the Dazhinn once and for all. They would pay dearly for taking her from him—for condemning him to a life of nothing more than memories of her.

Then, as he stood there, staring into the black void below the fortress, he felt a sudden surge in the force of the spell. He stared in amazement as the night was suddenly filled with tiny pinpricks of light, as though a million tiny stars had dropped from the heavens to hover in the darkness of the valley.

From nowhere, a cold wind rose, whipping about him. That low hum that he'd felt ever since this had all begun grew louder and now became something heard through his ears, as well as felt by his body.

Running steps approached him, but he could not take his eyes from the scene below, where the lights danced in the darkness, mesmerizing him with their eerie, pulsating movements.

"Are all our troops out of the valley?" he asked without turning his head from the unnatural scene.

"Yes, Chief," one of his officers replied. "Does this mean that the Dazhinn are returning?"

Zach nodded. All but the one he wanted to return. And soon he would make them pay.

Rowena and Seitha hurried from cottage to cottage in the darkness, using back paths to avoid being spotted by Alma's allies. Seitha had learned that Alma had recruited what amounted to a personal army, who'd undergone a quick and intensive training in the use of the green fire. Under the guise of keeping order, they were roaming the valley, seeking Rowena. Alma didn't know for certain that she was here, but it was obvious that she was taking no chances.

Several hours ago, this ersatz army had shown up at Seitha's cottage—to the surprise of neither of them. Everyone knew that the two women were close. They'd told Seitha that they were simply checking on everyone and had made no reference to Rowena. But they'd invited themselves inside and quickly searched the cottage.

Rowena had hidden in a secret cellar beneath the cottage. Only a few of the cottages possessed them. They were left over from the time of their ancient battles with the Warriors, and existed only in the oldest of the homes, like Seitha's. Fortunately, the people who'd come hadn't known about it.

Rowena had to stifle her rage as she thought about it now. That she should be forced to hide from her own people was unthinkable! But she still didn't miss the irony of hiding from them in a place intended to protect her from the Warriors.

They were making their way around the village, telling the truth to those who could be trusted. People were frightened and as yet unwilling to let go of their ancient hatred for the Warriors, but they still listened. It was all Rowena could hope for at this point.

Finally, they reached the home of the one Council member they had decided to contact. He was first cousin to Rowena's and Seitha's mothers, and they decided that even if he didn't believe them, he still wouldn't tell Alma that Rowena was here.

They huddled in the shadows at the cottage's kitchen door, surrounded by the fragrance from the herb garden that his wife planted to use for her medicinal preparations. The woman herself answered their knock, opening the door a mere crack until she saw who was there. Then she flung the door open and drew them quickly inside, at the same time calling for her husband.

"Rowena!" he cried, embracing her. "We had feared that you might be lost in the Gateway—or that you'd gone back to . . ." His voice trailed off uncertainly as he released her.

"To my Warrior lover," Rowena finished for him. "That was my intention, but I couldn't get through."

"Then where is he?" he asked, casting a nervous look at the door.

"He has returned to his people," she said, hoping that was true.

Then she launched into her story as both people listened intently. As with others, she saw doubt in their faces, but not outright denial.

When she had finished, she asked the question uppermost in her mind. "Is it true that Alma has sent Abner to make an alliance with the Atanians?"

His eyes wouldn't quite meet hers as he nodded. "Many of us had grave reservations about the wisdom of such a thing, but Alma was very persuasive. They are the enemies of our enemy."

"The Warriors are no longer our enemy, Jared. The world has changed. But if we ally ourselves with the Atanians, the Warriors will destroy us. I've seen their weapons—weapons you cannot begin to imagine. Our magic won't help us against guns that can fire great distances, or against gases that fill the air and kill those who breathe it."

"But the Atanians, too, have such weapons," he protested uncertainly.

Rowena shook her head. "They have some—but not as much—and their numbers are smaller. Besides, their ruler is an evil, corrupt man, and even if he should somehow be victorious, he could not be trusted."

"And you believe that this Warrior chief can be trusted?" Jared asked skeptically.

"Yes. He's a good man—and a man of peace. But he is still a Warrior, and if you become his enemy, he will crush you. The king is a good man as well, for all that he is weak. And unlike the Atanians, they have a parliament—like our Council, only much larger. And they gain more power each day."

"The Warrior chief permits this?"

"Yes, he does. Unlike us, he understands that times have changed."

"You make him out to be a most extraordinary man, Rowena."

"He is. Otherwise, how could I love him? You have to persuade the others to give up this alliance, Jared. It's the only way to save our people."

Jared sighed heavily. "We have granted temporary powers to Alma to do as she sees fit. She must consult with us, but that is all."

"How could you do such a thing?" Seitha cried, interjecting herself into the conversation for the first time. "This goes against everything our people believe in!"

"That's not true," he protested. "In centuries past, when we were faced with war, it was customary for the leader of the Council to be given such powers."

"Perhaps we had better leaders then," Rowena replied, though she doubted that, given what she now knew of their savagery.

"Nevertheless, it is done."

"What is done can also be undone," Rowena stated angrily. "I want to meet with all of you. I want the opportunity to confront Alma with her lies."

Jared nodded. "That is fair enough. I will see that—"

He stopped in midsentence as they heard shouts from outside. And then they all felt it: deep, powerful vibrations that seemed to touch every part of them with its force.

"It is happening!" Seitha said, her voice a hoarse whisper. "The spell is breaking."

They all rushed outside—even Rowena, who no longer cared if she was spotted. Thin, jagged bolts of lightning crisscrossed the heavens, but there was no thunder. The deep vibrations now became audible and many people clapped their hands over their ears as the sound swelled still more. Then suddenly, the lightning dissolved into a shower of sparks: millions of tiny, pulsating lights that floated in the darkness.

The entire village stood transfixed as the lights danced above them, knowing what it must mean. The enchantment of 500 years was coming to an end. But what would happen to them now?

Rowena's thoughts were on Zach. Tears streamed down over her cheeks as she clutched the memory of him to her: the great gentleness of his hands on her body, the passion of his kisses, the feel of him deep inside her.

Then suddenly, it was over. The lights winked out and a canopy of stars could be seen in the heavens. The vibrations died away, leaving them all with only a tingling memory. People began to ask if they'd returned to their ancient home. How could they know?

Her eyes blurred by tears, Rowena turned to the east, scanning the darkness. Then she drew in a sharp, quavering breath.

"We're home!" she said, pointing. "That is Ashwara."

The name was passed from one to the other in hushed tones as they all stared at the cluster of lights atop the distant hill. Rowena knew that the sight must be striking terror into the hearts of all, but it brought hope to her: a hope that Zach was there, perhaps even standing on the rooftop and watching as the Dazhinn returned to their valley at last.

Zach faced the most difficult decision of his long and illustrious career. With the dawn came confirmation of the Dazhinn's return to their valley. After a largely sleepless night, he was on the rooftop of the fortress when the first fragile light tinted the sky, and saw, spread below him, the village and fields green with crops. With his powerful glasses, he could make out figures moving around within the village. Even with the aid of the binoculars, he couldn't see their faces, but he imagined that as he looked down at them, their gazes were fixed upon Ashwara.

There was no sign of the enemy down there, but he knew that they could be hiding in the thick woods at the far end of the valley, near the Gateway. Or what had once been the Gateway, he reminded himself.

The guns at Ashwara and the guns on top the cliffs were all trained on the valley. Zach knew that no magic the Dazhinn possessed could match them. Magic belonged to a vanished world. But how did he dare use those guns now, when Rowena might be down there?

He desperately needed to get someone down into the valley—someone who could be accepted by the Dazhinn. The only possibility that came to mind was Paulena. Duncan certainly wouldn't like the idea of sending her into the valley—but he thought that Paulena just might do it.

He summoned an aide and told him to send a messenger back to the city. If his old friend didn't yet know that Paulena was Dazhinn, he would soon find out.

When she stepped out of Seitha's cottage shortly after dawn, Rowena's eyes went automatically to the stone fortress on the distant hill. She imagined Zach up there—but what was he thinking? He could be no more certain that she was down here than she was that he had returned to Ashwara.

Others were gathering in front of their houses, staring at the imposing fortress. From here, it was impossible for them to see the big guns, or the other guns at the far end of the valley scattered along the cliffs. And even if they had been able to see them, they wouldn't truly understand their significance.

There is nothing to be done about them, she told herself. All I can do is hope that Zach is still leading his army and will not order his men to fire upon us.

By now, everyone knew of her return, and she'd spent an uneasy night worrying that Alma might send someone to kill her. But the hours of darkness had passed peacefully, and now Jared would be trying to convince the Council to let her confront Alma and her allies.

Rowena wanted to be hopeful about the outcome, but her conversations last night with various people had proved to her just how unlikely it was that she could convince her people to ally themselves with their ancient enemy.

She had just fortified herself for a long, difficult day with a cup of strong tea when a Council aide knocked at the door and informed her that her presence at Council Hall was expected. She let herself hope just a bit. At least Jared had succeeded in getting her a hearing.

All the members were there when she walked into Council Hall, past the Sandor tapestries. She wondered what her mother and grandmother would think of her now. Would they believe she had betrayed her people?

Alma's gaze was fixed unwaveringly upon her from the moment Rowena entered the formal chamber. The silence was tense. Most of the members looked as though they'd slept as badly as she herself had.

"I have been persuaded to let you have your say, Rowena—but I warn you that I will not tolerate your lies." Alma shifted her glance from Rowena to the Council members.

"Remember that this is a woman who has taken the Warrior chief as her lover."

Rowena looked from one to the other. Some were openly hostile: Alma's allies. Others wore neutral expressions. A few, like Jared, seemed to be sympathetic. It was the best she could hope for.

"I will not tolerate your lies, either, Alma," she stated firmly. "I know that you lied about what happened at the Gateway."

Then, ignoring the woman's protest, Rowena explained why she'd brought Zach through the Gateway, and what had transpired when they were met by Alma and the others.

"She would have killed us both. Zach didn't draw his weapon until she showed the fire. He came in peace, to offer an alliance, and she tried to kill him."

She paused, once again ignoring Alma's protest, then explained about the guns at the fortress and along the clifftops. "If they wanted to destroy us, they could do so easily. Our magic is useless against such weapons. And if they believe that we have allied ourselves with the Atanians, they *will* use them."

A horrified silence greeted that statement. Then Alma sneered at her. "We have no need to fear those guns. Your Warrior lover wouldn't risk your death."

"He doesn't even know for sure that I'm here," Rowena pointed out. "For all he knows, I could be dead—or lost in the mists of the Gateway.

"And even if he knows I'm here, he may still use them. He is a man of peace, as I told you— but his first loyalty is to his people. If he sees us as the enemy, he will use those guns."

And as she spoke, she felt sick, thinking about the terrible decision that Zach might be facing. But he was honor-bound to protect his people— even if that meant killing her.

"If we ally ourselves with him, we will still face his weapons when the battle has been won," one of Alma's allies stated. "We have no guarantee that he would not turn on us."

"Of course you don't have that guarantee," Rowena replied angrily. "Alma tried to kill him when he came here to give you that assurance."

"The word of a Warrior chief means little," said another member, and many heads nodded in agreement.

The argument went on for nearly an hour. Jared and a few others wanted to ally themselves with Zach, or else remain neutral. Others pointed out that neutrality wasn't possible, given the fact that they were caught between the two enemies' positions. Alma's allies said that they had the personal guarantee of the Atanian king that they would be allowed to live in peace in the valley.

Rowena asked that a delegation be sent to Ashwara to meet with Zach—assuming, of course, that he was there.

In the end, the old hatred held sway. Alma coldly reminded them that she had been granted full authority to make such decisions, and although some were obviously regretting that, they remained silent.

What can I do? Rowena thought. If I leave the valley now and go to Zach, then he will surely destroy the valley. How could she convince him that most of them were good people who were simply frightened and willing to go along with a bad leader?

She was still debating this when the guns began to fire. The others stopped talking and frowned, perhaps thinking they'd heard thunder. But Rowena knew better. She'd heard that sound before—at Shemoth.

"They're firing the guns," she said as numerous pairs of eyes turned in her direction. "Probably the guns atop the cliffs near the Gateway."

They all rushed outside, just as still more booms echoed through the valley. Rowena saw immediately that she was right. A pall of smoke hung over the cliffs, and even as she watched, yet another gun fired.

At least, she thought, they haven't yet begun to fire at the village. No one had seemed to know for certain, but it was believed that the Atanians had taken up positions near the old Gateway. And as she watched, the woods near the Gateway seemed to explode.

The others saw it, too, and from the expressions on their faces, Rowena knew that despite her descriptions, they hadn't fully understood the power of those weapons.

She scanned the hillsides between the Gateway and the fortress, and drew in her breath sharply. There were more guns there now. Zach had brought in reinforcements. Even as she stared in horror, she saw more of the big guns being wheeled into place. The entire valley was now at their mercy.

Zach trained his glasses on the far end of the valley, where shell after shell exploded in the

359

thick forest. There was no sign of the enemy, but he knew they must be there somewhere—unless they'd sneaked into the village itself under cover of darkness.

He didn't want to think about that possibility. As long as they limited the shelling to the far end of the valley, there was little chance of his hitting her or any of her people. He'd been there, and he knew the area was uninhabited. But if he were faced with the decision to shell the village itself . . .

Zach wanted desperately to believe that she was still alive and down there with her people. But that hope clashed violently with his oath to protect his people. If the Atanians gained control of the valley, the war would spill out into the town of Ashwara and the surrounding countryside that was filled with numerous small towns and villages.

He still had his glasses trained on the far end of the valley, where the usual mists hung over the trees, mixed now with fires started by the shells. But when he lowered the glasses, he saw that the mist was spreading, pouring through the broad valley. Was it only the wind, blowing the smoke and fog toward the village? There was no wind where he stood, but conditions could be different down there.

After watching the scene for a time, Zach concluded uneasily that what he was witnessing wasn't natural. The gray-white fog was behaving like a living creature as it swallowed up the fields and then the village itself, drawing an impenetrable curtain over the entire valley.

He left the rooftop and spent the day making plans, positioning his newly reinforced troops and some of the artillery at the ends of the two roads that led from the valley. If the Atanians had taken the village or formed an alliance with the Dazhinn, they would meet devastating resistance when they tried to exit the valley, which remained invisible below its curtain of fog, despite the fact that the day was sunny and clear everywhere else.

They could still feel the force of the spell, even though it had subsided. He wished that he'd learned more about the talents of the Dazhinn. Rowena had said that none of them now possessed the great magic of their ancestors, but he wondered about that. She wouldn't have lied to him, but how could he be certain that others didn't have secret knowledge?

He had just finished his evening meal and was about to journey to the rooftop once again, when Duncan and Paulena arrived. Zach had only to look into the eyes of his old friend to know that he was still trying to assimilate the knowledge that his beloved wife was a Dazhinn sorceress. It occurred to him as he grasped Duncan's hand in welcome that it was probably worse for Duncan than it had been for him. As Rowena had said, the knowledge had always been there inside him. Still, Duncan had been spared the sight of his wife wielding her magic fire.

He told them of the situation. Paulena gasped when he explained that he didn't know Rowena's whereabouts, and feared that she might have been killed by her own people—or by her ancestors.

"No!" she cried. "Not even Alma could do something like that!"

Zach reminded her that Alma had in fact tried to kill them both, but Paulena shook her head emphatically.

"No Dazhinn can turn her fire on another. The way you described it is just as we've always been told. Some have more power than others, but the most they can do is what Rowena did to Alma. The fire is Dazhinn magic and cannot be used to kill another Dazhinn."

"But she could have killed her by conventional means," Zach pointed out.

"She wouldn't do that," Paulena insisted. "The people wouldn't stand for it, even if they did believe her to be a traitor. Your mistake is in believing that Rowena could have prevented an alliance with the Atanians. I'm sure she tried, but she may not have succeeded. The old hatreds still live among the Dazhinn. They've been locked away for so long, with only their history to feed upon—and a one-sided history at that."

"But if she's alive, why hasn't she left the valley and come to me?" Zach demanded.

"She may be staying in the valley because she believes that her presence there will prevent you from destroying our people," Paulena replied.

Zach slammed his fist against a table in frustration and pain. "I cannot let the Atanians escape from the valley—even if it means shelling the village."

"So you want me to go down there and persuade her to leave," Paulena said, making it a statement, not a question.

He nodded, fearing her response.

"I will go, Zach—but I cannot promise you that she will return with me."

"Polly!" Duncan said, his voice shaking. "I can't let you go down there! What if they won't let you leave, either? From what you told me, they'd regard you as a traitor, too."

Paulena put a hand on her husband's arm. "I must do it, Duncan. They wouldn't kill Rowena, but they might be holding her prisoner. And if so, perhaps I can set her free. However, the decision to leave the valley must be hers."

Zach nodded his understanding and avoided looking at the stricken Duncan. "What magic do they possess, other than the fire?"

Paulena frowned. "That's impossible to answer. Over the centuries, we've lost much of our magic because we had no need for it. I myself don't know how to call upon the fire. As far as I know, no one else did, either—until it became necessary again.

"But there have always been scholars among us who have kept themselves well versed in all the lore of our people. I've no doubt that the mists you described were the result of someone's learning an old spell."

"What about the spell that can rob a man of his mind?" Zach asked.

"I never even heard of that one until Rowena told me about it. It's possible that that was done with herbal potions, rather than by means of a spell. Or perhaps I just don't want to believe that we possess that kind of power." She shrugged.

"Our powers are not uniformly distributed, Zach. Some people have talents that others don't have. Rowena, for example, can draw off the power from thunderstorms—as she did that day we went boating. But it is, as she says, largely a useless talent."

She frowned in thought. "But she demonstrated another talent that day that I hadn't known she possessed—when she saved our servant from falling overboard."

Zach remembered that: how he'd seen the man being suspended in air and then lifted toward the railing. At the time, he'd thought his eyes had lied to him.

What else can she do? he wondered with an inner shiver.

"The truth is, Zach, that most of us probably don't know what we're capable of—until it becomes necessary to call upon those powers."

Chapter Fourteen

Fear traveled through the village with the speed of gossip. Everyone could see the smoke from the guns above the cliffs and the thicker smoke arising from the forest near the Gateway. The word "guns," until now unknown to the Dazhinn, was whispered in horrified tones. "Warrior magic," they called it—a magic far superior to their own.

But there were those cooler heads among them that reminded others of old magic, long unused by the Dazhinn. The scholars among them were surrounded by eager listeners. Bleary-eyed from having spent days and nights studying old books, the scholars spoke of this forgotten lore—especially of times when the Dazhinn had acted in concert, combining their talents and powers to defeat the Warriors.

Absent from all these hurried discussion was Alma. Neither she nor her allies were anywhere to be seen. Instead, it was to Rowena that the people turned. If any of them still considered her to be a traitor, they kept it to themselves. Her presence there in their time of great danger seemed to soften any harsh feelings, as well as give them hope that the village itself would be spared from the Warrior chief's guns.

Seitha whispered to Rowena that it must be for this reason that Rowena had been turned back at the Gateway, and Rowena could not dispute that even though she continued to believe that Zach would in fact turn the guns upon the village if it was the only way he could prevent the war from spreading to his own people.

As the big guns continued to pound away at the forest near the Gateway, several farmers joined them. They'd gone out in the first pale light of dawn to check their crops, then retreated in haste to the village when the artillery fire started.

They reported that they'd seen no sign of the enemy in that area, leaving everyone to wonder just where the Atanians were. Had they retreated from the valley completely, forsaking the alliance offered to them by Alma? No one knew, since no one could find Alma to question her.

Rowena listened to all this, wondering not just about the Atanians, but about Alma as well. Could she even now be meeting somewhere with the Atanians, plotting against Zach?

Spurred on by their fear that the shells could start falling on the village at any time, the people listened carefully to the scholars, then began, clumsily at first, to link up and call upon ancient talents. To everyone's surprise—including Rowena's—she became the "channel" the scholars had spoken of: the one among them in whom all their powers could be concentrated.

At first, Rowena wondered if it might be possible to cast a spell on the big guns that would prevent them from being fired. But either the guns were too far away or Dazhinn magic was useless against Warrior "magic," because the guns continued to fire from the cliffs into the forest.

So Rowena did the next best thing. Using the energy given to her by her fellow Dazhinn, she called upon the mists, drawing them from their hidden valley beyond the cliffs and bringing them slowly over the entire valley. It was an imperfect solution at best, though, since the soldiers already knew where the village was and could still fire blindly into the blanket of fog if they chose to do so. Still, she hoped it could buy them some time.

Then she and Seitha set about to find Alma, and soon discovered that not only the Council leader had disappeared. None of her allies could be found, either.

Thwarted in her attempt to find Alma, Rowena decided to risk a trip to the Gateway, to see if there was any evidence that the Atanians were nearby. Together with Seitha and several others, she rode through the misty valley, knowing that the very fog that protected them against the Warriors could also be concealing the presence of the Atanian soldiers.

The guns atop the cliffs had stopped firing long before they reached the Gateway, but they soon came upon the results of the shelling. At the bottom of the valley, the mist was thinner, and that allowed them to see the still-smoking craters in the ground where crops had been thriving only hours before.

This devastation had a far more powerful effect upon the others than upon Rowena, who had already witnessed the havoc that could be wreaked by artillery. Still, she was not immune to the scene. This was *her* valley, her people's home, and she understood now as she hadn't before that they were no longer safe in their enchanted place—far beyond the reach of men who made war.

They entered the forest near the base of the cliffs, where the fog mixed with smoke and huge old trees were no more than blackened stumps. All of them were very much aware of the soldiers high above them, and once or twice, Rowena thought she could hear the muffled sounds of men's voices. Could Zach himself be up there—so very near and yet so very far away? She found herself straining for the sound of his voice even as she fought down the terrible pain of her separation from him.

They tethered the horses in an untouched part of the woods and made their way cautiously beneath the cliffs into the Gateway. Seitha was the first to remark upon what they all noticed: the powerful forces that all who approached this place had always felt were gone now. The final remnant of their ancestors' crowning achievement was gone, either because it had ended with the spell or because the guns of the Warriors had destroyed it.

It soon became obvious that the soldiers had concentrated their greatest fire on this small area. Even the stones Rowena had trodden so frequently these past days were no longer in place. But neither here nor in the fields and forests did they see any trace of the Atanians.

"Perhaps they've retreated," Seitha said hopefully as they turned back and once again passed beneath the cliffs.

Rowena nodded. It was a possibility, but that didn't explain why Alma and her allies were missing.

It was late afternoon by the time they returned to the village and reported what they'd seen. The big guns remained silent, which made everyone there less fearful. But when Rowena learned that Alma and the others still hadn't been seen, her own fears escalated.

She returned to her cottage deep in thought. And then suddenly she remembered something she'd read in the ancient volumes at the library in Ashwara. There'd been several mentions of caves. The Warriors had believed that the Dazhinn might have fled their valley and hidden there at the time of that last battle. But no caves had ever been found, even though many attempts were made—some even centuries later.

Now she had a sudden rush of certainty that she'd hit upon the reason for Alma's absence. If the caves existed, they could hide not only the Dazhinn, but also Atanian soldiers, who could secret themselves there and then swarm out after the Warriors had given up the search they must be conducting for them even now.

If she was right, and Alma knew about those caves, then at least a few others must know as well. She left her cottage quickly to seek out the scholars as the most likely source of that information. She herself had read a few of the ancient volumes contained in their library, but she'd never been all that interested, and there were many books, handwritten in nearly illegible letters.

The library took up a large portion of Council Hall, and it was there that she found their most eminent scholars still poring through books they must surely know by heart. She inquired about the caves.

"Yes," one of them said slowly. "There are such caves, high in the mountains. No one has gone there since the spell was put on the valley, because they lie too close to the boundaries."

"But you know where they are?" Rowena asked eagerly.

One of the group had gotten up and was already searching through the shelves. "Yes, there are maps that show their locations—two of them."

She stopped her search and frowned at the others, pointing to an empty space. "It was here. Has anyone moved it?"

The others all shook their heads, stating that none of them had used that particular volume for many months.

"Could Alma have known about the caves?" Rowena asked.

"Oh, yes, she certainly could have. Alma has always had great interest in our history. She might have been an excellent scholar if she'd applied herself a bit more."

Or if she hadn't become obsessed with power instead, Rowena thought, now certain that her thoughts were correct. "Do any of you remember where they are?" she asked hopefully.

They did—or thought they did. Rowena listened carefully as they described it as best they could. There was no road or path, since the Dazhinn had always regarded the caves as being a last refuge if their enemies should somehow manage to overpower their magic and enter the valley.

Rowena explained that she'd read about them in the library at Ashwara, and she saw the scholars' eyes light up at this possible source of new work for them. They began to pummel her with questions about that library, but Rowena gently put them off. She hoped they could one day go there and see it for themselves, but for now, she needed some answers.

"How will I ever find them if the Warriors never found them?" she asked, imagining herself roaming through the mountains on a fruitless search.

The eldest of the scholars smiled at her. "You will find them because you're Dazhinn. The Warriors and others could not find them because a spell has been cast to hide them from all others. But why do you want to go there?"

"Because I think that's where Alma and the others have gone—to hide the Atanian soldiers. Do you know how big they are?"

"No description of their size was ever written down, but they must be large enough to hold all our people. And there's one other thing." He frowned thoughtfully, glancing at the others.

"There was one phrase in the account of them that has caused some disagreement among us. I think the writer was suggesting that the caves led *through* the mountain—and not just into it. But others have interpreted it differently."

"*Through* the mountain?" Rowena echoed. "You mean that it comes out on the other side—that it's another way out of the valley?"

"So I believe." He nodded. "But as I said, others have disagreed with me. It's a very old argument."

Rowena thanked them and left, her mind spinning. If the caves did have an outlet, she could be wrong about Alma's plans. Instead of just hiding the soldiers, she might be helping them to get out of the valley and *behind* Zach's army. They still wouldn't be able to capture Ashwara itself, but they could certainly take the town—and the other towns and villages beyond. The big guns at Ashwara were trained on the valley, and if she recalled correctly, they were mounted in such a manner as to be incapable of being repositioned.

She hurried to Seitha's cottage and explained it to her. "I must find those caves, and if I'm correct, then I must warn Zach."

Seitha wanted to go with her. Rowena resisted the idea at first, knowing the danger involved—especially if she was right. But then she relented.

"You can come with me to help me find the caves, but then you must return to the village. If the Atanians aren't there, it could be a place for our people to hide, and you can lead them there."

They went to the stables and got the best horses they could find, then set out for the mountains, knowing that their mission would be made even more difficult by the mists and the fact that only a few hours of daylight remained.

It was dusk by the time they found the entrance to the first cave, and they wouldn't have found it at all if it weren't for sensing the spell that kept it hidden. They stood in the mouth of the cave and stared into the impenetrable darkness, their voices echoing eerily.

"We should have brought flint and torches," Seitha said. "But I don't think anyone has been here."

Rowena nodded. The passage of so many soldiers would have surely left some traces. "Let's find the other one," she said, unwilling to let go of her belief that Alma had led the Atanians here.

Even in the near darkness, they began to see evidence that many feet had trampled the brush near the other cave, which wasn't far away. Rowena felt some satisfaction in knowing that she'd been right—but she would rather have been proven wrong. Alma could have led the Atanians here last night, in which case they might already have passed through the cave and be sneaking up on Zach's army. She turned to Seitha.

"Go back to the village. I'm going to see if the cave does have another entrance."

Seitha stared at her in horror. "But you can't go in there! See how dark it is? And what if they're still hiding in there?"

"If they're there, I'll surely hear them. Listen to how our voices echo. And I won't be traveling in the dark." She raised her hand and let the magic fire encircle it.

"This has uses beyond striking down the enemy."

"But you still can't fight them," Seitha protested. "You're only one person."

"You're right." Rowena nodded, thinking back to earlier, when she'd acted as a channel for their combined powers. "When you get back to the village, ask Tovar to try to reach me. Maybe he can help me become *more* than one person if the need arises."

Tovar was their most powerful 'path, and while Rowena herself had never demonstrated any talents along those lines, she'd already seen that she had powers beyond her previous imagining.

Seitha tried to dissuade her, then gave up and turned back toward the village. Rowena summoned the fire again and stepped into the cave.

"There's no sign of them, Chief. The scouts are pretty sure that they didn't return across the borders."

Zach frowned. Where were they? Even in these mountains, it was impossible to hide an entire army, not to mention their horses. He'd had scouts out all day, looking for them.

"Could the Dazhinn be hiding them?" the captain asked.

Zach thought about Paulena, who'd gone, against Duncan's wishes, into the valley. He desperately needed to know what she'd found there, but she wouldn't be back before tomorrow morning at the earliest. And with the accursed fog hiding the whole valley, it would have been easy for the Dazhinn to have concealed the Atanians.

"They could be," he answered reluctantly. He knew what the man's question implied. Even with the fog, they could still shell the village and destroy the enemy if they were there. But that meant destroying the Dazhinn as well. He swore again that he'd do just that if they'd killed Rowena, but he wasn't yet willing to concede that horrible possibility.

"We will wait until tomorrow before we do anything," he told the man, then dismissed him and went to find Duncan.

His old friend was still badly shaken by the discovery that his wife was a Dazhinn sorceress. But the fact that he was also frightened for her safety told Zach that he loved her nonetheless.

They talked in that careful way men do about the women they love. Zach knew that things had forever changed between Rowena and him the moment he'd seen her magic fire—but he also knew that he loved her anyway.

"Do you think they've ensorcelled us into loving them?" Duncan asked after his third cup of strong wine.

Zach shook his head, still nursing his first cup. He couldn't afford to be muzzy-headed in the morning. "No, I don't think that, although I think that we might have fallen in love with them at least in part because they're Dazhinn. You have Warrior blood in you, too, and something in us knew all along what they were."

Even in the midst of his fears for Polly, Duncan still thought about Zach. He seemed to have convinced himself that Rowena was alive, but if he was wrong . . .

Duncan repressed a shudder. Without Rowena, Zach would be no more than a shell of a once great man. And even beyond this war, his country needed him badly.

Rowena made her way as quickly as possible through the cave. The glow from the magic fire illuminated the damp walls and warned her of the many twists and turns. In the mucky floor of the cavern, she could see the imprints of many men and horses, but she could hear no sounds other than the steady dripping of water from the weeping walls and ceiling.

When she saw the first faint light, she didn't quite believe it. Then she thought it must be the Atanians, camped out for the night somewhere in the depths of the cave. She proceeded cautiously, but still heard nothing. And then she realized that the glow was moonlight, streaming in through the other entrance to the cave!

She closed her fist, putting out the fire, and moved swiftly to the mouth of the cave. Overhead, the moon was nearly full, casting a silvery light on the scene below her. Directly beneath the steep mountainside lay a small village, surrounded by croplands. Off to her right, nearly out of sight, were the lights of the town of Ashwara— and of the mighty fortress on its hilltop.

A perfect spot for them to mount a sneak attack on Zach's army, she thought as she stared at the scene. They're probably down there now, concealed in the woods at the edges of the fields. Or perhaps they've already captured the village.

She was wondering what she could do when she felt something. At first, she was frightened by the feeling that came over her, but then she realized what it was as Tovar sent soothing thoughts. He'd managed to reach her, after all.

Following instructions that she felt, rather than heard, Rowena let him see what she was seeing and sent her explanation. Ashwara was too far for her to make it there before morning, and she was quite certain that the Atanians, with the aid of Alma and the others, were planning to attack at dawn.

"Try to reach the Warrior chief," said Tovar in her head. "There are several hours yet before dawn."

"How can I do that?" she asked doubtfully. "I'm not a 'path."

She felt his smile. "But you *are*, Rowena, and this is a man you love. We are all agreed that we must stop Alma. Many of us still have doubts about the Warriors, but we do not wish to see the Atanians, led by one of us, attack them and kill innocent people as well."

"The Council has agreed to this?" she asked in surprise.

"Yes," came the response. "They are all with me now."

Rowena's head began to ache and Tovar seemed to sense that. "Rest for a few minutes, and then try to reach him. You can do it."

Rowena felt him withdraw and she sank down to the rocky ground in front of the cave to wait for the headache and the dizziness to pass.

Zach's eyes flew open and immediately began to search the shadows in the corners of his bedchamber. He'd turned the lamp low, but had left it burning, thinking it was unlikely that he'd sleep.

Rowena! He was sure that he'd heard her voice calling his name. He whispered her name now as his eyes continued to roam around the room. She'd materialized before his eyes another time and he was half-convinced that she would do so again.

But long moments passed and nothing happened. He groaned and dropped to the pillows again, knowing that it must have been merely a fragment of a dream. He didn't think that he'd actually been asleep, but rather had been in that half-light between wakefulness and slumber where the mind plays tricks.

Then, as he drifted with his thoughts of her, it came again. But this time, her voice seemed like a feather-soft brush against his mind, something he felt rather than heard.

A feeling of uneasiness stole over him. Could it be some sort of Dazhinn trick—not Rowena at all, but rather someone else, like Alma, trying to distract him with thoughts of her?

In spite of his uneasiness, Zach began to drift closer to sleep as the first tentative light of predawn touched the world beyond his window. He felt the breeze stirring and could even hear the soft rustle of the heavy drapes, and yet his mind was moving toward a different place.

He was standing on a rocky ledge, staring out at a dark world below and a lightening sky above. Directly beneath him lay a small village, one he thought he recognized but couldn't quite place. Surrounding it were vast expanses of farmland, broken by stretches of forest that reached up the side of the mountain where he stood.

He turned his head slowly. It was a strange sensation, as though it wasn't really his head that was turning. But it must be, because he was now staring at something very familiar in the distance: Ashwara. The town itself lay wrapped in darkness still, with barely a light showing. But the fortress was outlined against the lighter sky, clearly recognizable.

Now he had his bearings. He'd hunted in these mountains years ago when he'd been a student at Ashwara. Something about them nagged at him, a memory he couldn't quite retrieve.

Then he was turning again, this time to look behind him. And that half-buried memory came back in a rush! These were the mountains that legend said held caves in which the Dazhinn might have hidden from his ancestors. Like many others before him, he'd searched for those caves—but on the other side of the mountain, the side that faced the valley.

Instead, the cave was here, its dark mouth yawning before his eyes. Here—and possibly in the valley as well? The thought came to him as Rowena's voice had earlier. And then he knew what he was seeing.

He leapt from bed and flung open the door, calling out to his young aide who was sleeping on a cot in the anteroom. Then, after ordering him to summon his senior officers, he dressed hurriedly. He knew now why they hadn't found the enemy, and he was fairly certain that they must be hiding in the woods or in the village itself, waiting for dawn to mount a rear attack on his troops.

Not until his officers had assembled did it occur to Zach to question how he had come by this knowledge—and then he knew it must have been Rowena. What he'd seen must have come to him through her eyes. She'd told him that there were those among her people who possessed the ability to send their thoughts across the Gateway, but she'd denied having that ability herself.

Quickly, he explained the situation to his men, offering no explanation for how he'd come by the knowledge and leaving them no time to question it. There might still be time to move the artillery from the hills above the valley to a perimeter around Ashwara, but it would be up to the troops to save the village and farms between Ashwara and the forests where the Atanians must be hiding.

As soon as he'd issued the requisite orders, Zach called for his horse and set off with his hastily assembled elite troops for the village he'd seen in his dream. And as he rode flat out through the gray light of dawn, he hoped that Rowena would have enough sense to remain up on the mountain and therefore out of harm's way.

Rowena began the treacherous descent from the mountain as soon as she could see well enough. Tears stung her eyes, but she brushed them away. She hadn't been able to reach Zach, but that didn't necessarily mean that he was dead. He might have gone back to the city. Or she might simply have lacked the talent to get through to him.

It was all up to her now. Sooner or later, word would get back to Ashwara that the Atanians had outflanked them, but by then, many people would have died and the town of Ashwara itself would be in danger. And blame for all those deaths would fall quite rightly upon her people, thanks to Alma's treachery.

She knew that she couldn't hope to stop an entire army, but if she could just frighten them and slow them down, the villagers would have time to flee—and to send someone to Ashwara. It was a desperate, nearly hopeless plan, but it was the only one she had.

By the time she reached the base of the mountain, the sky was red with the approaching sun. How she wished she had a horse, so that she could more quickly find the Atanian troops.

Then she saw a small cabin through the trees, and even as she approached it, hoping she could steal a horse there, a man emerged from the little log house, stretching and yawning.

Forgetting caution in her desperation, Rowena ran toward him. He turned and frowned at her, blinking a few times as though he couldn't quite believe his eyes. Without preamble, she asked if he had a horse.

"Two of them," the man said, still staring at her as though she were an apparition beyond his wildest dream.

"Even better," Rowena replied. "You must give me one of them, and then take the other one and ride as fast as you can for Ashwara. Go to the fortress and tell the guards that you must speak to Commander MacTavesh—or whoever is in charge.

"Tell him that the Atanians have come through the mountain—through caves from the valley."

The man blinked a few times. "Atanians—here?" He looked around him and then back at her. "Who are you?" he asked suspiciously, as though a possibility might be just now dawning upon him.

"My name is Rowena Sandor. I'm Dazhinn. I followed them through the caves. Hurry now, man. They'll attack the village down there anytime now."

The man shrank back from her. "Dazhinn?"

"Yes." She raised her hand and let the fire arc into the air between them. He stared at it, swallowed hard, and then gestured to another log building at the edge of the clearing.

"All I got's two logging horses."

"That's fine," Rowena said, hurrying off in that direction, then turning to urge him to follow her. When he still didn't move, she sent a silent message that brought him to her and set him to the task of bringing out the huge animals.

She leapt upon the back of the first animal. "Go to Ashwara as fast as you can and warn them."

She waited until he had climbed on the other horse, and then rode off herself to find the Atanians.

*   *   *

Zach was less than ten miles from the village he'd seen in his "dream," riding ahead of his troops with only his aide and one other officer. So far, they'd seen no sign of the Atanians, but it was only now becoming full light, and if he was right, the enemy would be on the far side of the village.

Then he saw someone riding toward them, raising a cloud of dust that indicated he must be riding hard. Zach came to a halt, his hand already on his pistol. The other two did likewise.

As the rider drew closer, they could see that his horse was a large draft animal of the type used for plowing and logging. The rough-clad man didn't appear to be armed, but he was surely in a hurry. Zach's fears escalated as he wondered if this was someone who'd escaped from the village when the Atanians attacked.

The man slowed down and then stopped and stared at Zach. "It's Commander MacTavesh, isn't it?"

When Zach acknowledged impatiently that it was, the man's story poured out in nearly incoherent fashion. He'd just awakened and gone outside when a woman came down the mountain to him: a Dazhinn sorceress. He'd seen her magic fire, the kind they were supposed to have. She'd taken his other horse and told him to go to Ashwara and warn everyone there that the Atanians had come through the caves in the mountain.

This made no sense, the man said, shaking his head. He knew those mountains. There weren't any caves there. It must be a Dazhinn trick of some sort.

Zach cut him off with a demand that he describe the woman, then was barely able to restrain himself when the man described Rowena. She was alive!

"You said she took one of your horses. Where did she go?"

The man shrugged. "Toward the village, far as I know."

Zach's heart sank once more. Surely she couldn't be foolish enough to believe that her magic could stop the Atanian army!

People were just beginning to stir as Rowena rode into the village. Some of them had come to draw water from the community well, and they stared at her as she thundered into the village square.

"Listen to me!" she shouted. "This village is going to be attacked at any moment by the Atanian army. Is there somewhere you can hide?"

A tall, gray-haired man stepped toward her. "Who are you?" he asked.

Once again, Rowena showed her fire. Screams and gasps came from the small crowd as they shrank away from her. She closed her fist quickly and soothed her nervous horse.

"My name is Rowena and I'm Dazhinn. But I've come here to help you. I've already sent someone to Ashwara, but they won't get here in time to save you. Is there somewhere you can hide?"

"The mine," the tall man said. "But most of us have guns. We can fight."

"Fine. Then send the others to the mine."

Within moments, people were scurrying away, carrying babies and small children, and men were hurrying into the square with their rifles. Rowena pointed to a steep hill she'd passed on her way into the village.

"I think they might come from that direction. I'm going to wait for them on that hilltop. You stay near there and hide in the bushes."

The man she'd spoken to first eyed her hand curiously. "Are you going to use that on them?"

Rowena nodded. "But I don't know how much I can do. That's why I need you there, too."

He peered at her steadily. "'Tis said in Ashwara that Commander MacTavesh has got himself a Dazhinn woman. Would that be you?"

Rowena nodded. "Have you seen him—recently, I mean?"

"Aye. I was in Ashwara just yesterday, 'cause we'd heard that the Dazhinn had come back to their valley. And I saw him myself, riding through the streets with his men."

Rowena smiled through her tears of relief. "Thank you. That's the best news I've heard for a long time."

Then she turned her horse and rode back to the edge of the village, where she tethered it out of sight and began climbing the hill. Zach was alive—and soon he would be coming here. All she had to do was hold back the Atanians, with the help of the villagers, until his troops could get here. If Tovar could help her, she was sure she could do it.

She was tired by the time she reached the top of the hill, but it was all she'd hoped for, commanding a perfect view of the road and the farmlands beyond a brief stretch of woods. Then, even as she narrowed her gaze on the distant woods where she thought the Atanians might be hiding, she saw them! They swarmed out of the woods, their horses raising huge clouds of dust as they rode toward her.

Rowena felt fear knife through her. There were so many of them—far more than she'd expected. How could she possibly hold them off? It would be hours before Zach's army arrived, and even with the assistance of the villagers, she couldn't hope to stop them.

Desperately, she reached out with her mind for Tovar, and almost immediately felt that strange touch of his mind against hers. She let him "see" through her eyes the size of the advancing army and her position atop the hill. And she told him about the villagers.

"It is in our history," he told her, the words touching her silently. "There were times in the past when one person or a few held off an army of invaders. It can be done, Rowena."

She wanted to feel reassured, but as she watched the soldiers come closer to the base of the hill, her doubts grew. But so did her determination. She would not allow people to die because of treachery by a Dazhinn. The Atanians wouldn't be here now if it hadn't been for Alma. If they were to live in peace with their neighbors, it had to start now.

She called upon the fire as the first of the soldiers entered the stretch of woods just below the hilltop. And as she did so, she felt a surge of power that nearly knocked her off her feet!

The fire arced above her and then downward with a brilliant flash. The first men to see it shouted and their horses reared up, snorting. They seemed at first not to know where it came from, but then one of them looked up and spotted her. He began to shout, and then all faces were turned to her as they sought to control their mounts and others behind them pressed close upon them.

The first shot whistled past her, so close that she could feel the disturbance of the air. But by the time the second man had raised his rifle, she was ready for him. The magic fire leapt toward his gun and he screamed and dropped it.

Others began to fire, and Rowena retreated farther back on the hilltop until she was out of sight. But still the green fire flowed from her fingertips, curving high into the air and then dropping beyond her range of vision—right in front of the troops.

. After a few moments, she decided to risk returning to the edge of the hilltop, and moved a short distance away so that she wouldn't reappear at the same spot and immediately draw their fire.

She gasped when she saw what had happened. A wall of shimmering green fire had been erected in front of the troops. Several men dismounted and approached it cautiously. But the instant the first one touched it, he fell heavily to the ground, and his companion beat a hasty retreat.

There was now nothing more than a soft glow around her hand, but the force of the energy flowing through her seemed to increase with every moment. Or perhaps, she realized, *it is I who am weakening.* It felt as though something of her was being drained away even as the ancient magic flowed through her.

Below her, the soldiers began to dismount and move up the steep hillsides on both sides of the wall of fire. Rowena reached for still more magic and extended the wall on both sides, until the top of it was nearly level with the hilltop on which she stood.

They would get through sooner or later; she knew that. And she also knew that she lacked the energy to escape or to make herself invisible to them.

Drained and utterly helpless from the forces flowing through her, she sank to her knees. Tovar's mind touched hers in question, but she begged him not to break contact. As long as she was conscious, she could still hold them off.

She let Tovar see her situation and his words whispered soundlessly through her mind. "Leap into the fire if they come for you, Rowena. The fire will save you."

She had no idea how long she stayed there, half-sitting and half-lying on the ground. But then she heard sounds, and raised her head to see two soldiers making their cautious way toward her, their guns aimed at her. It took every ounce of strength she possessed, but she rolled herself over to the edge and leapt off just as gunfire sounded behind her.

She stopped falling almost immediately, and instead hung suspended in a shimmering green mist. Remembering her journeys through the Gateway, she rolled herself into a ball to fight the strangeness of the feeling. She could see nothing, but she could hear men's shouts quite close by as they made their way across the hilltops, slowed but not stopped.

I've failed, she thought miserably when she heard the first shots being fired a short time later. The villagers will never be able to defend themselves, and Zach must yet be far away. The Dazhinn would be blamed for this once the truth came out, and her people would never be allowed to live in peace, even with Zach's help.

Suddenly, the green mist parted and she floated gently down until she was lying on the now deserted road. She lacked the strength to get up—or even to think very clearly. She tried to reach for Tovar, but felt no response.

The last thing she heard before blackness carried her away was the sound of gunfire. So much gunfire, she thought. They must have found the villagers who were hiding, and now they were killing them, too.

Rowena awoke slowly, slipping in and out of sleep for an indeterminate period of time. She ached too badly to stay awake for long. And once, when she tried to open her eyes, the pain became even worse and she closed them quickly.

A low, soothing voice that sounded vaguely familiar asked her to say her name. She thought that was a strange request, but it seemed easier to comply than to question.

Once, she came to that semiwakefulness to find a large, callused hand holding hers. It felt familiar, too, but she didn't know why. A different voice spoke now: a man this time, saying her name.

She gave no thought at all to where she was, or how she had come there, or what had happened to her. Thinking required too much effort.

But then a time came when the pain eased and the memories began to flood her brain, tumbling through it as though a dam had burst. She opened her eyes to find Seitha bent over her, holding a hot, steaming bowl of fragrant herbs whose scent tickled her nose.

Seitha smiled at her and set the bowl aside. "You're back!" she whispered. "Tedda said the herbs should do it when you were ready to come back."

Rowena saw that she was in her own bed and smiled for a moment. Then she frowned. "Why are you whispering?" Surely there could be no danger here. She was back in the valley.

Instead of answering, Seitha backed away from the bed—and then Rowena saw him. He was sprawled in a chair, his head drooping on his broad chest as he slept. Instead of softening his harsh, aquiline features, the flickering firelight emphasized the sharp planes of his face and the stubbly beard that darkened his cheeks and jaw.

Seitha set down the bowl of herbs and gave her a quick hug, then left the cottage. Rowena got carefully out of bed. She still ached, but at least she could move.

She sat down on the rug in front of his chair and stared at him. She had so many questions, but for now, she wanted only to be near him. Carefully, she reached out to touch his hand which dangled over the arm of the chair. She hadn't really intended to awaken him, but she felt guiltily happy when she saw his eyelids flicker and then open.

"Are you all right?" He was awake instantly and out of his chair, dropping to his knees before her.

"I will be—as soon as you hold me," she said, smiling.

He accommodated her very quickly, lifting her into his arms and carrying her back to her narrow bed, where he put her down carefully and then joined her.

For a time, she said nothing as she let him fill her senses and the certainty of his love fill her heart. Then she asked him what had happened.

The village had been saved. Not one life had been lost, although several men were wounded. She had managed to hold back the enemy just long enough for him to get there.

He'd found her lying in the road outside the village and had decided to bring her back here, rather than to Ashwara. The villagers had told him about the wall of fire, and he knew that whatever had happened to her had happened because of Dazhinn magic.

The Atanians had been routed, and their king was suing for peace, claiming that he'd let his generals get out of control.

Alma and her allies had sneaked back into the valley through the caves. But she was no longer the leader, or even a member of the Council. Instead, she would spend the remainder of her days living in disgrace. Zach didn't think that it was punishment enough, but Rowena knew that it was.

Abner and those who'd accompanied him had not yet been found, but Zach had men out searching for them, and when they were found, they would be returned to the valley to be dealt with by the Council.

Secure in the strong circle of his arms, Rowena drifted off to sleep as Zach talked about protecting the Dazhinn from the inevitable curiosity seekers until such time as they chose to leave their valley, or permit others to enter it.

393

The last thing she heard was about not one, but two weddings: one in the palace and one here in the valley, honoring both his tradition and hers.

TIMESWEPT ROMANCE

TIME OF THE ROSE
By Bonita Clifton

When the silver-haired cowboy brings Madison Calloway to his run-down ranch, she thinks for sure he is senile. Certain he'll bring harm to himself, Madison follows the man into a thunderstorm and back to the wild days of his youth in the Old West.

The dread of all his enemies and the desire of all the ladies, Colton Chase does not stand a chance against the spunky beauty who has tracked him through time. And after one passion-drenched night, Colt is ready to surrender his heart to the most tempting spitfire anywhere in time.

_51922-4 $4.99 US/$5.99 CAN

A FUTURISTIC ROMANCE

AWAKENINGS
By Saranne Dawson

Fearless and bold, Justan rules his domain with an iron hand, but nothing short of the Dammai's magic will bring his warring people peace. He claims he needs Rozlynd—a bewitching beauty and the last of the Dammai—for her sorcery alone, yet inside him stirs an unexpected yearning to savor the temptress's charms, to sample her sweet innocence. And as her silken spell ensnares him, Justan battles to vanquish a power whose like he has never encountered—the power of Rozlynd's love.

_51921-6 $4.99 US/$5.99 CAN

LOVE SPELL
ATTN: Order Department
Dorchester Publishing Co., Inc.
276 5th Avenue, New York, NY 10001

Please add $1.50 for shipping and handling for the first book and $.35 for each book thereafter. PA., N.Y.S. and N.Y.C. residents, please add appropriate sales tax. No cash, stamps, or C.O.D.s. All orders shipped within 6 weeks via postal service book rate. Canadian orders require $2.00 extra postage and must be paid in U.S. dollars through a U.S. banking facility.

Name_____

Address_____

City _____ State_____Zip_____

I have enclosed $_____in payment for the checked book(s).

Payment <u>must</u> accompany all orders.☐ Please send a free catalog.

TIMESWEPT ROMANCE
A TIME-TRAVEL CHRISTMAS
By Megan Daniel, Vivian Knight-Jenkins, Eugenia Riley, and Flora Speer

In these four passionate time-travel historical romance stories, modern-day heroines journey everywhere from Dickens's London to a medieval castle as they fulfill their deepest desires on Christmases past.

___51912-7 $4.99 US/$5.99 CAN

A FUTURISTIC ROMANCE
MOON OF DESIRE
By Pam Rock

Future leader of his order, Logan has vanquished enemies, so he expects no trouble when a sinister plot brings a mere woman to him. But as the three moons of the planet Thurlow move into alignment, Logan and Calla head for a collision of heavenly bodies that will bring them ecstasy—or utter devastation.

___51913-5 $4.99 US/$5.99 CAN

Three captivating stories of love in another time, another place.

MADELINE BAKER
"Heart of the Hunter"

A Lakota warrior must defy the boundaries of life itself to claim the spirited beauty he has sought through time.

ANNE AVERY
"Dream Seeker"

On faraway planets, a pilot and a dreamer learn that passion can bridge the heavens, no matter how vast the distance from one heart to another.

KATHLEEN MORGAN
"The Last Gatekeeper"

To save her world, a dazzling temptress must use her powers of enchantment to open a stellar portal—and the heart of a virile but reluctant warrior.